The Case of the Open Drawer

By Luke Allan

First Published in 1936 by Arrowsmith

This Edition by **Stillwoods** of Canada

Stillwoods.Blogspot.Com

http://www.lulu.com/spotlight/lulubook22

Catalogue Information:
Author: W. Lacey Amy; aka Luke Allan.
First Published: 1936
Title: The Case of the Open Drawer
ISBN: Canada 978-1-988304-00-7
Published by: Stillwoods. Doug Frizzle (1949-
Website: http://www.lulu.com/spotlight/lulubook22
Blog: Stillwoods.Blogspot.Com
This file dated 2016Mar10.

This edition dedicated to my wife and partner, Gail Kelly, with my love.

AMY, W(illiam) Lacey. 1878-1962.
By David Skene-Melvin
Wrote as "Luke ALLAN".

One of Canada's finest delineators of her own land, an indefatigable traveller who began his peregrinations at home before venturing constantly abroad, and Canada's first home-grown war correspondent whose dispatches on the home front in Britain during World War I still stand as some of the most perceptive commentary on that period, William Lacey Amy, who eschewed the use of his praenomen, was also from the 1920s for 30 years until his death one of Canada's most prolific writers of crime fiction with his immensely popular "Blue Pete" series that appeared pseudonomously as by "Luke Allan".

Although one can understand the disappearance of his crime fiction written as it was for lending libraries and before the academic respectability of popular culture, and "Luke Allan"'s consequent obscurity, it is a matter of regret that Lacey Amy the social commentator is not better remembered.

~ ~ ~ ~ ~

Even if he had never written any novels, Amy would still deserve a place in Canadian writing for bringing to urban and literate Canada such an evocative and telling description of the lives of residents of the country's small towns and outports as he did with his pre-World War One travel articles, articles that fully deserve re-publication.

I A Scream of Terror

IT was a wasted evening, and what made it more mortifying was that I knew Larry was as conscious of it as I. But Larry's manner of evincing it differed from mine.

I sulked, pained that Jack Ponting had let me down, annoyed that I had argued Larry into going, worried by the certainty that Larry was not likely to give me a chance to explain.

For Larry just whistled.

That was Larry's way—he just whistled. Larry whistled under any condition. I have seen him lounging before the wicket, his lips pursed to a whistle, having carried his bat for hours—with four runs to tie the score. I have seen him whistling in perfect tune the latest popular song as his fist crashed into the teeth of a street rowdy engaged in kicking a fallen foe; and he continued to whistle as we bolted from the scene to escape police annoyances. And those same lips would pucker to a soundless whistle in the court-room where I sat, perspiring and restless, while the jury debated a case that threatened to make or break me in my profession.

I had induced Larry to accept my estimate of Jack Ponting's taste in drama, and for three long, dull hours we had endured the second night of *The Silver Spoon*. Three hours on my part of a vain struggle to support my respect for Jack as a critic, three hours of Sphinx-like apathy in my companion.

Perhaps it was in part due to the way the evening opened. A respected and valued client had come to me with a case against Vance Horton, a nasty case that was certain to involve a lot of dirty linen— the sort of case that, so far as Vance was concerned, would occasion no surprise or shock. But in my short career at the Bar I had avoided such exposures of laundry abominations, partly because I have never known laundry washed in court, despite the filth exposed, to emerge one whit whiter; partly because I happen to be in the fortunate position of not being forced to take a case I dislike.

Besides, Vance Horton and I had attended the same school— and had never been friends since. As everyone knew.

I had refused the case, and probably lost a client.

So that I had entered the Olympia in the wrong mood.

And as we drove homeward—it was half-past eleven—with some dim relieving thought of Cuddy's sandwiches and whisky awaiting us, I continued peevish. Both of us were silent.

You see, *The Silver Spoon* was a problem play, one of those artificial problems so beloved of unimaginative playwrights and scenarists—and of typists and schoolgirls, I suppose: the two-day infatuation of a silly schoolgirl for the man to whom, unknown to her, her mother was engaged. And the mother, loving the man and wholly loved in return, felt compelled to dismiss him for the sake of her daughter's happiness. The woman behind me blubbered.

The plot, bad as it was, suffered, too, from an unlover-like lover, from a sentimental heroine born to self-sacrifice, from a daughter who was certain to fall in love again with the next good hair-cut that crossed her path.

Silent? No, Larry whistled, lounging low in the seat beside me.

We were running along Figmore Street. Figmore Street is one of our show streets. The houses are large, ancient, and imposing, and the effect is heightened by the exclusiveness of high stone walls and thick shrubbery. With the exception of three or four the houses remain in the original families. But the new generation is not like the old; and not a few have lost the means to maintain more than artificial exclusiveness. Here and there extensions and alterations have been made, and taste and fortune have seldom improved together.

A few lighted windows twinkled at us through the trees as we bowled along, but the street was dark and deserted.

It was Larry spoke first:

"After all, Dill, women have a right to their little problems."

"But no playwright has a right to ask fifteen shillings to see the shallowest of them."

Larry chuckled softly. "It's your problem to decide whether to pay or not." He whistled a bar. "How happy they are, Dill—the women, I mean—in painting the tragic results of everything they do!"

"And," I grumbled, "how simply they solve their problems—a colour, a smile, the cut of a coat, a tear, a kiss! Bah!"

"A kiss." Larry heaved himself upright in the seat. "After all, Dill, what shouldn't a kiss solve?"

I made a sound of disgust and pointed ahead to a two-storied range of lighted windows, from which, even at that distance, sounds of revelry played havoc with the outdoor peace of the street. "Then Vance Horton has his niche in the world. It's the first defence I've heard of him and his ways."

Larry's eyes followed my pointing finger. He laid a hand on my arm.

"Let's stop here for a minute or two, Dill. Laughter there, light-heartedness, irresponsibility—I've never been able to attain to a din like that. How do they manage it?"

"You and I, Larry, thank God, have never been able to attain even to patience with Vance Horton's method of attaining it."

I had drawn in to the curb. Through the trees and the darkness came the raucous hilarity of maudlin men and unrestrained women. Through a couple of open windows came a discordant duet in the very song Larry had been whistling; in another room someone thumped an accompaniment with two fingers to some outlandish instrument that sounded like a kazoo.

Suddenly Larry stirred. He opened the door and thrust a foot to the running-board.

"What the devil are you thinking of doing?" I growled.

"How do I know?" he replied blandly, and vanished into the darkness across the road.

I had stopped the car at the upper end of the garden, and the last I saw of Larry for the next few minutes was his dim form crowding through the hedge.

Vance Horton was one of the newer generation, not only in age but in manner of living. He had advertised that by calling in an architect on the day following his mother's death. The stone wall so favoured of the street was torn down and replaced by a hedge. In due course, too, there rose a long single-story wing, euphoniously called a billiard-room. True it was fitted with appropriate equipment, but gossip had it dedicated to less reputable entertainment.

The fact of the alterations, their callous haste, did nothing to improve Vance's reputation in the city.

But Vance, even as far back as the old days at Cortwright, had shown how indifferent he was to a reputation he did not seek.

He had friends, of course, though few in Figmore Street. Some in the city danced to his tune, and from London he brought every week or so a houseful to shock the neighbourhood with their carousals. Such as on that night as Larry and I stopped to comment on it.

Vance was handsome in a reckless way, and he had a way

with him that accounted in part for his amours. He was, too, a free spender. That was expected, for his mother had been a Bowman, of the big distilling firm, and Vance had fallen heir to all she possessed.

From her, too, he must have inherited certain traits not so negotiable as her money. From which side he inherited his perverted mind and callous conscience was never quite clear. Even to his schoolmates at Cortwright that had always been a matter for speculation. It expressed itself on my part in an unbroken antagonism that climaxed in a spanking I gave him at school, literally a spanking, for a foul thing he had said to a junior. He had never forgiven me. Indeed, he had gone out of his way more than once to harass me, and I, in my turn, had lost no opportunity to express my contempt.

Larry, too. At school Vance had started false stories about Larry, and my friend, half as big again and twice as strong, dare not take it out on his hide. Larry's strength always laid him open to a charge of bullying.

For a moment or two after Larry left me I sat listening. The scene interested me—the quiet, deserted street, the bright windows from which emanated the raucous clamour, Larry's odd curiosity and his stealthy disappearance within the dark grounds. Slowly I coasted the car along the curb, until, directly opposite the billiard-room, I pulled up and shut off the engine.

Only a dim light, as from a solitary bulb or, at most, two, came from those six tall French windows. It surprised me, for the billiard-room, at least in local gossip, had always been closely associated with Vance's orgies.

As I stared at the lighted house a gale of drunken laughter, noisier than anything that had gone before, filled the night.

But it was not that that sent the blood leaping in my veins and my hand to the door beside me. From the heart of the laughter, the discordant singing, the crazy music, something had cut like a knife. It was a woman's scream.

II A Corpse

EVEN now I fail to understand how I picked it out. The clamour of a score of tipsy voices must have been louder, and my attention was fixed on them. Yet in that moment I heard only the scream.

I leaped from the car and raced across the street.

But as I scrambled through the hedge, too excited to go on to the gate, a hand fell firmly on my arm. It was Larry.

"Easy, old thing, easy," he whispered.

"But—but, Larry, you heard? You must have heard that scream."

He held me like a vice. "I heard it. . . . And when I hear a woman scream from Vance Horton's house, Dill, I go on my way whistling. This is no time for chivalry."

I struggled, but he was too strong for me.

"It's their playful ways, Dill, that's all. They've probably stripped another one—or smashed the piano. Some trifling horse-play or other."

"Not to make a woman scream like that," I protested. "Let me go. I'm going to see what happened, anyway."

"You're too late, Dill. If it's tragedy, better keep out of it. If it isn't, don't give our mutual friend such a chance to jeer. He's never forgotten—or forgiven you."

I scarcely heard the words he used, but from the tone I read an uneasiness in my friend equal to my own.

And suddenly something else far back in my memory, something that had but dimly registered at the time, came to the surface. It was not alone the scream that had brought me on the run, for a dozen women were screaming in the house. No, not that, but its sudden interruption, its arrest. A picture flashed through the mind—a brutal, or terrified, hand clapped suffocatingly over the lips that had sent that cry of terror into the night.

Brutal or terrified? It was to obtain the answer that, with a sudden jerk, I wrenched myself from Larry's clutch and hurried toward the billiard-room. But Larry was on me before I had taken three steps.

"You're not going in there, Dill, *not you,* if I have to carry you home."

The grimness of it stilled my hysteria. "I'm not a fool. I'll just have a look—into the billiard-room there. If you're frightened—"

"I'm frightened for you." But his grip slackened. "Go ahead. I'll toddle along."

Straight before me was the billiard-room, and from the house on my left came the clamour of Vance's guests, a large party. I had been in the house three or four times, fearful of the implications of refusing Vance's intermittent invitations. Upstairs and down were large sitting-rooms, luxurious to sensuousness—Vance Horton himself in material things.

The scream I had placed in the billiard-room, though, even as I crept toward it, I knew it must be nothing but a guess, probably directed by the continued gaiety from the house, and the dim lights in the room before me. Not a sound came from it.

As I advanced I scanned the windows. Every curtain was drawn, but a line of light cutting across the flagged walk that extended along that side directed my steps toward the second window from the end. It was, I saw, slightly ajar.

Even as my foot reached out to touch that line of light a stab of fear cut through me, a strange, inexplicable dread that rooted me momentarily to the spot, and made my knees shake and a cold sweat break out on my forehead.

Yet all I could see was the perpendicular line of light in the opening, and, beyond, a foot or two of billiard-table; farther still, a rack of cues on the other wall. But the stillness that reached out to me was deathly, unnatural, an almost tangible thing that blocked my advance. For I knew then, as surely as if I had stood there and watched, that the scream had reached me through that narrow opening.

I drove myself forward.

Easing the window back, I advanced my head into the opening.

I do not recall now that my eyes took in anything else at the moment, anything but that one spot of life to my left.

Life? Scarcely.

There before a mahogany table sat Vance Horton, his chair turned slightly toward me. His left arm hung over the arm of the chair; the other, palm down, lay on the table. His head dropped limply over his right shoulder, as if staring at the floor beneath the table.

But it needed only a glance to tell me that Vance Horton was dead.

A shock, of course. But something vastly more startling, more urgent, more terrifying. Vance and I had always disliked each other, and at the moment I could think of little else. Swiftly I retreated.

Conscience. More than once I had pictured my world without Vance Horton on my heels. His goading, threatening presence had made me in fancy a murderer. And so, in the moment when I saw him dead before me, I became his murderer.

It was Larry's strong hand on my shoulder, whirling me about, that brought me sharply back to realities. The light through the open window fell on us, and in my face he must have read what I had seen, for he drew a quick breath.

"Larry! Larry! He's—dead!"

With a fling that almost threw me from my feet he had me back in the shadows, his hand over my lips.

"Shut up!" It was more than a command—a threat.

And then, as he held me powerless to move or cry out, I felt him jerk about and stand for a moment as if listening. The next moment he was dragging me toward the street.

"Come on, for God's sake!"

At the hedge he halted to peer up and down the street.

"Damn you!" he snarled. "What did you bring the car down here for?"

I was dazed. As he drew me into the shadows an ugly thought had popped into my head. It hung there now, blanking out everything else, though I fought flabbily against it. Shaking from head to foot, I shrank away from him.

And then he had me through the hedge, and we were running across the street to the car. Opening the door, he thrust me in, flew around to the other side, and climbed in beside me.

"Step on it!" he ordered. "Quick! And as silently as you can."

Automatically I obeyed.

At the corner he jerked the wheel himself, and we spun into Tunham Terrace. Half-way down the block he ordered me to stop.

"Go on home, Dill." He climbed out. "Keep along here to Osprey Street, then cut across home. Don't stop for anything, not for anything."

"But—but, Larry—"

"Do as I say." He thrust his face through the open window and glared at me. Then, as I sent the car forward, I heard him whistling back up the street.

An involuntary shudder ran through me, but with a desperate effort I managed to expel Larry momentarily from my mind. Vance Horton dead! Vance Horton dead! Vance Horton dead! Tonelessly I kept repeating it.

But Vance Horton dead meant so much more, so much that was more horrifying. Where was Larry when Vance was—murdered? For I knew, as surely as if I had seen him struck down, that Vance had been murdered. By whom? It was the murderer, not the murder, that mattered.

For Larry Rockford was my best friend. Through the years at Cortwright, at Oxford, and since I had tested that friendship too often to doubt it. Large of frame, inclined to stoutness, Larry at times showed a tendency to indolence that irritated me. But when the call came for action he became a tiger.

And now my friend—a murderer!

It struck so hard as it came, fully worded, into my mind that the car jerked precariously. I managed to straighten it, and as I did something in the seat behind jarred against the door. My golf-bag, I reflected. On my return from the afternoon game with Jordan Fleming I had forgotten to remove my clubs from the car.

Understandable enough, since, for the first time in a struggling record of contests, I had beaten Jordan—and 88 as well. At his best Jordan was a 75 man, but to-day he had done everything one would never expect of him. And he had gone the round morose and silent, so absent-minded that at times I was forced to remind him to play. And, having beaten him, I had skipped into the house on my return, leaving my clubs in the car, to exult to Larry who had come to dine with me.

Automatically I had followed Larry's instructions. At High Street I was forced to a skidding stop by a car flashing past with shrieking horn. And as it flew along I slid lower behind the wheel, trembling. For in that fleeting glimpse I recognized Inspector Emerson behind the wheel.

As I crossed High Street my eyes lifted by chance to the small mirror above the windscreen—and a momentary dizziness swept over me.

For there in the small oblong of glass I saw something close to my back—the top of a head!

Instantly I ducked forward and swung the car to the curb. Murder was in my mind. Murder was in the air. But as I threw the door open a soft voice at my shoulder whispered: "Please, please, go on. It's—it's too light here." And a head of dark, wavy hair, and a pair of wide, frightened eyes appeared above the back of the seat.

I must have been too stunned to think, for automatically I sent the car on. Nothing now was visible in the mirror, though I kept my eyes fixed on it, almost to disaster, for I managed just in time to veer from the track of an oncoming car.

Presently I found my tongue.

"If you wouldn't mind—Oh, see here!"

It was too much, a nightmare of impossibilities, for a second head, a fair one this time, crept into sight. The dark one rose beside it.

"Please go on," she begged.

"If you wouldn't mind sitting up where I can see you," I begged in my turn, "it would seem less—less—impossible."

"It's all impossible." The girl's voice broke.

I had never seen a woman cry, and the thought of it sent me into a panic.

"I'm sorry about the golf-bag," I said foolishly. "If it's in the way, open the door and shove it out. Did you—stowaway at the theatre or—"

Impossible to finish the question, for suddenly I knew, and with the blundering, amazing, shocking revelation I stiffened.

"It happens," I declared grimly, "that I know where the police station is."

The two faces came abruptly into view.

"You wouldn't—do that?"

Just a glimpse of her face and I knew better than she that I wouldn't. For the girl was beautiful—beautiful with something more entrancing than fine features, behind that lovely face was intelligence, gentleness, honesty, but, above all, courage.

Perhaps she read in the mirror the admiration in my eyes.

"Please let us out now," she murmured. "It's darker here."

Instead I pressed the accelerator.

"Madame," I said, "this is not a taxi. If I can't take you to your own home you're coming to mine."

10

EVER since Cortwright and Oxford I have longed for a home of my own. The meals foisted on us at Cortwright as "selected, individualized diet" cured me for life of any patience with menus; and Oxford did little to weaken my craving. Then, too, I have whims as to hours, and certain unusual ideas about service, and personal comfort, and furnishings. What bachelor hasn't? But, mind you, I was in no sense an "old bachelor." Whatever foundation my habits might provide for such an accusation my age repudiates—twenty-eight.

Thus my *ménage*. A house of my own, ridiculously large, perhaps, but I like untrammelled space, and to be able to sleep my friends; and I could afford it. For service Cuddy, dad's batman in the Great War; and Mrs. Beaton from eight to eight. A gardener, Hodges by name, completed the list, but Hodges counted little—except in those isolated moments when the technicalities of his profession enabled him to gloat over me, gloating the more visibly as I became more peevish about it.

Cuddy had come to me with dad's estate. He could look like a travelled French chef, and he could scrub and wash and iron and garden—handle me and my affairs with the subtle certainty of a diplomat. And his hours were immeasurable, at least by me, for I had never succeeded in catching him in bed.

Cuddy met us at the front door. I had never entered the house at that time of night by the front door, if I had my car out. But then, neither had I ever before brought home with me even one of the other sex, let alone two. But Cuddy's face expressed no surprise. Had I returned with wings I believe Cuddy would merely have rearranged the feathers when he accepted my coat and hat.

Still, knowing Cuddy's active mind as I did, and prepared to find him waiting up for me, I found the moment embarrassing.

"You'd—you'd better," I ordered, struggling to duplicate his composure, "make up more sandwiches."

"Yes, sir. And tea, sir?"

I never took tea as a nightcap, but Cuddy anticipated that. I thanked him with my eyes and turned to the elder of the two girls, the dark one.

"Tea?"

"Please—and so strong." She sighed.

For a moment I thought of suggesting something stronger, but Cuddy would know what was best.

He bowed. "In nine minutes, sir." That was Cuddy, staking his reputation on a second. Had the gas gone off, I hate to think of Cuddy's shame.

With military stiffness he wheeled and set off down the hall. As he passed the library door he reached in and switched on the centre lights. I had thought of another room at the front, a stiff, formal, cold room, reserved for state occasions. But again Cuddy knew best.

The library was my favourite room. There I always returned after my household browsings. I was a little proud of it, and my friends had always been kind about it. But as I stood aside to let the two girls precede me, it seemed to fail me. A man's rooms—and a dull bachelor's at that. At night, too, there was not the pleasant vista of garden visible through the door I always left open on reasonable days.

I waved helplessly to the chairs. "Please sit down, that is, if you can find a comfortable chair. I—I didn't think of women when I bought them."

A wan smile appeared on the face of the dark one. Her arm was around her slighter, younger sisters waist, and she led her to the most comfortable of the chairs and gently eased her into it. With a sigh she dropped into another beside it.

A lump rose in my throat. "Yes, you must be tired," I murmured.

She raised her eyes to mine—to look far away through me. "Tired? If it was only that!"

She glanced at her sister. I did the same.

Hitherto I had avoided it. The younger girl's eyes were wide, glassy, and unfocused, the pupils enlarged. She seemed to move in her sleep. But as we turned to her, with a pitiful cry she dropped her face in her hands on the arm of the chair and sobbed.

Instantly her sister was on her knees beside her.

"Don't, Willo, don't!"

"Oh, Barby, Barby, how could you?" wailed the weeping girl.

Barby pressed her sister's face to her shoulder and turned slow, guilty eyes to mine. "Sh-sh, dear, sh-sh!"

I crept from the room.

Cuddy was in the pantry, slicing a fresh loaf with almost

ludicrous care. From the kitchen beyond came the hiss of gas at full pressure. He did not turn as I entered. His back was very stiff.

I laughed nervously.

"A new experience for us, Cuddy."

"For me, sir, yes." It was the nearest to criticism he had ever permitted himself.

"Hell, Cuddy!" I groaned, "you're the only one of us all with nothing to worry about."

"Yes, sir. As you say, sir." Another paper-thin slice of bread fell away.

I caught him by the shoulders and whirled him about. "Cuddy, if you knew what I've been through, what we've all been through— yes, the girls in there, too—you'd make the best sandwiches you ever made . . . and tea like lye, as they wish it."

"Yes, Sir" He held a slice of bread on his knife. "I'm doing 'em. They're my business, sir."

"And," shaking him, "what's my business is yours, and you know it. And what happened to-night is so much my business that I may have run my head into a noose. And that's more than a metaphor. . . . Cuddy, I saw a corpse a murdered man—and no one knows it. No one," I added, with a shudder, "but Larry Rockford."

The lump in Cuddy's throat rose and fell as he stared at me. "You mean you mean—you—murdered someone, sir?"

"Not I. I didn't have—"

Cuddy's face cleared. "If it's Mr. Rockford, sir, he'll manage." He returned to his sandwiches.

"It wasn't either of us, I tell you." I heard my voice rise angrily, and I blushed.

"If you don't mind, sir, there's the kettle boiling."

"Damn the kettle! In that room a girl is weeping her heart out."

"They do, sir. . . . And sometimes they're a bit tardy about it."

I could have struck him. "Do they look like that sort of girls?" I demanded fiercely.

Cuddy cleared his throat. "If I might say, sir, speaking as man to man, I'd say I couldn't blame you."

I laughed and gave it up. "All right, Cuddy. But get this into your thick head: I'm hiding those girls."

"If I knew who from, sir, *what* from—But it doesn't matter."

"Indeed it does. That's all that does matter. Only—only I don't know myself what I'm hiding them from. Blast you, Cuddy, you're cold-blooded as a snake!"

Cuddy started for the kitchen. "They're not *my* friends, sir."

I followed to the door and watched him making the tea. "They'll have the yellow room, Cuddy. When you have served us get it ready."

"Yes, sir."

I returned to the library. Willo had recovered herself. But there was that in her eyes that warned me. She was still dazed. I preferred not to understand. She sat now with her face averted.

"Cuddy," I said, lightly as I could, "will be ready in time. . . . We have two minutes alone—two and a half."

Barby had not taken her eyes from my face. Now her lips twisted to a lifeless smile.

"Yes," she agreed, "an explanation. I know it's due to you."

Willo whirled on her. "Don't tell him, Barby, for God's sake don't!"

The elder sister reached out and laid her hand on Willo's, but the latter drew away.

"It's all right, Willo." Then to me: "You know when we climbed into your car. . . . You saw—in that room. Doesn't it—explain?"

I nodded miserably.

"Thank you." She sat for a moment or two staring at the carpet. "You—saved us. It's more than we can ever repay."

"You owe me nothing." Nothing, I said to myself, but—the whole story. It left me more unhappy than ever. These two beautiful sisters—or Larry?

Cuddy stalked in with the tray and placed it on a table beside me. He waited.

"That will do, Cuddy."

He bowed and strode from the room, his very back accusing. Not so much as a glance had he cast at my two guests. I lifted the tray and set it on a table between them.

"Will you pour, Miss—Miss—"

Barby threw a quick, nervous glance at her sister and made no reply.

I hurried on, embarrassed, for I had not thought to secure their names by any such conventional subterfuge.

"Cuddy seems to have done himself proud. He was taking infinite pains."

Barbara arranged the cups. Overhead Cuddy trudged along the hall to the yellow room.

Willo refused the cup handed her, but her sister insisted, and she took it listlessly without raising her eyes. A deep silence fell over the room, while I stirred and stirred at the sugar in my cup.

"I'm so sorry." It gushed from Barby's lips. "We dragged you into this, but there seemed no other way. If you can keep us just to-night—that was so thoughtful of you." She regarded me anxiously over the rim of her cup. "No one saw you there. Please, please, keep out of it."

"But—but I saw—in that room—"

"Don't, don't!" The cup fell from Willo's hand with a crash, and she sank her face in one arm over the back of the chair. I swept the fragments out of sight with my foot under the tea-table.

"I'm sorry," I apologized. "I'll get a cup."

I hurried from the room. When I returned Willo's weeping had ceased. But her chin continued to quiver threateningly.

"I hope," I said, rising, when the sandwiches were gone, "you'll find your bed comfortable, more comfortable than this room. I never realized before what a bachelor's house must be to a lady. You see, I can't even imagine what a lady likes."

A fleeting smile crossed the older sister's face. "I'd risk it," she said. And I felt myself blushing.

When I escorted them to their room there was Cuddy, standing stiffly to attention outside the door. And once more I felt myself blushing. Cuddy, the chaperon.

Closing myself in the library, I called up Larry's rooms. But there was no response, and I sat down to consider the situation.

Only then, with nothing to do but think, did I realize the full horror and gravity of the night's events. Hitherto so much had intervened to distract my attention. But everything that had happened, I knew, hung on Vance Horton's dead body back there in his own billiard-room. That the focal-point, as well as the danger. After that? What but the murderer? A woman had screamed in that room—and here were two who had fled the scene in my car. And Larry, too, had been there. Larry, with those quick ears of his, had heard the flight of the two sisters as he stood holding me silent and helpless.

Theirs the terror of guilt, surely. But did that free Larry from suspicion? For Larry hated Vance even more than I, because he could hate harder.

And then my own peril occurred to me, all the greater that I felt compelled to shelter the other three. The whole city that knew us knew that Vance and I were not friends, that, indeed, we were open enemies. If the police knew that I could not deny being the first—after the murderer, of course—to see the dead body, where would I stand? There was, too, my duty as a citizen to tell what I knew. But in that case how could I explain my flight?

In desperation I tried once more to get in touch with Larry, only to meet the same silence as before. And just as the awful thought entered my head that, realizing his peril even more keenly than I, he might have fled my telephone rang. It was Larry.

"Thank God!" I breathed, as I recognized his voice. "I've been trying—"

"How's everyone?" he interrupted cheerily "Get 'em home all right?"

"What—what—do you—mean?"

"Your two guests, Dill. I hope they didn't frighten you."

"You knew?"

"And so I left them to you. I'm not a lady's man. But remember, I'm blind as a bat—about everything. And you, too, must be."

I had one question that would not wait. "Larry do you think they—they could have—"

"What do *you* think?" he broke in. "You've known them longer than I."

I<small>T</small> was the violent clanging of the knocker that wakened me next morning. And as my senses returned, I knew it had been weaving into my slumbers for several seconds. Surprised that Cuddy had not answered, I looked at my watch. Seven o'clock.

Slipping from the bed, I threw on slippers and gown, and hurried to the hall. As I opened the door Cuddy rushed past toward the stairs. I called to him, but he pretended not to hear.

And then, as I stood in the hall, depressed and uncomfortable and not long enough awake to understand the reason, the incidents of the previous evening flashed into my mind. And with the memory that impatient, mandatory clatter at the front door assumed a portentous significance. I leaned over the balustrade, steadying myself by the grip of my hands on the rail, conscious that a broken night's sleep had done nothing to prepare me for further trouble.

Cuddy had reached the door. I saw him straighten his shoulders and pull down his jacket. Which proved that Cuddy, too, was alarmed.

Then he turned the knob. Instantly the door flew open and three police officers pushed in.

I clung to the balustrade. My knees felt weak, my heart pounded painfully. In the yellow room beyond the hall slept two girls I had made up my mind to protect, whatever they had done to require it. And there below me was the very peril from which I must protect them. A momentary thought came to me of rushing back to warn them—of locking their door against the police, perhaps of letting them out of the window by the bedclothes. But could I move without those keen men below hearing me?

As I hesitated one of the officers—Inspector Emerson it was fired a question at Cuddy. Where was his master? To which Cuddy replied calmly that I was upstairs, probably still asleep.

"Get him," snapped the Inspector.

I knew Inspector Emerson. In a way we were friends, but I knew him best as a stickler for duty. Officially he knew no friend. To prove it, as Cuddy hesitated, he started up the stairs, brushing my servant aside.

As quietly as I could I turned toward the yellow room, but my foot caught a spindle of the balustrade. The Inspector lifted his head sharply.

"Oh, Mr. Fullerton!" He stood three steps from the bottom, holding my eye. "Shall we come up, or will you come down?"

My answer was to hurry down to him. Probably I hurried too much.

"I had no idea you kept such late hours," he said, eyeing my *négligé*.

"And I," I retorted, "had no idea you kept such early hours— for paying calls."

"It depends on conditions, Fullerton."

"And is this a condition," I asked, "to justify pushing your way into a private house at such an hour—or at any hour?"

"What do you think," he murmured, tilting his head and smiling. "Before you answer, let me tell you that your car was seen last night in the vicinity of a house where a murder was committed— at approximately the moment of the crime. Don't misunderstand. Perhaps you'll tell me where you were last night."

"*Certainly. At* The Silver Spoon."

"And *The Silver Spoon* was over at a quarter past eleven."

"Probably." I waited.

"You returned by Figmore Street."

"I believe I did." I wondered how long I could maintain the conversation at the level of question and answer. For I had a story, such a story, that I dare not tell.

"You would be near Vance Horton's house about—h'm— about eleven-thirty."

"Look here," I demanded, "what does it mean? Has something happened—this murder—at Vance Horton's?"

It was a futile assumption of innocence, with those two sisters trapped upstairs and unprepared, and I knew it. But I was too nervous to think clearly.

But Inspector Emerson showed no sign of suspicion. "Mr. Horton was murdered—found dead a few minutes after your car had passed. He was shot to death in his billiard-room."

"Vance Horton—shot! But—but—"

The Inspector looked away. "I wish to ask a few questions. Did you hear or see anything that might be of use to us in tracing the murderer?"

I considered. "One doesn't pass Vance Horton's house on the

night of one of his orgies without hearing a great deal. Last night was noisier than ever, a riot."

"You heard no shot?"

"No." It was fortunate that my reply came instantly, for the next moment some recess of memory opened. But I had not lied.

"Mr. Fullerton," formally the police officer, "I've an unpleasant duty to perform. I have a warrant to search your house."

"What for?" I tried to make it indignant, but it was not indignation that made me reach out to the newel-post to steady myself.

Inspector Emerson shrugged. "For anything. Please don't make this more unpleasant for both of us. Had my own brother been in your place last night it would be my duty to do the same to him."

"You think," I began hotly, "that because Vance Horton and I were not friendly—"

He stopped me with uplifted hand. "The less said about that the better. . . . Vance Horton had more enemies than friends, I believe. You needn't feel lonely."

Over the Inspector's shoulder I caught a glimpse of Cuddy's face, stiff and still. But as I looked one eyelid closed and opened. It was almost ludicrous in the formal, expressionless mask that served my servant as a face, and in my nervousness I could have laughed. Cuddy was trying to reassure me.

I stepped back against the wall. "Would you prefer to start at the garage or the basement?" I inquired sarcastically.

Inspector Emerson on duty was impervious to sarcasm. "With your permission we'll start upstairs." Clever fellow.

"Isn't it unusual to obtain a warrant to search the house of one who merely happened to be in the vicinity of a murder? I profess no grief at anything that might happen to Vance Horton, but, as you say, I needn't feel lonely about that. For years he's been hounding me. For years he's been digging his own grave. I only wonder—"

"Fullerton"—he laid a hand on my arm—"let's start, please."

He drew me gently toward the stairs. Cuddy stepped before us and climbed. He might have been showing the house to a prospective tenant—one he did not like.

"Stay here, Bullock," the Inspector ordered, addressing one of his companions. And at the head of the stairs: "You stay here, Rankin."

To my consternation Cuddy had turned along the hall toward the yellow room. The Inspector followed. I too, unstrung, helpless, furious. We reached the door, and Cuddy threw it open. I hastened up behind the Inspector, glaring at Cuddy as I passed.

The room was empty.

Not only empty but showing no sign of having been slept in. Somehow Cuddy had saved the situation. And then I knew why he had delayed so long answering the knocker.

Inspector Emerson glanced about. "Why," he asked, "did you bring me here?"

Cuddy replied stolidly, his gaze fixed on the wall above the Inspector's head: "Starting at the end, the most likely room."

The Inspector studied my servant for a moment and seemed about to speak, but his lips closed without a sound.

My confidence had returned. "May I ask again, Inspector, what you hope to find?"

"I hope to find nothing. . . . But a man has been murdered."

"Shot, you said. Did you find the gun?"

The quick glance he shot me warned me to be careful.

"No."

"The bullet, of course."

"Of course. It's in the body. Doctor Millbrook will deal with that."

Doctor Millbrook was the police surgeon, a quiet, retiring, studious man, with a wide local practice. But his reputation was based more on his uncanny work for the police. Though in manner—and, I believed, in inclination—unfitted for his official duties, his skill had solved many a crime. As a result his life had been attempted more than once, incidents that had done little more than provide the Doctor with a fund of chuckling stories, when he could be induced to talk.

"May I have the room to myself?" the Inspector demanded.

I had crossed to the dressing-table, foolishly reassured and somewhat reckless by the turn in events. Cuddy stood near me. I happened to glance at him, and I thought I caught a swift flash of alarm in his ugly face.

"Certainly," I said, and started for the door.

But Cuddy did not follow. Instead, he turned to the dressing-table and commenced to fuss with the cover and the accessories that lay on it. I saw him pick up a scrap of paper, crush it in his hand, and drop it carelessly in the waste-paper basket. Then he pivoted on his toes and marched after me.

In the privacy of the hall I studied his face, but Rankin was there at the head of the stairs, and I could not speak. Cuddy was nervous. We set off along the hall. I hoped to get him alone for an explanation. But as we passed the Policeman Rankin cleared his throat.

"The Inspector would wish you to stay here, sir," he said.

I seated myself. "So I'm a prisoner, am I?"

"Oh, no, sir. It's just the formalities; sometimes they're annoying."

Inspector Emerson appeared. I grinned into his face.

"You found the gun, of course? If you did, I'll pay you to keep on with that search warrant. You may find something valuable."

"You have no gun?" So far as the Inspector was concerned I had not spoken.

"Not that I know of. I took the house partly furnished—and I had no search warrant."

Again the Inspector ignored my insolence. "There are other bedrooms?"

"Of course. Just wander about and make yourself at home. I'll dress, if I may. If you feel like resting—the beds are comfortable, I believe." I turned my back on him and vanished into my bedroom.

To my surprise—and alarm—the search was completed in a few minutes, and the three officers trooped from the house. What, I asked myself, as I dressed, could they have been looking for? Except the girls? But then, how could they know of them? . . . How did they know of my car in Figmore Street? One answer would probably serve both questions.

Dressed, I hurried down to Cuddy. I remembered that I had heard nothing of him since he left me in the upper hall. Had he, disgusted with the events of the past eight hours, scandalized, too, by the presence of the police—had Cuddy taken flight? Old servants such as he have peculiar ideas of the respectability of their profession.

Softly I opened the pantry door. Mrs. Beaton was just entering the kitchen from the rear. But Cuddy?

Cuddy was there. He was seated in the pantry on the high stool he used for his work, his head dropped forward on his arms against the lower shelf of the china cupboard. My heart leaped into my mouth. Only a few hours before I had seen such another limp body.

"Cuddy! Cuddy!"

But Cuddy was not dead. With a jerk he was on his feet, standing to attention, ashamed, apologetic. But I saw then how heavy were his eyes, how haggard his face.

"Sorry, sir. I must—have dropped—asleep." With difficulty he controlled a yawn.

I drew him after me to the library and pressed him into an easy-chair.

"Cuddy, you ass, you weren't in bed last night."

Cuddy looked furtively about. "Are they gone, sir?" he whispered.

"Yes, it's all over."

With a bound he was on his feet, racing for the stairs.

After a moment of speechless surprise I plunged after him. But Cuddy twenty years my senior, was half-way to the hall above by the time I touched the first step.

"Cuddy! Cuddy! What the devil—!"

At the top of the stairs he turned and beckoned me to follow. But he had disappeared into the yellow room by the time I reached the upper floor. I hurried after him. In the middle of the room stood Cuddy, grinning as I had never seen him grin before, feet spread wide; and in one lifted hand he held a ruffled scrap of paper.

"He didn't find it, sir," he crowed.

I looked toward the waste-paper basket. The scrap Cuddy had carelessly thrown into it was no longer there. I took the paper from him and smoothed it out.

"So sorry," it read, "that we could not stop to thank you. You've done more for us than you can ever know. God bless you!"

It was signed "Barbara and Willo."

I looked at Cuddy, and his eyes fell before mine.

"Cuddy, you rascal, you knew they'd gone."

"I saw them go, sir. I was up all night, watching."

"Saw them go," I said, "and helped them go." I was inclined to be annoyed.

"Well, sir, it looked foolish to waken you. They—wished to leave. I didn't consider it my place to argue, sir . . . not when you had such confidence in them."

Clever Cuddy, faithful Cuddy. I took his arm, and side by side we returned along the hall. At the head of the stairs he tried to withdraw, but I drew him to his own room opened the door, and thrust him in.

"My breakfast is ready, Cuddy. Mrs. Beaton will serve lunch. If I see you before tea I'll fire you."

VI The Compact

But, even with Mrs. Beaton's best toast—on which she concentrated to convince me that Cuddy was not the only breakfast cook in the world—I was worried. I even forgot to exult at my escape from a major calamity. For I had an idea that Cuddy had not only watched the two girls leave the house, had helped them, but had even urged them to go. And, though to that alone I owed my escape, I felt that my servant was overacting the part of chaperon.

Worst of all, they had gone without leaving an address. Indeed, I did not even know their last name. Not having seen them before, it was part of my folly concerning them that I concluded they were new to the city.

I bit savagely into the last slice of toast. They hadn't beaten me yet.

I had just risen from the table when the knocker sounded again, a familiar tat-tat, and a few moments later Larry and I were seated in the library comparing notes. I had welcomed him with open arms, but Larry had not so much as smiled.

"Why the blazes," I demanded, fighting the foreboding his gravity roused in me, "didn't you come last night?"

"You had your hands full without me." There was a suggestion of a smile on his bronzed face. Then, soberly: "I want to keep out of this."

Again that wave of foreboding washing over me. "Where were you?"

"With the corpse."

I stared at him; but there was no flippancy in his face. "You mean you—you went back to Vance's house?"

"Certainly. It seemed wise. I waited till the police showed up, and then I strolled in on them. You see, Dill, you and I have to walk a narrow plank . . . and I want to know where the edges are—and every knot and splinter."

"You and I!" I laughed harshly. "Why bring *me* in?" And with a gush: "My God, Larry, it's awful!"

He leaned forward to peer into my face. "Don't you think we'd better change the conversation, old thing?"

"How can we?" I groaned

Larry leisurely struck a match and helped himself to my

cigarettes.

"All right, Dill; but leave *me* out—for the time being. . . You know that nothing so promising to your future ever happened to you. We both hated him and he us . . . but he didn't really matter to me, one way or the other. And so," puffing a long spiral of smoke, "and so you and I have a task before us."

"You bet we have."

He nodded. "You and I, Dill, have to find the murderer of Vance Horton."

"But, Larry, we—we—"

He glowered at me through the smoke. "We nothing. You and I, I said, have to find the murderer of Vance Horton. Now, tell me what happened here. I saw the police leave. I'd have come in sooner, but I wanted to make sure they'd left no guard. Did they find the girls?"

I told him the whole story. At the end he sat for a long time with shaking head.

"Who the devil saw us in Figmore Street?"

"Emerson didn't say. He seems to know only that my car passed at that time."

"Emerson is sly, Dill. He doesn't tell all he knows. Better get your affairs in shape for sudden flight."

"Damn it!" I exploded. "You don't think I'm going to skip out—as if I were the murderer?"

"There are a number who may. A bold front isn't innocence, not in this case. . . . And I might do better without you . . . if they suspect you."

"What about you?" I demanded. "You were there—right there at the billiard-room when—"

Larry said calmly: "They seem to know nothing about me yet. I could hardly afford to give you the alibi you need. Dill, they're spreading a wide net. I'll be surprised if Scotland Yard isn't called in."

"Do you think they know of the girls?" I asked.

"We'd only be guessing if we answered that. Besides—"

"But, Larry, isn't it silly to go about pretending to look for the murderer when we know—about the girls?"

He frowned at me. "We know nothing about the girls. . . . And we're not pretending. Do you find it so impossible, Dill, to imagine those beautiful girls there only by accident—like ourselves?"

"If you'd seen their eyes, Larry!" I moaned. "If you knew their terror, the horror—both of them—"

"They saw a corpse, as you did."

"But they ran away."

"So did we."

I drew a long, strengthening breath. "Larry, it was Willo who screamed."

"So would you—if you hadn't been too frightened. You felt too guilty to scream. But how do you know it was she we heard?"

"I know it, Larry."

"Did she scream for you again?" he asked.

I ignored it. "If they told me themselves that they shot Vance Horton I would not believe it."

Larry clapped me on the knee and grinned. "That's the spirit. Blind and deaf—nothing like love to induce such afflictions."

"Don't be more foolish than you can avoid," I replied shortly, feeling myself blush.

But Larry had no eyes for me. He rose to pace the room, flicking ashes from his cigarette as he walked. He whistled tunelessly.

"Dill, if it was Barbara or Willo who shot Vance it would be too easy, much too easy . . . and much too silly and hopeless. . . . Because in the murder of Vance Horton there's a real mystery. You see, I was there for the preliminary investigation. And do you know how many potential murderers were in that house last night—can you guess? *Just—as many—as there were guests!* Every one of that rowdy crowd seemed to have reason to hate him. Vance was like that, as we know. His friends were his worst enemies. . . . And now it's his *open* enemies—you and I—who must find who murdered him. We must, in self-defence."

I asked: "What if the police find out you were there last night—there right near the billiard-room?"

Larry blew a funnel of smoke toward the ceiling. "I've been thinking of that. It's why I'm here. . . . Had the occasion seemed propitious last night, as I stood there beside the body in that billiard-room, I'd have told all I know. It wouldn't have sounded so convicting, I'm thinking—returning from the theatre—the disturbance in Vance's house—my curiosity—all that. But the longer I listened to what was said the more inopportune it seemed. It wasn't the time to talk, for, Dill, there wasn't a clue, not one. And, of course, I had no idea the police knew you were there."

He took a turn the length of the room.

"Did I say no clue? There were too many clues; that was the trouble. . . . And I can't deny that the one there would have been against us would have topped them all. I didn't see the point in providing it. Dill, you and I walk—well, I said a narrow plank, but it's narrower than that. First of all, we can't even admit we saw a corpse. To have seen it and run away—well, what would *you* think? I'd just as soon not face a jury with that to answer for."

"And next, we must protect Barbara and Willo," I put in.

Larry turned to glance quizzically over his shoulder at me.

"I try to think I'm a gentleman," I declared indignantly. "I wouldn't give up a dog that took refuge with me."

"That's fine." Larry rubbed his hands together. "Then you'll guard with your dying breath that I was there?"

"I'd take my oath you weren't."

"H'm—I don't know that even I am as good a liar as that . . . if they ask me about you."

Larry narrated in detail the scene in the billiard-room after the police arrived. He told the story with many long, thoughtful pauses, as if in the telling new glints of light filtered through the dark confusion of denials and evasions.

He had lingered in a doorway until the police car rushed up, and then he had gone in. Larry stood in well with the police, having shown more than once that his amateur interest in crime was something more than critical of official aptitude.

"What puzzles me," I said, "is who called the police. That drunken gang was too intent on itself to know what happened in the billiard-room."

"That," said Larry, "is the impression they all tried to give. . . . Answer your question by asking who told the police your car was there. . . . So far as you and I are concerned that's the puzzle we must solve; it's as important as the murderer himself."

"Probably one and the same," I suggested.

"Probably you're right . . . But I've an idea, from the questioning last night, that there were many in that crowd none too drunk to pull a trigger—not too drunk to wish it. . . . But we mustn't let ourselves be side-tracked."

Was Larry trying to get something across to me, to take my mind from his own position at the time of the murder? I dare not look at him.

"I don't believe," I said, "either of us is concerned in the murder of Vance Horton, except to clear ourselves."

"And isn't that enough?" he shot back.

He studied me for a long moment through half-closed eyes.

"Dill Fullerton, I've an idea that when we come to the end of the trail there are going to be surprises."

As Larry pictured it, with all his Celtic sense of drama, it must have been a tense scene in the billiard-room after the police arrived.

They had entered directly through the open French window and until the preliminary investigation was finished none in the house knew of their presence. All the time the music and laughter continued, a hideous, shocking incongruity.

So far as Larry could see Inspector Emerson found no real clue. Vance had been shot through the heart, and the bullet was still in the body. Doctor Millbrook and the finger-print expert had been called immediately, but there was nothing for a doctor to do but to pronounce the victim dead. The finger-print man had not told what he found, though Larry thought he looked unsatisfied.

Then one by one the guests were brought into the billiard-room and faced with the dead body.

There followed a couple of hours of confusion. Not one of the guests was too drunk to realize what had happened, and the effect of that recumbent, lifeless body, with the blood-stained shirt (coat and waistcoat had been removed by the Doctor for the examination) was varied. Most of the men had been grim about it, frightened by the accusing murder, a few defiant, not one indignant at the questions Inspector Emerson fired at them. Two of the women had fainted, three or four had attempted hysterics, only to be brought up sharply by an unsympathetic officer and a few had attempted defiance and cold indifference.

"It was when they came to answer questions," said Larry, "that they gave themselves away. They hated Vance Horton to a man. It required no detective to deduce that. And their hatred accused them. . . . And so they muddied the water, confused the trail. Dill, there wasn't a clear conscience among them."

He paused for a moment with shaking head.

"The men? Well, you know why Jordan Fleming would have given his right hand to have Vance out of the way."

My heart gave a leap. For my memory had gone back to our game of golf the day before. "Jordan Fleming? My God, Larry, that golf game! I beat him—easily. He—"

"That's scarcely an alibi, Dill."

"An alibi? It's the opposite. All through the game Jordan had something on his mind, something important something desperate—"

"Just because," said Larry sharply, "Nora Fleming's been seeing too much of Vance Horton of late you can't call her husband a murderer."

I shook my head sadly. "You don't know it all, Larry, two days ago Jordan got me to start divorce proceedings"

Larry whistled shrilly. "Jordan—seeking—a divorce! He leaned eagerly toward me. "Has it gone too far to keep it secret?"

"I don't know. It depends—"

"It's not for Jordan's sake," Larry broke in. "It's for Nora.

Nora, too, was there."

"I don't see how—"

"Dill, Nora Fleming's madly in love with her husband, as madly in love as the day they married. All this philandering with Vance Horton was nothing but protest at the way Jordan's been neglecting her for business. She may be feather-brained, but that doesn't lessen her capacity for love, her need of loving. It only explains the limit of her allowance for Jordan's business worries."

"I still don't see the connection," I said.

"Only this: If I were asked to pick the murderer from last night's evidence I'd say Nora Fleming killed Vance Horton. . . . And don't think Inspector Emerson hasn't his eyes open. Absurd? Not a bit of it. Nora must have known of Jordan's plan to divorce her, and the one way out would be—well, you see?"

"And still absurd," I contended; but it failed to convince even myself.

"Jack Ponting, too, was there."

I forgot the Flemings. Here was something I could understand—revenge, security—a wife and four small children to keep from the poor-house. There was a time when Vance had an ambition to become a playwright. He had written a play, and, after several refusals from managers, he had set about producing it himself. It cost a lot of money, but after a week—with Jack Ponting's two line review in *The Planet*—it had died of inanition. For Jack had simply written: "Vance Horton's venture into the realms of art is what one might expect from Vance Horton."

Vance did not have to wait long for his revenge. A friend of the more or less disreputable owner of *The Planet,* he had had Ponting turned into the street.

But Vance was still unsatisfied. When Jack got on with *The Guardian* Vance had quietly set to work to obtain control of the stock. And only a week ago he had boasted openly that Jack's number was up. And Jack loved his family.

"Jack Ponting," I defended stoutly, "would never do a thing like that."

Larry only smiled. "The fidelity of friendship never cleared a guilty man yet. Not one of Vance's guests last night but could produce a hundred friends as loyal as you." He eyed me under his brows. "You'd even swear *I'm* incapable of it, wouldn't you, Dill?

Though, after last night—" He shrugged his wide shoulders. "Oh, well! You'd have to be there with me at that investigation to realize the horde of enemies Vance had. Had he planned to get even with them he couldn't have done it so effectively in one stroke in any other way as by inviting them to a feast and committing suicide in the midst of it."

"You don't think he'd do that?"

"Not Vance. He was murdered. . . . The parade continues: Effie Shannon. Even Inspector Emerson must be aware of how Vance has treated her. Effie hated Vance too thoroughly to hide it last night even from the Inspector. . . . Then after her came a long line of discarded flames of Vance's, jealous, still hopeful—each murderous with her hopes killed. You know the proverb of a woman scorned.

"Vance had gone even to London to round them up—these enemies of his. They were the drunkest, men and women . . . and the most incapable, mentally and physically, of committing a crime like that. . . . And there was—you'd never guess—Peter Davenport!"

"Peter Davenport!"

I found it hard to believe. Six months before Sally Davenport, Peter's sister, the prettiest girl in the city, many of us thought, had disappeared. And all her friends—and Vances—knew why. Except in whispers no one mentioned her name. Then, two weeks ago had come word of her death—in Belgium somewhere, it was said.

"Larry," I said impressively, "there's something wrong there. It's only a week since Peter horsewhipped Vance openly in the street. And you and I know Vance escaped something worse only by running away. Peter has sworn to get him. If Peter was Vance's guest last night—oh, it's all mixed up, Larry. It's uncanny, a nightmare."

"That's what I've been thinking—a nightmare. . . . The only difference is that the horror remains after the awakening. . . . Something odd about the way Inspector Emerson handled Peter, too—just a question or two—unimportant—then he let him go. I don't like it; it worries me."

I said: "If Peter did it I'll lead the cheering."

"At the hanging?" He saw me shudder and went on: "Peter did his best to get himself into trouble. He was defiant and rude to the Inspector."

"Perhaps he was sore that someone got ahead of him."

"That's worth a thought, too," mused Larry . . . "After him

came Lee Moshier."

"The one exception," I said, "to the list of enemies. Vance's death will leave Lee out in the cold. How'll he live now? And a damned luxurious living it was!"

To my surprise Larry shook his head. At Cortwright Lee had been Vance's bodyguard, an evil sycophant. And he had never relinquished the post. He was Vance's companion in his most disgusting dissipations, a goad to further excesses. Poor, he had lived on Vance and for him.

"Then," said Larry, "you're not up to date. For months Vance has been cutting down on Lee. Indeed, a few know he was about to kick him out—and Lee was one who knew it. Of all that miserable crowd he was the most uneasy. At first he feigned drunkenness, but Inspector Emerson is too old a hand for that. He ordered him to the police station—and Lee sobered at the shock of it. . . . He cringed when the Inspector charged him with forging two large cheques in Vance's name. It seems that Vance discovered it only a few days ago; he was still undecided whether to prosecute or not. But the Inspector had the cheques on him; he flashed them before Lee's frightened eyes. . . . I'm wondering if Vance hadn't it in mind, as one of the refinements of his cruelty, to have Lee arrested right there before the whole crowd."

"It would be like him," I said. "Did they find the gun?"

Larry did not answer. His eyes were fixed blankly on the carpet at his feet. I repeated the question, and he looked up quickly.

"Strange that, too," he murmured.

"What's strange?"

"That we heard no shot. Can it be that Vance was not murdered when we thought he was? It's impossible to tell to the minute from the body—"

"But I did hear the shot, Larry."

He furrowed his brows at me. "You heard it?"

"I heard it without noticing it in the excitement of that scream of terror. It just came to me when Inspector Emerson asked about it— one of those freaks of memory—a flash that returns days afterwards sometimes, brought to the surface of memory by some inadvertent word or incident. We not infrequently come across it in court."

"But I didn't hear it."

"You were too near the other noises. They drowned

everything else out in your ears. Besides, some sounds carry farther than others, though they may not be so loud close by."

Larry glowered at the carpet. "That—makes it—nasty."

Again that dreadful thought swept over me "I didn't tell the police," I assured him hastily.

"It's not that, Dill. I was hoping—for a way out—for them."

"Who are you talking about?"

"The two girls, the two pretty sisters who spent the night with you." He stopped my indignant protest. "You were right, Dill. It was one of those girls who screamed. And the scream came from the billiard-room."

I felt sick. "Perhaps—perhaps we're mistaken."

"Don't you see what it means, Dill? Either they shot him, or they saw who did it."

"Did anyone—mention them last night?" I asked.

He shook his head. "That's what I don't understand."

"I don't," I declared, "believe they were in that gang at all. They're not that kind."

"Then why were they there?"

"I don't know. . . . I'll ask them."

"So you *do* know where they live?"

"No. But we'll meet again. I know we will."

Larry laughed. "You're determined to make your life uncomfortable, aren't you, old chap?"

We sat for a long time smoking in silence. Larry had crushed out his third cigarette, when I asked:

"By the way, what did they find in that drawer?"

"What drawer?"

"The drawer in the little table. It was open a few inches, as if he'd been putting something in or taking it out."

Larry stared at me with the oddest expression on his face.

"Hold on, Dill. Let's have it again—and think, think hard. You say there was a drawer in a table—you mean the little one to the left of the window, I suppose—and that it was open?"

"Why, yes, of course."

"But, Dill, there was no drawer in that table."

I let my mind run back to the scene. "I tell you there was. I'm positive. I remember it distinctly. It seemed even then to have something to do with the crime. It was the only small table I saw."

Larry lunged to his feet and commenced to pace the room, whistling dismally. Suddenly he spun about and faced me.

"Are you game, Dill, for a bit of private research?"

"I thought that was what we had in mind. We're going to find—someone to blame the murder on." I said it defiantly, but he seemed not to notice.

"But this is real adventure—with a spice of danger thrown in."

"I'm game for anything that will clear my head of a lot of horrible suspicions."

"Never mind your head," he laughed, and his eyes danced with excitement, "except what the law will do with it if we're out of luck."

I rose. "Going now?"

"No, not now. This little adventure requires the cloak of darkness. But if you are dying for action—h'm—how would you like to pay your respects to an old friend?"

The "old friend" was Vance Horton. I knew it only when we drew up before the mortuary. Knew it so uncomfortably, so disgustedly, that for a time I refused to leave the car. But, as usual, Larry had his way with me.

When we reached the door, however, our way was blocked by a big policeman—Rankin.

"You can't go in now. Doctor Millbrook's in there."

"The autopsy?"

"The post-mortem, sir. Muckin' about, I call it."

"By jove, Rankin," said Larry enthusiastically, "that's just where I'd like to be. I'm a prize mucker."

"Maybe, but it's against the rules, sir."

"Thank God!" I breathed. "Now and then a rule shows sense—if you don't, Larry."

We walked about in the corridor outside. Twice I silenced Larry's desecrating whistle, and once Rankin himself coughed suggestively into his hand when Larry forgot.

"It isn't *our* funeral, you know, Rankin," said Larry. He added to me, out of Rankin's hearing: "And I don't feel a bit solemn."

"Ever see an autopsy—a post-mortem, Rankin?" he asked.

"Never lasted one through," replied the policeman, with a wry face. "I looked in there once," jerking his thumb over his shoulder. "Muckin', I call it, fair muckin'." He cheered up and grinned. "The only one I lasted through was the one the doctors did on me after an East End riot two years ago. Pretty bad it was—but it wasn't nothin' compared with this in here." He shivered and hugged his arms together.

And just then the door behind him opened and Doctor Millbrook hurried out. He was white and shaken, and his hair hung wildly beneath his stiff hat. His lips worked oddly, as if he might be sick with little effort. In his hand he carried a small black bag, holding it away from him, almost as if it smelled.

It was a surprise to me—Doctor Millbrook, a well-known surgeon, unnerved by an autopsy! My surprise was no greater than his when he saw us. He pulled up sharply, and a stiff smile wrinkled the corners of his eyes behind his glasses and twisted his lips.

"Hello, Rockford! How do, Fullerton? Doing the vulture act,

eh?" His lips smiled, but his tone was full of disgust. "You're welcome to it—if only you'd take it off my hands. It's beastly. Ugh! I hate it."

I said: "One would expect you to get hardened to it."

"Never. In my college days it threatened to put me down. Oh, those dead bodies! A live body, now, with promise of new strength, new health, with flesh throbbing under the knife—that's different. I can wade through that and not turn a hair. See me now."

He set down the bag, and with a whimsical smile swept off his hat and mopped his face with a handkerchief. "After the bullet, I suppose?" asked Larry.

"Chased it all over the place. The damned thing turned downward—Heaven alone knows why, for it missed the front ribs— and lodged up against one at the back. I had to go in from the front, of course. An awful mess."

"You got it?"

"Of course. That was my job. Did you think he'd digest it? Here it is."

He opened the bag and took from it an envelope. From the envelope he dropped in his other hand a misshapen piece of lead that bore little resemblance to a bullet. He held it out to Larry.

"A .25 automatic, I should say, though it might almost be anything from the shape it is now. I'll check up at the lab." He bent over it. "Think I can make out the six grooves right now."

Larry took it in his hand. Doctor Millbrook watched his face eagerly.

"I'm curious about that bit of lead, boys. Something about it . . . or is it the general mystery of the murder colouring my reflections? What do you see, Rockford?"

"It certainly got itself into a jam," said Larry.

The Doctor nodded. "Yes, and how the devil did it manage it? I never knew a rib before to mushroom a bullet so completely, especially with the rib itself scarcely marked. See here." He reached into the bag.

I stopped him. "I'll take your word for the rib, Doctor. I usually eat in an hour or so—and I enjoy my meals."

The Doctor grinned. "You should have my job—and save on your board. You see, one would naturally think that, if the bullet failed to shatter the rib, it must have lost all its force passing through the body. Then how did it mushroom like that? It's not soft-nose, either."

He returned the envelope to the bag and sighed. "Well, that's where my job ends, thank goodness. I found it. Ballistics always interested me. That's why this has me guessing. It's why I work with the police. You see, I like to follow the bullet from the gun—yes, from the very mind of the man who pulls the trigger—to where its force is spent. And it doesn't need to be Exhibit A to interest me."

He picked up the bag.

"I envy you your job, Doctor," said Larry.

"Do you, now?" The Doctor beamed. "Say, if you're interested, you boys, drop around this evening to my house. My lab's there. I'm going to work on that bullet to-night. All the same," as he started away, "it's a beastly job." With a shudder he left us.

We watched him go, his short, quick, sturdy strides carrying him swiftly to his car. Larry remained so long that I touched his arm.

"There, Dill," said he, "goes the ace card of the police game. Without him and his skill in cases like this they'd play deuces. God, what an interesting job!"

"If you asked me," I replied, "he'd willingly hand over parts of it. Post-mortems—br-r-r!"

Larry laughed. "Something granitic must have been inserted in me for a heart, I guess. But a corpse—well, it's just a corpse. Now let's go in and see the job that shocked him so."

He took my arm, but I held back. "You cold-blooded brute! Go on, if you must. I'm staying right here."

"You're not much help as a detective, are you, Dill?" He sighed extravagantly.

"I leave the muckin' to you," I said.

He must have been gone twenty minutes. When he returned he looked little happier than the Doctor.

"Have a nice gory time?" I jeered.

He shook his shoulders. "Doctor Millbrook was right. These carvings would take the cream from the job. . . . And what a carving it was! They'll almost have to shovel him into a coffin."

I said: "I'd hate to see you less affected than a police surgeon."

"But, Dill, Doctor Millbrook's an unusual chap. I've heard that the police think him too soft-hearted for the job."

"And that," I maintained, "stands to his credit. Now, what good did it do you to muck about in there?"

He did not reply for some seconds. "One never knows. . . . Oh, yes, Dill. You and I had better get rid of any .25's we have."

"Never owned a gun in my life—a revolver or automatic, I mean."

"The usual story—after a murder. I'm just warning you."

I laughed scornfully. "The police have nothing on me. At the time Vance Horton was murdered you can swear I was—" I stopped in some confusion.

Larry chuckled. "Exactly. Those unfinished sentences! The rare occasions when that ponderous mind of yours gets to work! At the time Vance Horton was murdered you and I were—there at his house, there at the billiard-room where he was shot—and a window was open. The police know some of it, at least. But how much? The last you saw of me—before the murder, I mean—I was pushing my way through the hedge toward that billiard-room. The last I saw of you—well, you might have got anywhere by the time Willo screamed. I thought you understood this act we're putting on is safety-first. Then, there's the fair Willo—and the dark Barbara. Oh, well! Now to lunch. And we've a full day before us."

I inquired his plans.

"I'm curious about Peter Davenport. I'm more than curious— I'm concerned. Peter's a reckless young fool, reckless enough to run his head into a noose. . . . Peter wouldn't look well in a necktie like that."

We lunched at the Ardmore. We took our time at it.

Peter was an executive in his father's department store and would probably take a couple of hours at lunch. Larry was unusually silent as he ate, and afterwards he sat smoking fitfully. That he had something in his mind he did not wish to discuss with me did nothing to ease my discomfort when, as frequently happened in spite of myself, my thoughts came round to Larry's position.

At last some of it came out:

"I can't get that mess at the mortuary out of my mind, Dill. Not that it ruined my appetite, as you see, but imagine a jury being forced to view that body as it is now! What would it tell them? Only that the autopsy had been effectively carried through."

"Doctor Millbrook will fill in the rest," I said.

"But my conception of a jury's duty, at least in viewing a corpse, is wider than to hear what someone else saw in it."

I made a sound of disgust. "Everyone knows that the mind of a jury is the one natural vacuum known to man. Imagine a few farmers, and clerks, and mechanics being asked to decide life or death on the technicalities of the average case!" I glanced at the clock over the cash-desk. "Peter should be in his office by this time."

We passed out into the street. And one of the surprises of the day was Larry's absent-minded indifference to who paid the bill. I paid and followed him out. He was trudging along, whistling dismally, as if he had forgotten my existence. I overtook him and fell into step. I was thinking of Peter Davenport. Peter was, as Larry had said, so reckless. He was also hot-tempered, and to face him on the day following a murder of which he might well be suspected was not my idea of a good time.

Larry had parked his car around the corner, and we decided to walk to Peter's office. As we reached the corner a car slid up to the curb at my side with a shrieking of tyres, and Jordan Fleming leaped out and clutched me by the arm.

He was breathless, his face alight, his eyes so wide and bright that for a moment or two I thought he must have been drinking. Drawing me away from Larry, he said—and his voice rang exultantly as he spoke:

"Dill, you loafer, I've been looking for you. Call off the divorce."

I shrank away from him. My mind had raced, with amazing swiftness and lucidity, to the inferences. I could say nothing. He shook me almost angrily.

"Do you hear? I said to stop divorce proceedings."

"But—but, Jordan—"

"Hell! there aren't any 'buts.' It's off, I tell you. Nora and I, we're—well, we don't want to be divorced."

I looked sternly into his flashing eyes. "You mean, after what happened last night."

"I mean," he said, suddenly grim, "there's going to be no divorce—and it's none of your damned business why!"

But I could be as grim as he. "It suits me," I said. "I'm going to be busy. Larry and I are out to find the murderer of Vance Horton."

He had turned to leave me, but my tone broke through his

exultation. And at the end he whirled on me, his face crimson with anger. But Larry strolled between us, whistling carelessly. And Jordan, after one quick, half angry, half fearful look from Larry to me, dashed away and climbed into his car.

I turned to Larry. His head was shaking ominously.

"Bad business, Dill."

"Oh, shut up! Jordan Fleming couldn't be guilty of a crime like that."

"I meant bad for *your* business," said Larry. He whistled for a few steps as we passed along. "All right, have it your own way. Say Jordan didn't do it. What about Nora? A woman can pull a trigger as well as a man. . . . I wonder what the police will think when they know of this."

IX   A Fruitless Interview

At the Davenport Department Store Larry and I were shown into a long room where four more or less pretty girls were at work. Two typed steadily and rapidly, not so much as looking up as we entered. The other two bent over steel files ranged along three of the walls. The rear wall was broken by several glass doors bearing the names of store officials.

The girl at the nearest typewriter finally raised her eyes, and Larry asked for Peter.

"He's not in." She looked at a clock on a pillar beyond the low glass partition about the room. "He should be back at any moment. Please sit down."

We had been seated only a few seconds when a large man of about sixty-five entered. He bustled in, his aggressive manner accentuated by heavy, unkempt eyebrows and bristly iron-grey hair. Larry and I knew Peter Davenport's father by sight. He planted himself before us.

"Who'd you wish to see?" he growled.

Larry told him.

"My son is very busy to-day. Besides, he may not be in. I don't think he can see you."

All the time his keen eyes bored into us, and at the end he turned, as if to pass on, with a movement so expressive of dismissal that involuntarily I rose. But Larry did not move.

"We'll wait—if we may," he said with an innocent smile.

Instead of going on to his office Mr. Davenport wheeled about and passed back out to the store.

Larry shook his head dubiously. "At least he couldn't say Peter's dead. . . . I'm afraid we'll wait a long time, Dill. Daddy doesn't intend Peter to get himself into more trouble this day."

I pointed to a door that bore Peter's name. "Then he can't get back to his work. He has to pass here."

"Yes . . . yes," Larry agreed. "And we must fortify our courage and patience by the altruistic thought that it's for Peter's sake. Not," he added, "that I hope to convince him of that. Is it permitted to smoke?" he inquired of the nearest clerk.

She smiled apologetically. "I'm afraid not. Mr. Davenport doesn't like it. We don't sell tobacco or playing-cards. But," glancing about to see that no one else was within hearing, "if you require anything in the way of bridge prizes, or score-pads, or cigarette cases, or lighters, or ash-trays, or—"

"Sh-sh!" Larry hissed the warning from the corner of his mouth. Then to me, intent on the back of one hand: "Talk, you duffer, say something."

I contrived a remark about the steel files, pointing to them as I spoke.

"Peter," said Larry, in a low voice, following brightly my pointing finger, "has just looked us over from the outside through the glass. Poor Peter!"

Evidently Peter accepted the situation, for a few moments later he stormed in on us. Planting himself before Larry, his face a thunder-cloud, he jerked out a single word.

"Well?"

Larry's face was a picture of geniality.

"How're you, Peter? Got over the affair last night yet?" The smile remained, but it was fixed and meaning, as he looked straight into Peter's angry eyes. "Got a minute to spare?"

Peter hesitated. Then, jerking himself about, he made for the door that bore his name. Larry was close behind him, though I never saw a franker dismissal. Peter opened the door and stood aside.

"Come in."

The door closed behind us with a slam that convinced me my reading of Peter's manner had been correct. But Larry had taken the bold course, and Peter dare not openly rebel.

"Never in here before, Peter," Larry drawled, looking about. "Real business place."

"You bet it is," said Peter, dropping with a thud in the chair behind a flat-topped desk and leaning his arms on it to glare at us. "Well?" he demanded.

Larry lounged himself into a chair and held out his cigarette case. But Peter almost struck it aside.

Larry smiled. "Ah, yes, I forgot." He returned the case to his pocket. "You're a busy man, aren't you, Peter?"

Peter half rose from his chair. "Look here, Larry, what the hell—"

"At least, Dill," said Larry, in his laziest tones, "they don't permit *smoking* in the store. All right, Peter. We just came to tell you that you need us."

"Need you? Like hell I do! I saw you snooping about there last night, Larry Rockford, keeping your ears open. You're the last man on earth I need, the last I wish to see."

"Naturally," agreed Larry. "Except, of course, the police." As Peter's face paled a little Larry went on: "Yes, you saw me. But you didn't see the others who were brought in like yourself to be questioned. I was there through the whole performance. And so, Peter, I repeat: 'You need us.' I think we can be of service to you."

His voice had grown gentler, more friendly, at the last. And Peter, his armour of fear and anger pierced, sank slowly back in the chair and eyed us beneath his brows.

"I don't see—what you can do," he murmured. The sound of his own submissiveness must have shocked him, for he stiffened. His face twisted to a contemptuous smile. "You can be of service, you say. On what terms?"

Indignant, I made as if to rise, but Larry held me back.

"The only terms, Peter," he said, "are that you accept our services. You haven't a thing we want. You haven't enough to buy what we plan to do for you."

"And what is that?" asked Peter, struggling vainly to maintain his independence.

"Dill and I are going to find who murdered Vance Horton."

For a long moment a heavy silence fell over the room, broken only by the tap of the typewriters beyond the door.

"Amateur detectives, eh?" Peter tried to sneer, but it was badly done. "And what do you think the police are for?"

"To report our discoveries to," answered Larry calmly.

"But what can you do?"

"We have—certain information not yet available to the police."

Peter had dropped his eyes to the desk, where one hand moved restlessly among the papers.

"What is it you want of me?" he asked warily.

"The truth."

"What can I tell you—more than what you heard last night? You saw," vehemently, "what a fool I made of myself before Inspector Emerson. All I cared was that Vance Horton was dead—dead!" His voice rose, his eyes blazed. "I wanted to cheer—except that I'd rather have done it myself. Where's the God who let him live so long?"

A shudder ran through his big frame, and his fists clenched on the desk.

"Don't you think the Inspector let me off easily, Larry, considering how I showed my elation?"

"Too easily, suspiciously easily."

Peter's eyes widened. "What do you mean?"

"Not quite what you think. Does anyone think Inspector Emerson a fool? If you'd been in my place you'd feel less satisfied. I saw how he treated the others." Larry stopped, waiting for Peter to speak.

"Go on." No anger now, no defiance—no satisfaction.

"I intend to. Don't imagine Inspector Emerson is unaware of what you felt for Vance, and why. Just bear that in mind, Peter—and ask yourself why he would be so easy on you. . . . He didn't even inquire how you came to be a guest of a man you'd sworn to get."

"I wasn't a guest," said Peter. "I wasn't invited."

Larry whistled softly. "Then how the devil—"

"Listen, Larry." He leaned his arms on the desk, his hands clenched together, his eyes boring into us, appealing. "All right, boys, I'm going to talk. I'll take you at your word. I've a knack for getting myself into a mess, and this time I excelled myself. . . . To all intents and purposes I killed Vance Horton."

Larry, I could see, was by this time as confused as I. Peter smiled wanly.

"No, I was not invited. I invited myself. This—all this—that everyone knows—about Vance, I mean, and—and why I swore to get him—it's hung over me all these months till I can't sleep, can't eat, can't work. For months I could think of nothing but that smirking fiend playing his way through life, trampling everything decent under his brutal feet. And hell was too distant to punish him adequately."

He drew a long breath to steady himself and his working hands.

"You don't know that yesterday he met me on the street and smiled—smiled straight into my face. If he hadn't been in his car I'd have torn him to pieces there and then with these hands. . . . I couldn't stand it." A sob shook his body, and he raised a hand to conceal his wet eyes. "I suppose I went temporarily insane. I went straight home and tried to drink myself stupid, but all it did was to further inflame me. I knew of that party last night. I think it was Effie Shannon told me. She was going. That was the last straw: Effie—Vance's guest, after the way he treated her! Vance was never to suffer for his crimes. I put my gun in my pocket and, in the height of the revelry, walked into that house."

"You were going—deliberately—to kill him?" I questioned.

"Deliberately to kill him," Peter repeated coldly.

"The gun—it was a .25 automatic," said Larry casually.

This was a mistake, for Peter Davenport's eyes narrowed.

"Have I talked too much?" he asked, through tight teeth. "Have I made an ass of myself once more?"

Larry replied: "Not in what you've told us but in what you haven't. Never mind the gun."

"Did they find it?" Peter inquired anxiously.

"No."

"And Vance let you in?" I puzzled.

"Vance didn't see me. He was not in the rooms with the crowd. I searched for him. Most of the guests were too drunk to notice me, but two or three recognized me and were frightened, I think. I suppose I looked the murderer I planned to be. I was going to shoot him down, right there among his drunken friends—to drive home to them the fiend he was. . . . It might have done them good, though I didn't think of that."

"Who saw you?" asked Larry.

"Jack Ponting was one. He didn't seem to be drunk, not so drunk as the others. Jack, I believe, was acting a part. He started for me, as if to say something, but I plunged on to another room."

He stopped there, and his hands shook spasmodically.

I said: "And you found Vance—in the billiard-room."

"Yes," he murmured, "I found him—in the billiard-room."

I glanced triumphantly at Larry.

But Larry only smiled—not at me but across the desk at Peter. "You found him, Peter—but—you did not kill him."

Peter started, as if he had forgotten our presence through those tense moments of memory.

"Thank you. . . . Yes, I found Vance in the billiard-room. But I did not go in. I had reached the door when I heard his voice. He was saying, in that sneering tone of his: 'And so you think you can tell me what I should do.' And then someone hushed him, and I heard no more.

"I might have shot him then and there, but that would not have satisfied me. Nothing but a crowd, standing agape about us, would do that. I turned away and walked to the other end of the hall. You've been there; you know how long that hall is. And between me and the billiard-room were two rooms of rioters; and from upstairs more noise swept down about me. Things were at their noisiest then. I stood there. I had a vision of Vance coming out—of me walking straight toward him along that length of hall—Nemesis, you see, and seconds of sheer terror as he watched me approach—and then, in the doorway of one of the fullest rooms I would shoot."

"Do you mean you don't know when he was shot?" Larry asked gently.

Peter did not answer for a time, and his face worked as if the words would not come.

"I do know, I do know," came from his white lips in a burst. "I was too impatient to wait long. My fury was eating me up. I returned along the hall. . . . I was only a few steps from the billiard-room door when he was shot."

He looked into our faces, as if trying to drag from us whether we believed him or not.

"Then you saw who shot him?" I had to ask it, but I dreaded the answer. The terror-stricken faces of the two sisters rose before me accusingly.

"I did not see. I didn't wish to. The door was closed. . . . The sound of the shot struck through my madness, and I realized my danger. Perhaps it was not so much the shot as the scream that went with it—a woman's scream of utter terror."

Larry and I looked at each other.

"Which came first?" Larry asked.

Peter's brows met. "God, I don't know. What does it matter? I can't separate them. It seemed fitting that a woman should be there when he paid for his treatment of them, even if it was not a woman who shot him. All I thought of was the peril I was in, and I raced back to the upstairs rooms and mingled with the boisterous crowd."

Larry murmured: "It's a wonder you didn't run away."

"I had sense enough to realize how that would convict me. Several had seen me there. I still think I did the saner thing to stay and face it out."

Larry nodded. "What did you do with your gun?"

Their eyes met for a moment.

"Wouldn't the police like to know?" Peter jeered.

"So long as the police fail to find it, better not tell us anything about that. We're out to find the murderer—but we'd prefer that it wasn't Peter Davenport."

Peter jumped to his feet, his big figure towering over us. He pointed to the door.

"You'd—better—go!" he hissed through clenched teeth.

"So where does that land us?" I asked, as Larry and I descended in the lift.

"Just here—clearing out, Dill, as he ordered. . . . But we've done our duty—we've warned him. . . . I'd hate to give evidence against Peter."

"Did you believe his story?"

Larry grinned into the face of a woman who seemed to resent his whistling into her ear.

"It did sound a trifle rehearsed. I'd no idea Peter has such a sense of drama. . . . I'd no idea Peter Davenport could be confidential and frank with anyone. Perhaps he needed no warning. Perhaps we do him an injustice in thinking he does."

"Perhaps," I said, "he owes us something for the opportunity we gave him of rehearsing his story before the police have him cornered."

Eight o'clock that night. Larry and I gliding along past Doctor Millbrook's house in second gear.

The Doctor's house stood in a quiet street, an unpretentious building set in large grounds surrounded by a stone wall except across the front of the building itself. A quiet man in a quiet house in a quiet street. I found myself marvelling that he had made such a name for himself in the city. I stopped the car just above the gateway.

As I opened the door Larry touched my arm. He was lounged back on his spine, in his favourite lazy position, and I saw that he was examining the house.

"Modest chap," he murmured. "The sort of modesty that instils confidence. You'd trust Doctor Millbrook with your appendix—and the ensuing bill. You'd even trust him to prescribe, if he considered it best, and forgo his surgeon's fee. And that's the absolute limit of commendation for a surgeon. And," he added, as he dropped a foot to the running-board, "damned uncanny when it comes to a police case."

We climbed the four steps to the front door, and Larry rattled the heavy brass knocker vigorously. As we waited the soft strains of a piano reached us from somewhere far back in the house. A wiry old woman opened the door a couple of inches on a burglar-chain and showed a single weak eye in the opening.

"Go round to the office door," she growled, and pushed the door against us.

But Larry had his foot in the opening.

"This, madam," with his deepest bow, "is not a professional visit. Doctor Millbrook asked us to come."

"Are you the police?" she demanded, still with the chain in place.

"Didn't you hear what my friend said?" I replied shortly.

It worked. With a grudging snort she released the chain.

"Stay here," she ordered, and set off along the hall, leaving me entranced by the music that floated to us from somewhere toward the rear.

The woman had taken only four or five steps when the music ceased abruptly.

"It's all right, Mrs. Jaggers." Doctor Millbrook's voice came cheerily out to us from an open doorway at the end of the hall. "Bring them here." A pair of skilful hands touched the keys again.

I looked at Larry in wide-eyed surprise. It was not the music alone, and Larry understood. We were near the doorway, and Larry pointed to a mirror set high in the frame, at the same time making a zig-zag movement with his other hand. Mrs. Jaggers stood at the side of the doorway, waiting for us, and as we entered I saw a second mirror in the wall, facing the first one.

Across the room, before a piano, sat the Doctor, smiling up into a third mirror on the wall before him. With a glide of his fingers the music ceased, and he slid round on the bench.

"Simple, isn't it, Rockford? I saw you pointing. Three mirrors, set at the proper angles, and I can see anyone entering the front door. Another over there," pointing to a mirror over a desk not far away, "with its complementary pair, and I can see the office entrance."

"The inside story of a reputation for clairvoyancy," laughed Larry. "And mum's the word."

The Doctor laughed with him. "The inside story, you might say, of my whole skin. It pays for a police surgeon to see his—visitors before they see him."

I noticed then that his voice was more brittle than the ordinary English voice, betraying his Canadian education, though he had it well under control, and the gentleness of the man softened it.

The room in which we found ourselves was not unexpected. A long room, with a door and a window at the far end, and other doors opening from it on opposite walls, it was a muddle of books and ornaments, of tables and chairs. A large grand piano filled one corner just inside the door by which we had entered; and though the rest of the room was littered, its top was bare. Apart from those agile fingers I would have known the owner of that piano was a real musician. To the right, a few feet distant, stood a desk, and beyond it a tier of open shelves filled with books worn by frequent consultation.

"Please go on," I pleaded.

The Doctor's eyes lit up. "That's so nice of you. It's poor melody I attain now; I'm out of practice. But I manage to wring a lot of pleasure from it still. I haven't played for anyone but myself for years. You see, I dream while I play."

"If you can dream over the Second Liszt Rhapsody you needn't be afraid others will fail to take pleasure from it."

"You recognized it?"

"More: I recognized the hand of a master."

"Now, now!" But he flushed with pleasure as he rubbed his nose whimsically. "I wish you could convince Mrs. Jaggers of that, Fullerton. You should hear the competition we set up—my piano against her pots and pans. A sort of domestic symphony—or dissonance. She usually wins. I'd get rid of her, only I haven't the courage. I guess you saw why. The only solution seems to be to neutralize her—I mean, to get some pretty assistant in the house. I really should, you know someone more attractive than Mrs. Jaggers to answer the door."

He shrugged and threw out his hands. "But you're not interested in my domestic troubles. I gabble on. You see, I don't have a chance to talk to friends, not often. With my patients I'm strictly professional, and with the police—" He made a wry face. "Won't you sit down? Or would you rather go straight to the laboratory?"

"As you wish, Doctor," said Larry.

The Doctor stood pondering the situation, looking like a small boy in a difficulty. "Let's get the lab. off our minds first. Business before pleasure."

He trotted to one of the doors at the end of the room, and we entered directly into a businesslike laboratory. Unlike the room we had left, it was planned to the last inch.

The windows were high in the walls, leaving unbroken space all around for the work-tables, except at one side, where stood a heavy safe and a large electric refrigerator. On the work-tables stood test-tubes in their racks, various instruments also in racks against the wall, spirit lamps, blow-pipes, pads of litmus paper, a large camera, syringes, glass jars, and the rest of the paraphernalia of his job.

Above the table at the far end was a rack of fire-arms and to one side a sheet of steel marked with bright spots where bullets had struck at close range.

The Doctor waved his arm about. "Most of it police work," he said. "My collection of fire-arms there—I'm proud of them. That's what I'm most interested in. The refrigerator—over there—where I keep my perishable specimens. The safe—just a safe, but a necessary part of the equipment."

He had turned on all the lights, and now he crossed to the safe, spun the knob a few times, opened a heavy door, and returned with a sheet of white paper on which rested the mushroomed bullet we had seen in the morning outside the mortuary.

"It's a .25 all right. I've weighed and tested it. . . . If only I'd got it in better condition! As it is I'm afraid it's going to be difficult to trace the gun that fired it. From the post-mortem, however, I was able to deduce a few important facts. The gun was fired on a level with the dead man's chest. The bullet entered straight and, for some reason, turned downward. Bullets do strange things. They'll puncture flesh like paper, at times. That is, at first; but the passive resistance blocks them at last, sometimes quite quickly. It didn't in Horton's case. That cotton there"—he indicated a large roll of white fluff in the corner—"it'll stop almost any bullet, yet it's softer than flesh.

"Well, that's about all the service I can give the police in this case—which isn't much. We know the time of the murder, of course, at least to a few minutes, so that there was no need to examine the stomach."

He returned the piece of lead to the safe and twirled the knob. "Now you see one use for the safe. That bullet is valuable. Over here is my toxicological section. Poison cases keep cropping up all the time, and they're usually the easiest to get a conviction on. Poison is a silly weapon. That Edmondson case—you may remember it. There's the whole story in those tubes. Don't know why I kept them. But the guns are my pet—the target to get velocity and power, the cotton for a whole bullet, to get the landmarks and grooves. Every gun has its own, you know, like finger-prints.

"Along that wall my microscopes, perhaps the most important part of my work. All those microscopes—one of my dissipations. Cost me a lot of money—and I should have them insured, I suppose. Now, let's drop business. The other room's more comfortable, if no tidier."

The sitting-room gave me a somewhat different impression when we returned to it. Perhaps I had grown accustomed to the litter, perhaps the Doctor himself had worked the change. With all its seeming disorder it breathed a certain cosiness, a homeliness that was apt to escape one. But there was the piano. I was thinking of that Second Rhapsody.

Several moments of impatient rummaging in table drawers, and the Doctor produced an unbroken box of cigars. "And I bought them only this afternoon," he laughed. "But, being English, perhaps you prefer cigarettes. I got into the cigar habit in Canada—though I smoke little now. I think—I think I forgot cigarettes." He stood thinking for a moment, finger to lip. "Yes, I'm quite sure I forgot."

I accepted a cigar, though I do not care for them. Larry lit one of his own cigarettes. Doctor Millbrook did not smoke, but he could relax, without the twining of smoke before his eyes, more completely than either Larry or me—and Larry had always been to me the acme of lazing. The Doctor sank back in his chair, legs widely outstretched, his hands clasped over his stomach, a smile of perfect peace on his round face.

He beamed on us.

"You don't know what this means to me—to have someone to talk to, and anything but business. Really, you know, I'm a gregarious creature. And here I have only the police—and Mrs. Jaggers, of course. . . . Yes, the more I think of it, the better the idea appears. I'll hire a nice-looking girl to have about the place. I'll make a note of it."

He swung about to the desk and made a swift note on a pad.

"And I don't think," he resumed, turning back to his former position, "I've made a mistake in you boys. I hope you won't mind if I let down the bars. I may talk twaddle, but when a chap's had only the robot police—But then, I mustn't say that. But I'll confess there've been many times when I'd like to have had someone unofficial to unburden myself to even about what may seem official business. The police are so—so unimaginative, so—stupid, one might say, in a way. A hundred little flashes crop up here, a fanciful deduction there, a wondering thought now and then; but if I discussed them with the police they'd sign me up for the asylum. Already they think me foolishly sentimental." He sighed.

"And," he went on, "perhaps they're right. But I ask you how a man could wade through that gory business this morning and retain his humanness without sentiment. If I hadn't any I'd go berserk."

He studied us through the smoke.

"That's why I invited you here to-night. No, I begged it, though you may not have known it. I saw you were interested in this case. You knew young Horton, I believe. And there are features about it I can't bring myself to discuss with the police."

"We certainly knew Vance Horton," I said. "Fact is, Doctor, Larry and I are so interested we've made up our minds to find his murderer. We've just got to."

Larry was scowling at me, but I ignored him. The Doctor's face had lost its smile.

"You knew him—well? Close friends, perhaps."

"No, we—"

Larry interrupted brazenly. "It's not that, Doctor. Dill and I have concerned ourselves in several recent cases—sort of amateur detectives, you might say. This case is a little different because we did know the victim."

"And so," said the Doctor thoughtfully, "you're doing some sleuthing of your own. Odd, that. Seems as if Providence led me to you." He smiled his boyish smile. "Because I may be able to help you. Anyway, I'm going to tell you all I know . . . some, probably, that I will never tell the police. Please understand that I've no intention of concealing from them anything essential, anything that might lead to the murderer, but I've certain thoughts about the case that would be meaningless to them, even, perhaps, misleading. They wish only facts from me."

He shoved the box of cigars toward me, and took a chair nearer us, where he might talk in a lower tone.

"As I told you, Vance Horton was shot with a .25 automatic, and the gun was fired from the level of his chest. Horton was standing straight before the gun, and if his murderer held it so as to aim he must be shorter than his victim. Horton was six feet. That for what it's worth.

"By the way, Rockford, you saw the body there on the floor, and the evidence of a struggle. It means that Horton was not shot unawares. Connecting it all up, it points to a friend—or one accepted as a friend; certainly not a stranger.

"The struggle might occur after the shot, were it not for the instant death—comparatively instant, for there's no such thing as instant death—that would follow a bullet through the heart. That he died like that"—he snapped his fingers—"is proven by the absence of blood. After death the leakage is only by gravity."

He pinched his lip thoughtfully. "But I've a feeling about the affair—as if everything is not as it seemed. This is outside my duty as a police surgeon, and any self-respecting detective would not thank me for mentioning it. That's what I want to talk about."

He removed his glasses and wiped them on his handkerchief, then cleared his throat. He wished to talk, yet questioned the wisdom, the correctness, of talking to us.

"Of course, you know there were a dozen possible murderers among that gang Horton happened to be entertaining. At least, that's what the police think. I knew the dead man only by sight, but I'd heard something of his record. What I ask myself is: Would any of his guests, knowing they would be under suspicion, risk murder last night, especially when there are so many ways of effecting it without suspicion?"

"That," I suggested, "might be their cleverness. With so many to suspect—"

The Doctor shook his head doubtfully. "I thought of that. But everyone there was bound to be under police suspicion, to be questioned on the spot by Inspector Emerson, a past master in piercing any mask. I doubt if any murderer would risk facing him so soon after the crime.

"I may be wrong," he continued, after a pause, "but I don't believe that open French window was the blind the police think it was. How much cleverer for the murderer to have taken advantage of a time when so many who had reason to hate young Horton had it in their power to kill him! He could enter by the open window and you see, we have evidence that Horton was called away by a telephone message."

I said: "You were there, Doctor, for the preliminary investigation. You must have formed your opinion from the questions asked and the answers given. But, apparently, the police deduced something different."

But the Doctor was not to be drawn. "Have I told you what the police think? I've spoken, I hope, only of what can be no secret. You can't expect me to be more specific than that, Fullerton. I'm still a police officer—if I do gabble. . . . The problem for the police to solve is the very number of Horton's enemies. He seems to have had a penchant for making them. But I don't need to tell you that. . . . Strange life he led—so unfortunate, so needless. With money, and good looks, and leisure, what might he not have made of himself! But from what I hear he didn't seem to have the—the character, one might say, to utilize his advantages except for evil."

He paused, and a heavy sigh filled the room. Larry lay back in his chair, his lips pursed to a soundless whistle.

"You know his history, Rockford," said the Doctor, with a

suddenness that brought Larry upright.

"To some extent—what Public School companions know. There were stories at Cortwright, many of them. We boys made them blacker, I suppose, because we had no use for Vance. . . . Lee Moshier was almost the only friend he had there. Lee was a long-sighted chap."

"Lee Moshier—Lee Moshier. Wasn't that the surly big fellow the police—" He stopped in some confusion.

"I talk too much. But I can't see how it matters. The police had him at the station at noon while I was there. I didn't like him. He and Horton might well be friends. Did himself well with Horton, it seems."

"Lee never," said Larry, "had two pennies of his own to rattle. Everyone knows Vance kept him."

"H'm—Inspector Emerson seems to have a story that Horton was through with him—getting weary of grub-staking him."

"I believe that's so."

Doctor Millbrook shrugged. "There you are—one of the many who might have fired the shot. The others?" He glanced sideways at us and smiled. "Perhaps the police are aware that you were among the many who had no use for Horton."

"I suppose," Larry drawled, "that's why they made an early call on Dill this morning."

"Did they do that? I was just giving you a sly dig."

"It was something more," I said, "than knowing I had no use for Vance Horton. Someone told them my car was there in Figmore Street about the time of the murder. I'd give much to know who saw me."

"Wouldn't the Inspector tell you?"

"No. Do you know?"

"Now, now!" The Doctor lifted a fat finger. "Haven't I answered that? But even if I did know I daren't tell you."

Larry said: "Vance, in all his miserable life, did nothing more miserable than to kick out at a time when his enemies were gathered where they would all be under suspicion. He had, as you say, a penchant for dirt like that."

DOCTOR MILLBROOK removed his glasses again and wiped them absent-mindedly. That he had something to say, something he found it difficult to say, was apparent. He cleared his throat.

"I wonder if we aren't a little uncharitable. I've had his family history from the police. It's not a pretty one. The case interests me psychopathically, apart from my official capacity. He represents a rather new type to me, though I knew it existed. Vance Horton lived under a grave handicap.

"You must know some of the story; you may even know more than they told me. Young Horton had an unfortunate background. It inclines me to be—well, a little bit tolerant of the vices he developed. His father, it seems, was a bad egg . . . and his mother not only was no saint, but she, too, had an unfortunate background. She had the money, and when they married she made her husband give up his business and live on her. No wonder he turned out bad.

"A bad start. And as the years passed, and the children came, things went from bad to worse—a dependent, disgruntled father, and a nagging, disagreeable, irresponsible mother. I say irresponsible, because there's reason to believe that a strain of—irresponsibility, shall we say? cropped out now and then in her family. There were times when Mrs. Horton, they say, goaded herself to screaming hysteria. It must have been a hell on earth for the family, especially for her husband. At any rate, he disappeared. Whether he was kicked out or fled doesn't matter.

"His exit did not, of course, affect the resources of the family, except that Mrs. Horton had more to squander on herself and Vance. Thereafter she seems to have thrown herself into an orgy of extravagance and display. In this she was aided and abetted by the entire family, two boys and a girl—"

I interrupted. "At Cortwright we always thought there were three boys. One, a younger brother than Vance, was at Cortwright a year. He was expelled. He died soon after. I remember Vance going home to the funeral—and missing the train deliberately so he would not arrive in time. He called it a damned nuisance, a silly convention. It was one of the many shocks he persisted in giving us lads."

"I never heard of that brother," said the Doctor. "I suppose he died too early to figure in the essential history. The brother they speak of was older than Vance, several years older, I believe. He ran away, it seems—some money row, the mother's favouritism toward Vance. That was another misfortune for the unlucky young man. The brother that ran away seems to have resembled the father, perhaps the origin of his mother's dislike. . . . And yet, oddly enough, it was the news of that son's death to which is ascribed the death of the mother. Conscience, perhaps, or the tardy revival of the mother instinct. He was killed several years ago in one of those intermittent South American revolutions. It seems that he inherited only one thing from his mother, her taint of insanity. At least, Inspector Emerson tells me that—it was before his time—the police were called in one day to find the servants struggling with a half-demented young man, while Vance looked on, sneering, goading his brother to fury. It was after that the brother ran away."

Larry inquired what had happened to the father.

"I believe he ended in a French prison—some nasty love affair."

I said: "I remember the girl. She went insane, didn't she?"

"Yes, she's in an asylum now."

Larry looked interested. "Have the police checked up on her? She may have escaped—"

"No, they looked into that. The police also checked up on the father by telegraph to-day. He's still in that French jail—life term. In fact, all the family possibilities have been thoroughly canvassed—routine, you know. . . . But the phase of it that interests me is the terrible background young Horton had. That's why I can't be so cold-blooded about it as my friends among the police."

A slow smile twisted his gentle face. "I never saw the police so peevish about a case. They know they must work fast or lose the scent, yet there are so many clues to follow—rather, suspects to investigate. My own idea is that they're on the wrong tack. But that's between ourselves. If I were doing it I'd leave that drunken mob to the last. They can be investigated at any time. If it's someone else the trail will quickly cool.

"Of course, they did branch out—after you, Fullerton. But you're always available, and they needn't have been in such a hurry. There seems, too, to be another slant they're investigating—something about a couple of girls. I didn't get it all, but it seems someone saw them running on the street or somewhere near the house last night."

I had difficulty in controlling myself. But a glance at Larry's almost somnolent indifference steadied me. At the same time I steeled myself for new and shocking possibilities. Was Doctor Millbrook, even there in his own sitting-room, frank as he seemed, merely a cog in the police machine to trace the murderer? Were we being pumped, drawn on to an indiscretion that would convict us? I made up my mind to be more careful with the Doctor.

"I wouldn't be surprised," said Larry in his lazy tones. "I can imagine nothing more likely than that one of his many women victims—and his victims were his guests—reached the end of her patience and settled Vance's indebtedness to this world. I don't recall any evidence that any of his guests had disappeared before the police arrived."

The Doctor considered it ponderously. "In that case she must have gone prepared—with a gun, I mean. That would make it hard for her with a jury."

"She may have found Vance's gun," I suggested.

"It's possible, Fullerton. But we've found no gun. . . . And it doesn't fit into the picture that's been forming in my mind. However," raising himself in his chair and eyeing us with an interest that amounted to excitement, "it's the pathological side that centres my attention. And that's what I wished to talk about. I see Horton as the victim of heredity, of environment, of upbringing—surely the origin of incurable mental disease. At least incurable in the present development of therapeutics."

He rose clumsily and stumped to the end of the room, winding his way through the assortment of tables and chairs that littered the floor. And, studying him, I fancied the route showed the wear of frequent pacings.

It did not surprise me. In the hour we had spent with him, except for that flash of suspicion, he had lost his identity as a hard-boiled police official, a weapon of the law. He had become oddly humanized, entirely unfitted for the callous duties of his official task. I saw him as a lonely man, of tardy friendships, with suppressed and unprofessional emotions clamouring for expression.

And then, all in a few moments, I knew my reading of him was correct.

Suddenly he spun about and faced us. Behind his round

glasses his eyes blazed with a new eagerness, a new appeal, a new hope.

"I wish," he murmured, as if to himself, "I wish I could be certain."

"Of what?" Larry asked.

"That I can trust you."

Larry opened his eyes and rolled his head about to where he could see me.

"May I answer for you, Dill?" And when I nodded he continued: "Doctor, unless you tell us you murdered Vance Horton yourself we're dumb as that bookcase. With this qualification—that we're free to use anything you tell us in our search for the murderer. Because, you see, Dill and I are pledged to that."

The Doctor beamed on us. "Agreed—even delighted. And so—this: I found young Horton's diary."

Larry lifted his head sharply. More slowly it percolated through my brain how much such a diary might reveal.

"Yes," said the Doctor. "That's what I haven't mentioned to the police. I found it tucked away in a secret drawer in that large cabinet in the corner of the billiard-room. You see, I had the room to myself for a time when you were all gone last night. I can't tell you how glad I am of that now."

"Have you read it?" asked Larry.

The Doctor flushed, though Larry's tone carried no accusation.

"A few words here and there. Don't forget the boy's dead. The police would have combed its every page if I hadn't kept it from them, It's—it's the few words I read that incline me to be more charitable. It's a curious bit of writing." The lump in his throat moved up and down for a moment, and I looked away in some embarrassment. "Sort of—overcame me. If the rest is like the little I've had time to read, then Vance Horton was a pathological case."

"H'm—does it give any clue to the murderer?"

"Not a word, so far as I've read. Of course, if I find it does that I'll have to work some scheme to get it into the hands of Inspector Emerson. . . . I hope it doesn't. Is that wrong of me? I can't help it. I'd find it hard to bring myself to expose the diary to the unfeeling attention of the police."

His eyes moved quickly from Larry to me and back again.

They asked a question I did not at the moment read.

"That's where I thought you boys might help. The diary—well, it's too sacred to make public. But I thought—I thought maybe, in case it's useful in uncovering his murderer, we might be able to manage for you to find the necessary clues. It would serve the same purpose."

"May we," I asked, "see the diary ourselves?"

The Doctor hesitated, but after a moment he left us and disappeared into the laboratory. But in an instant he was back, smiling uncomfortably.

"No, I don't see how I could do that. It wouldn't be fair to show it to others and not to the police. You understand?"

We both nodded. One had to admire his decision, if not to agree with it. But one always excepts oneself in a question of propriety.

The Doctor reseated himself with a heavy sigh. "That's awfully decent of you. . . . And now, Fullerton, I'm going to try to be equally decent. I told you—or I gave you to understand—that I didn't know who saw your car last night in Figmore Street. That was true, but not the whole truth. Indeed, the police themselves do not know. The information came on the early mail this morning, in an anonymous letter."

XII Action

LARRY and I had much to occupy our minds on the way home. The Doctor himself had seen us to the door, his farewell so full of hungry gratitude for the visit that we eagerly accepted his invitation to come again as often as we could spare the time.

The anonymous letter worried us. I was really more indignant than worried, but Larry saw at once its dangerous significance.

"Someone was there, Dill," he mused, "someone we did not see . . . someone who does not wish to be brought into it. How much did he see?"

"He saw Barbara and Willo, too," I said. "It may have been a friend, one of those justice-at-any-price chaps. Naturally he wouldn't wish us to know what he had done."

"It may," said Larry sarcastically, "have been the man in the moon. Only the moon last night, at that hour, was somewhere over Australia—though I'm a dud at astronomy."

"All right, Sherlock Holmes, you guess."

"It might," he replied slowly, "have been the murderer himself."

It startled me. "You mean—"

"At least," he interrupted, "I don't mean Barbara and Willo. Better forget about them. We must work on other trails. You're no Vidocq, so let it go at that."

A sudden alarming thought burst in my head. "That's why Inspector Emerson searched my house this morning—the girls!"

"Hanaud!" drawled Larry. "Did you think they were looking for the gun? Did you suspect the Inspector of expecting you to keep the gun on the mantel? If they were interested in the gun there'd have been a squad of police; they'd have X-rayed your very innards."

I was still brooding over it when we reached Larry's quarters. As he climbed out a remark of Doctor Millbrook's recurred to me.

"By the way, Larry, the Doctor spoke of signs of a struggle in the billiard-room. I saw nothing of that. Vance was seated before that table as if he were asleep. One arm was—"

"Hold on! Hold on!" Larry climbed excitedly back into the car. "What's that you say?"

"There were no signs of a struggle—"

"And Vance was seated beside the table?"

"Certainly. He was turned slightly toward me." I described the scene; every detail was stamped indelibly on my memory. "I scarcely know why I knew he was dead. I didn't see the blood on his coat. . . . Or perhaps I did, without realizing it. Doctor Millbrook said—"

Larry broke in impatiently. "Describe it again, Dill, take your time. It's very important. For God's sake be sure you're right!"

I went through it all once more, my eyes closed. I stood once more in that open French window, peering in on Vance's dead body. . . . When I was through Larry whistled dismally.

"Dillon Fullerton," he declared, "of all the mysterious angles in this dizzy affair that tops the list. When the police arrived Vance was stretched on the floor."

I suggested that he may have fallen afterwards.

"Impossible. The body was a dozen feet from that table. The chair you saw him in was upset, and the back broken. Even the rug was puckered and kicked up at one corner, and his coat was half pulled from one shoulder."

"I'm positive there was nothing of that."

Larry whistled shrilly, and the echo returned from the house, struck the wall across the street, and came back to us.

"Stryke me dead, Dill, if that ain't a caution!" But he laughed a little hysterically. "Damn it! you've rushed us—pushed us into it. I was going to postpone to to-morrow night what must be done right away. Wait here for me."

He scrambled out. A couple passed, and Larry ducked around them, dashed up the stairs, and let himself in with his latch-key.

The man of the passing pair pulled up, staring at the door Larry had closed behind him.

"What!" he exclaimed to his companion, a woman who clung to his arm, tripping along at his side. "Larry Rockford in a hurry! Ye Gods! Something terrific must have happened. Well, my dear," looking down in her face, "where to? Have you decided yet?"

But as he spoke he swerved toward the car. I leaned well back.

For I recognized him. It was Jack Ponting—a Jack Ponting and his wife bubbling with joy! And only two days ago Jack had dined with me at the club, a silent, sombre, depressed companion who finally confessed he was "in for the skids again." he had learned of Vance's control of *The Guardian,* and he knew the reason.

I shuddered involuntarily. And then a ghastly thought entered my head. Jack Ponting! Starting out on a night of carousal just twenty-four hours after a murder that ended his troubles!

Larry came hurtling down the steps and leaped into the car. His pockets bulged.

"Drive on," he ordered.

"Where are we going?"

"To that billiard-room of Vance Horton's."

XIII A Night Visit

AT LARRY'S direction I parked the car in Southwold Street. Our goal was around the corner and two blocks distant, two blocks of the darkest streets in that part of the city.

"I don't like it," I grumbled as we climbed from the car. "This is dangerous, foolhardy."

"You have the hair bristling all over the back of my neck," Larry teased in a dramatic whisper.

"But the police are there. If they discover us!"

"You're a good runner, Dill. Here, you better have this." He thrust an electric torch into my hand. "No, don't creep along like an anarchist loaded with dynamite. These are public streets, my brave lad. We both pay taxes."

I was a little ashamed of how un-brave I felt.

"Jack Ponting passed when you were in the house," I told him, hugging up against him. "He was—I didn't like it, Larry—positively gay."

"You didn't expect him to wear crepe on his hat, did you?"

"He might at least lie low till he's out of the woods himself."

"Perhaps," said Larry, "he's waiting for us to get him out . . . We'll have a chat with Jack one of these days."

I scoffed. "The one we had with Peter Davenport didn't do much good."

We had reached the upper end of the Horton lawn, in Fraleigh Street. Larry stepped ahead, skirting the hedge.

"There must be a way to get through here without leaving too wide a trail," he whispered.

"And when you get through?" I questioned.

"Then we'll take to prayer. But stop gabbling. The police are not so all-fired omniscient. Don't forget Doctor Millbrook himself found a diary Inspector Emerson would give his gold stoppings to have discovered . . . I too. 'The Inside Story of a Libertine's Life'— imagine the spicy reading."

He pulled up and thrust his hand into the hedge.

"This feels possible. Get down on your marrowbones and poke your head through. If it doesn't brush your whiskers I may be able to make it."

We did make it, though Larry advanced by inches, easing the

rustle of his larger frame. Inside, he looked about.

"We may have to run for it. Keep the spot in your mind."

It was a lovely old-fashioned garden still. Vance had not had time to work havoc with it, to bring it more in accord with the new hedge that had replaced the stone fence of his mother's day. Or— remembering Doctor Millbrook's kindlier tolerance—perhaps Vance preferred it as it was.

With the utmost care we picked our way through the shrubbery toward the house, and in the shadow of a thicket Larry stopped.

"We'll know in a minute or two," he whispered, close to my ear. "If they have a guard *in* the billiard-room the expedition's off. I'm hoping he's outside. My bloodthirstiness stops short of shooting a policeman—though even that might be worth while."

We stood for what seemed hours, though it was probably only two or three minutes. I had never thought darkness in the open could be so black. From where we stood not a light was visible about or inside the house. Larry's hand fell suddenly on my arm.

"Listen!"

A heavy footstep thudded its way along the flag-walk at the front of the billiard-room, moving toward us.

"Allah be praised!" whispered Larry.

Those heavy feet, obviously a policeman's, halted at the corner for a moment, then passed on across the end of the billiard-room, and faded off up the far side.

"The conventional official routine," said Larry. "It suits us. We'll wait till he comes around again, to see how long the circuit of the house takes."

"I don't understand all this official watch-dog business," I puzzled.

"I don't myself—quite. But I'm accepting it in lieu of anything better to do. It's plain Inspector Emerson has a plan. I'm a little worried about its meaning, but we have to take a chance."

"Did it ever strike you, Larry, that we may have taken a big chance with Doctor Millbrook? We mustn't forget he's official."

"I'm not," said Larry. "I was on guard that we didn't bite at that hook. Silence now. Let's work over this way. There must be lights in the house."

We edged to the left. There we came in sight of three lighted windows on the ground floor. It was, I knew, one of the large lower sitting-rooms. The rest of the house was dark.

"Probably another bobby in there," Larry whispered. "Here comes the outer garrison."

The measured tread we had heard before became suddenly audible at the far corner of the house. Before one of the open lighted windows it stopped, a few words were exchanged with someone inside, and then the steps came on. The policeman passed—rounded the far side of the billiard-room.

"Come on!"

With a rush we stood at the end of the billiard-room. My eyes had opened a little to the darkness, and I saw the three high, arched French windows, with their fanshaped tops and small panes. Then I heard Larry's hand on a knob. With a snort of disgust he passed around the corner to the flag-walk.

"Not so much as a keyhole there—and they're bolted on the inside. It's more dangerous on the side here, but I know these windows open." I heard the rattle of keys in his hand. "It's a funny lock one of these won't open," he whispered excitedly.

He had moved with such precision, such certainty, that all my old dread returned. How did he know so much about the place?

"Get ready to run for it," he whispered. "Around the corner and into the shrubbery, till he passes again. Let's hope he stops this time for a longer exchange with his mate inside."

From where we stood we could see the light from the living-room shining across the lawn to a group of ornamental evergreens. It was so bright that it partially blinded us, so that we had to feel our way along the wall. At the first window Larry hesitated only long enough to try the knob, and a smothered oath betrayed his disappointment. We moved on to the next, the one through which, the night before, I had beheld Vance Horton's lifeless body.

"This one opens, we know," Larry whispered.

"Hurry!" I pleaded, in sudden panic.

Larry exploded into an oath so loud that I trembled with apprehension.

"Not a keyhole in the lot!" he exclaimed under his breath. "God!" His hand clutched my arm, gripping me so tightly that I could not move.

And at that moment round the corner of the billiard-room

came the sentry. He had reversed his course.

Not more than twenty feet away.

I tilted forward on my toes, prepared to run, but Larry's hand was still on my arm. And then I saw what he counted on—the light from the sitting-room windows that made everything else so obscure.

Slowly those heavy feet advanced. We were pressed tight against the window. The sentry passed—so close that I could have tripped him merely by extending a foot. At the last of the three lighted windows he stopped, and, leaning through, spoke to someone inside.

"Phew!" I breathed. "I've just got to sit down or tumble down."

Larry sighed. "And I counted so much on this."

I had taken hold of the knob to steady myself.

"Larry! Larry!"

He jammed his hand over my lips, for I had cried out more loudly than I thought. And well I might, for the door had yielded to my touch.

"It's unlocked, Larry."

He pushed my hand aside. "Allah be praised for the fourth or fifth time to-night! If only it doesn't creak!"

It didn't creak, and in a moment we were inside. Larry chuckled and blew a long breath of relief.

"Once more the police fall down, Dill. They forgot to lock that window. Stay here and keep an eye on that bobby. Let me know when it's safe to use a light."

I glued my eye to a crack in the window that was now a door.

"He's moved away," I whispered. "I can't see him."

But just then the front door slammed, and the voice of the sentry came booming down the hall. We stood in a tense silence. If he came on to the billiard-room!

But he stopped at the sitting-room and turned in. We could hear them talking. Larry whistled under his breath.

"Much more of this and I'll be a pukka Mahommedan. Keep your eye peeled, Dill, through that window. There may be another bobby. I'm going across to unlock one of the windows on the other side. We may need a different exit. If we have to leave in a hurry, make straight for the car."

I returned to the window. Across the room I could hear Larry moving with a confidence that revived a certain uncomfortable wonder in my mind. Then he was back.

"The table's still here," he whispered. I heard it slide over the carpet, and then Larry's excited hiss: "The drawer! It's here! It was turned around against the wall."

A ray from his torch shot out and vanished. Reappeared. Looking around, I beheld him bending over the open drawer. Then the light was shut off. When it reappeared Larry was on his knees beneath the table. I heard him whistle through his teeth.

"Go easy with that light," I warned. "Someone may see it from the street."

The drone of conversation continued from the sitting-room, with now and then a loud yawn or a lazy laugh.

Behind me I could hear Larry fumbling at the table. I could hear him breathing, too. Then the light moved to one side. It stopped on a metal ash-tray table.

"How long does it take to smoke a cigarette, Dill?" he asked. "Did you ever time one? . . . I wonder . . . is it possible Inspector Emerson missed this. I can't—"

He had closed off the light. "S-s-s!"

I too had heard it—the slightest of sounds outside the window where I stood.

NOT until that moment did the full eeriness of the place strike me. Hitherto the excitement, our unexpected success, and the lazy drone of the voices from the sitting-room had kept my mind from dwelling on the darkness and the perilous nature of our task. Larry's conduct in the billiard-room, too, had mystified me.

But now, there in that great dark room where Vance Horton had been shot down only twenty-four hours before, where police had been and gone, the scraping of that furtive foot not half a dozen paces from where I stood, the darkness was filled with creeping menace, a world of unseen perils.

The blood raced hotly through my veins, and tingles shot through my scalp. Retreat was cut off, at least by the way we came. I remembered Larry's precaution of unlocking another window, and I set out on my toes toward it.

But a large billiard-table blocked the way. Instinctively I turned to the right. In that ghastly darkness I dare not go the other way—where Vance's body had been. In some foolish way Vance and that stealthy footstep were one and the same—a ghost. For the moment I had forgotten Larry. I lived in the world of my own terror.

But Larry had not forgotten me. As I rounded the end of the table he came behind me. Had he touched me I should certainly have screamed. But he was wise.

"Steady, old chap, steady!" he whispered.

The calm tone quieted my nerves.

"Down behind the table, Dill, quick!"

He had hold of me then, and together we ducked beneath the end of the table.

In the few seconds since the first alarm nothing further had happened, but I knew those feet beyond the door were coming—coming. I raised my head above the table. Larry had left me and gone on. I fixed my eyes on the window by which we had entered. And in a moment, so soundlessly, so ghostlike, that I could have screamed, I saw the sky open above the trees.

Then it was closed off. Someone had entered the room and closed the door behind him.

A silence so intense that I could hear my heart thudding had settled over the room—over the world, for even the voices of the two policemen were stilled. I scarcely breathed. Keen as were my ears to the slightest sound, I could expect nothing less of that other there near the window. Listening, of course.

Then, so suddenly that I started, a ray of light shot along the carpet.

I dropped behind the table and slowly reached out until I could see around the end. The light had been cut off. It reappeared, lifting quickly until it steadied on the small table where Vance had been sitting—where Larry had worked so mysteriously only a few moments ago. Against the ray I saw a pair of legs for a fleeting second. My heart pounded painfully. I knew that only a moment away was some great and startling revelation. And I trembled to face it. I knew so many who might have murdered Vance Horton—so many I did not wish to suffer for it. And surely no one but the murderer would have taken such a risk.

Strange, that. Yet not so strange. I knew who had shot Vance Horton, yet Larry had in some way made two crimes of it. I found it impossible—yes, to the very end—to clear myself of that thought.

No one but the murderer would dare—And then, with a shock, it came to me that Larry and I, too, were there.

The light came and went, darting about, from table to carpet, like a will-o'-the-wisp. All the more that I could hear no sound. Outside a car rumbled by, and someone went whistling along the street. The policemen were talking again.

But where was Larry? What was he doing?

My muscles ached, for I was squatted on my heels. Cautiously I dropped to my knees. And just then the light focused on the table again, this time higher up, and I thought I heard a gasp. Darkness again—shuffling sounds.

In the middle of it I set out to find Larry. Far down the other side of the billiard table I came on him. As I touched his feet, he reached back and squeezed my arm. Then he moved on. I followed.

We reached the lower corner of the big table. We were then, I knew, almost on a level with the spot where I had last seen those legs. Larry rounded the corner. It seemed a desperately foolish thing to do, for if the torch were turned toward us we would be full in its ray.

But Larry must have a plan. He crept on. All was silence again.

And in the silence my head came in contact with the chalk-cup beneath the edge of the table.

In my ears it sounded like a gunshot. Recklessly I jumped to my feet. Larry, I could hear, did the same. And then a blinding ray shot straight into our faces. Larry turned on his own, but it was too weak. The other torch moved rapidly away toward the window, a ghostly thing, for there was no sound. The window opened—closed. The ray shut off.

Larry's torch struck the glass and, to our blinded eyes, went no farther. Beyond, the night was black. Larry snapped his light off.

"Did you see—anything?" he whispered.

"Just a light—and a pair of leg backs at the first."

Larry swore under his breath. "I hoped, when I turned on my light, you'd slide away out of his ray. The worst of it is he saw us. It may make another story of everything."

"If only we'd been able to do something!" I moaned. "Of course, it was the murderer."

"Was it? Perhaps . . . perhaps not. It may have been just a conscience—or someone wishing to protect the murderer."

"I'm getting out of this, Larry," I whispered.

"Yes, but we'll give our unknown friend time to get away first. Then—"

He drew a sharp breath. He had moved away from me toward the wall, and now his light came on in one quick flash and went out.

"Did you see that, Dill?" he demanded excitedly.

"What was it?"

"The table's been turned again. The drawer is facing the wall."

THE thing was getting on my nerves again. I felt suffocated, oppressed. Oh, for the open lawn and a chance to run. As I set out for the window Larry heard me.

"Not that way, Dill. The other window. He may be waiting out there for us. Go on. I'll lock this one."

In a moment or two he was beside me as I felt my way across the room.

"Have you worked out what all this means?" he asked. "Was that window missed by the police, or was unlocked by someone who wished to get in here? Another mystery. Here, I'll take you in tow."

He took my arm and led unerringly across the room. But we had no more than reached the end of the large table when one of the policemen in the sitting-room came out into the hall, humming sleepily, and strolled toward the billiard-room. Between us and the door stood a smaller billiard-table. Larry had just time to drag me down flat on the floor when the door opened, letting in a flood of light from the hall. But the shadow of the table saved us.

The policeman yawned. "Spooky place, this," he called back. "Big enough for a barracks. I'm glad the Inspector didn't make me stay in it. Well, I'm starting the round again."

A stentorian yawn, and the door closed. Then the front door slammed shut. But Larry did not move. His hand still pressed heavily on my back. Then his lips were at my ear.

"Don't make a sound, Dill. We must make that window somehow. If I say 'run,' get away for your very life. Never mind the car."

I quivered with excitement. Larry must sense some new peril. We reached the window. It opened without a sound. As Larry closed it behind us he whispered:

"Dill, there was someone in there, someone else. I felt it. Come on."

We ran for the nearest thicket. Larry, a few steps ahead, dived around it. I heard a violent rustle, then the threshing of branches. I stumbled forward.

"Be quiet, I tell you." That was Larry's voice, and he was not speaking to me. "Here's a policeman coming."

Round the corner of the house came the sentry, still humming.

He passed, and all was silence again.

"Now for the street," Larry ordered.

I felt my way after him, not understanding but too eager to escape from that menacing place to question him. We reached the opening in the hedge, and still I did not know what had happened. Beyond the hedge two figures rose before me.

And as we came within the rays of a street light I saw—a woman—Barbara!

Larry laughed as I gave an exclamation of surprise.

"Keep your hair on, old thing," he said. "Wait till we get inside."

This, the strangest of all the strange happenings of the night. Barbara—alone—there in the dark, ghostly garden! I struggled to concentrate on the courage of the girl. In part I succeeded.

"Your sister?" I asked vaguely.

"Willo's at home," replied Barbara.

We returned by a roundabout way. Cuddy, of course, was waiting for me. He admitted us without so much as a flicker of an eyelid. Perhaps he had given me up; perhaps Larry was chaperon enough for any foolishness of mine.

Barbara smiled at him. "I'm not a boarder, Cuddy."

"No, ma'am. As you say, ma'am." Which might mean anything.

He preceded us to the library and, instead of the centre lights, turned on only a floor light. Then he hurried to draw the curtains. Larry remained at the door, leaning against the wall, whistling softly. Cuddy paused before me.

"The yellow room, sir?"

I looked inquiringly at Barbara.

"I don't know why you brought me here," she murmured. "But if you wouldn't mind—"

"Prepare the yellow room, Cuddy," said Larry.

"And," I added, "for Mr. Rockford his usual room."

Cuddy bowed. "In nine minutes, sir—sandwiches and tea."

I pointed to a chair. "Please sit down, Miss—Miss—" There I was again, and I cleared my throat apologetically. "That chair, I think—"

"Barbara Venell," she broke in, a little defiantly I thought.

"And," said Larry, "the lady speaks the truth. Miss Venell, the name is safe with us."

We said little more until Cuddy had served us. It was Larry asked one of the questions that we all knew had to be answered:

"Do you live in the city, Miss Venell?"

Barbara did not reply to that, but in what she did say was the answer to several of the questions that hung on our lips;

"I daren't go home at this hour."

"No need," I assured her. "You're safe here. The police made their little raid this morning."

She started to her feet, her face white with fear. "They—know? They were after us? Oh, I knew it wasn't safe to stay."

"It's safe now, Miss Venell. Please don't let your tea get cold."

She ate and drank absent-mindedly. There seemed so much that must be said, that we were all embarrassed.

"For a young lady who dared to go into those dark grounds to-night—"

"I didn't dare not," she broke in. Then she sighed. "After—after last night who thinks of daring?"

"Hadn't we," I suggested, "better clear up some of this? My friend and I have only one thought—to protect you and your sister. But from what? If we do not know we may blunder you into trouble."

She made no reply—just kept sipping at her tea.

Larry said gently: "You need help, Miss Venell, need it more than you think. Scotland Yard has been called in."

She just looked at him with wide, staring eyes. I too. Was Larry trying to frighten her into opening her lips? If he were cad enough for that—

"Miss Venell," I asked, for I felt I must get it straightened out, "do you know who murdered Vance Horton?"

She turned slowly to face me, and tears were in her eyes.

"There's a story, Mr. Fullerton. And it's not all my story. I can't tell you—anything more."

"Your sister?" Larry's voice was gentle.

She nodded. Over our heads Cuddy passed along the hall to the yellow room. Larry lifted his eyes to the ceiling and smiled.

"I know, I know," she said miserably. "I know I can trust you. I knew it from the beginning. But it's Willo's story—Willo's and Vance Horton's. She was infatuated with him. We've lived here only two months, but I heard the stories about him. . . . Willo would never believe them. I saw what was happening—and Willo is my only sister. Ever since mother died I've been a mother to her. For months she has been seeing him clandestinely, here and in London, where we lived before. She would listen to no warning. And so I—"

Larry stretched rudely and broke into a whistle.

"It's after midnight," he drawled. "You must be tired, Miss Venell."

She turned startled eyes on him, as if she had wakened from an unpleasant dream.

"Thank you," she murmured, and rose.

THE inquest was held next morning. A great crowd gathered about the court-room, for the case involved so many well-known citizens. It was only Larry's acquaintance with the police that found us seats.

From the first it was evident that the police had everything planned. Just so much was to be revealed and no more. The jury had examined the body and come away with little inclination to curiosity. Two of the men were plainly "queer."

Neither Jordan Fleming nor Jack Ponting were called. It was significant, but from what Larry had told me of the course of the earlier investigation I was not surprised. Neither did Peter Davenport appear. The police, I decided, were out to bewilder—to frighten by that very bewilderment.

The one piece of evidence beyond what I already knew was given by Effie Shannon. Effie had learned her lesson in the meantime; she was no longer defiant, but told her story simply and calmly. I had a feeling that it, too, had been rehearsed before the police.

She had, she said, been talking to Vance not long before the police called them out. In the midst of their conversation he had been called to the telephone and had returned somewhat upset, or ill-tempered; she would not venture to say which. No, she could not recall who delivered the message to him, but it was not a servant. He had not returned to her, but had seated himself, if she remembered rightly, beside Mrs. Fleming. And after a time he had looked at his watch and left the room. That was all she knew.

Nora Fleming, called, admitted that she may have been the last to talk with Vance before the murder. She knew nothing of the telephone call, but Vance did seem out of sorts. And at the last he had looked at his watch and gone away. She had not seen him alive again.

The other witnesses had nothing of importance to add.

There was, of course, only one possible verdict: "Murder by person or persons unknown."

No revolver had been found, and there were unmistakable signs of a struggle.

Doctor Millbrook gave his evidence concisely, coldly, ascribing death to a bullet through the heart.

Larry and I discussed the evidence as we walked from the

court-room. The upset chair, the scuffled rug, could mean only one thing: The murderer was hidden somewhere there in the room when I looked in. (I was finding it easier every hour to exclude the two Venell sisters from the case.) The idea must have been to picture a stranger as the murderer. Yet, somehow, Doctor Millbrook's talk with us had fixed in my mind that the murderer was no stranger, though he may have entered by the French window. Of course, even then it may have been one of the guests.

Larry let me do most of the talking.

"Did you notice the stranger in the second front scat—behind Doctor Millbrook?"

I hadn't. "Why?"

"Nothing. I'm just curious, that's all."

It was in High Street that Jack Ponting overtook us.

"Been to the inquest?" he asked. The effort to make his voice sound casual was not a success.

Larry told him we had.

"And, of course, 'murder by person or persons unknown,'" said Jack.

I asked what else there was to find.

His eyes flickered to mine and fell away. Then he laughed shortly. "I thought perhaps Inspector Emerson might have found a victim."

"Inspector Emerson," said Larry lazily, "was too smart for that. He concealed all his evidence—except a word here and there, mostly between lines. . . . You should have been there, Jack."

Ponting had fallen into step with us. "Mind if I walk along a bit?"

"Come and have lunch with us," Larry invited. "We're going to Angelico's. An inquest's a hungry affair—if the police try not to be; and this is my spaghetti day."

"Thanks—thanks! Yes, I guess I can make it."

And all the time I knew that he would have made it in the face of anything.

"These coroners' inquests!" Larry yawned. "Nothing but official blinds. The one wish of the police is to conceal clues. For instance, they failed to call you."

Ponting missed a step. "Me? Why should they call me? I was only one of a couple of score."

"Number is unimportant," said Larry.

"What do you mean?"

"Just that it was most apparent that they wished to lull those they failed to call into a sense of security. That sort of thing has convicted many a murderer."

"Look here, Larry—" Ponting began angrily.

"I'm just telling you," said Larry easily. And just then we turned in to Angelico's.

Larry waved Ponting to the chair facing the windows.

"Effie," he said, unfolding his napkin, "gave the only evidence that might point to something. There was a telephone call, she said."

"But I was there," said Ponting hurriedly, and blushed and dropped his face over the napkin he fussed with.

"Of course. But a telephone call might mean nothing. . . . In fact, it probably did mean nothing or the police would not have brought it out. To the world—and probably to the police—it looks as if it was one of the guests murdered Vance Horton."

Ponting leaned suddenly across the table. His eyes were fevered, and a spot of red showed on either cheek.

"And first among them would be Jack Ponting. Is that it? God, boys," he burst out, the hand on the table shaking pitifully, "if you knew how it feels to feel like a murderer! Jack Ponting was the one there, the one of them all, with most to gain from Vance's death."

Larry reached across the table and touched his hand soothingly.

"All right, Jack. Let it go at that. Don't let the whole room hear you."

He sat for a moment, his eyes fixed on Ponting's.

"Then it wasn't you who shot him?"

Ponting struggled to his feet, upsetting his chair. Larry reached down and upended it, laughing easily. But under his breath he said: "Sit down, you fool!" For everyone had looked up at the noise.

Ponting slowly resumed his seat.

"You mean," said Larry, "you didn't do it. That's all I asked. Neither did I shoot him, nor Dill here, and if you asked us we'd say so. But, Jack, Dill and I are going to find who *did* kill him. We've reasons for wishing to know—no matter who it was. We can't afford to consider friends in this. Hovis bread, if you please," he demanded of the waiter.

Ponting wiped his forehead. "I'm all on edge," he sighed.

"We're all of us on edge," said Larry, "though some aren't foolish enough to advertise it."

"Yes . . . yes." Ponting's inflamed eyes flickered from Larry's face to mine and back. "I hope you find him," he said, and jabbed a fork into the plate of spaghetti before him.

Larry sampled his own plate with the air of a connoisseur.

"What else?" he asked.

"Why—why—" Ponting looked up, as Larry continued carelessly to wind a long string about his fork. "Of course you know I was there."

"Yes," drawled Larry, and there was a touch of contempt in his voice, "we heard about that."

"And you wonder, of course. But remember, Vance had lost me one job. You may not know that he was about to have me kicked from another."

Larry said: "That's what made me wonder. I'd mention it in a whisper if I were you."

"I'm explaining—to you," said Ponting nervously. "You know Vance. He was like a cat playing with a mouse. He took his greatest pleasure from seeing his victims squirm. While he tortured them he smiled. Take those guests there that night and you'll understand. Most of them hated him, yet they had reasons for accepting his invitation. I had."

He pushed his plate away; he had eaten almost nothing.

"There were varied reasons. Some daren't refuse. Some were too proud to refuse. Some may have hated him so intensely that they couldn't bear to lose sight of him—feeding their hatred. . . . And one went to kill him."

"And you?" Larry queried. "And keep your voice down."

"My reason was different. I went as a beggar." The blood that came so readily to his cheeks flamed there now. "I've a wife and four small children . . . And jobs are hard to find—in my line. And I haven't saved much—with Molly's illness and the kiddies . . . And— another operation for Molly as soon as we can get her strength up. I was willing to do anything to save my job."

The manner in which Jack was doing his job occurred to me. "I've seen *The Silver Slipper,*" I said.

He flushed. "Then you see what all this has done to me and

my work. I'm afraid to be honest. I daren't be. I can't afford to lose a friend."

Larry interrupted with his first sign of impatience: "You went as a beggar. Did you think for a moment that Vance Horton, surrounded by all those so-called friends, would do anything but sneer at you?"

"Wouldn't you take a chance," Ponting countered, "in my position?"

"In your position," said Larry slowly, "I might have shot him."

A spasm darted through Ponting's body, but he said nothing.

"Did you take the chance?" inquired Larry.

"Yes . . . I took it."

"And the result?"

Ponting's eyes were on his plate, as he poked among the spaghetti with his fork.

"He—promised to let me alone."

Larry gave an exclamation of scorn. "I hope you can get that to the police more convincingly. As a murder it was more successful than your lie."

To my surprise Ponting did not resent it. Instead, he threw a look of such abject terror at Larry that I kicked my friend under the table.

"Is this your method, Larry, of finding the murderer?" he breathed. Suddenly he stiffened, and a cold fury gathered in his face. "If it is you'll run into trouble."

He pushed his chair back and rose. "I don't need to thank you for the lunch, because I'm paying for it myself. I'm surprised that you'd eat with a murderer."

"Jack! Jack!" I pleaded, as he strode away to the cashier's desk.

I made a move to follow, but Larry held me back. "Let him go, Dill. We must avoid a scene—here."

"What the hell did you say that for? You know damned well Jack Ponting is no murderer."

Larry only smiled. "I do *not* know. Someone as unlikely as Jack did it. Besides, I only accused him of lying, and he was. Vance promised him nothing—unless it was further revenge. Jack has had that lie in his mind ever since the murder. He's had his warning now that it won't do."

"But you believe he went there to try?"

"What does it matter, Dill? It's what he did, not what he tried to do. Finished?"

He paid the bill. As we reached the street Larry asked:

"Did you notice the pair at the table in the corner?" I had noticed no one.

"You'll never make a detective, Dill. The one with his back to us was Inspector Emerson. The other was the stranger I noted at the inquest."

XVII A New Witness

WHEN I let myself in with my latchkey I was somewhat surprised to find Doctor Millbrook waiting for me. He had arrived only a few minutes before, and, to my surprise, Cuddy had shown him to the library and remained to entertain him. But Cuddy was less the servant with my friends than with me.

In a way, too, it made me uneasy. Had the Doctor been able to draw Cuddy out in my absence? I didn't trust him—the Doctor, I mean. Even if he had made no deliberate attempt to draw from Cuddy things I did not wish the police to know, if Cuddy had been indiscreet, I thought I knew the Doctor well enough to feel certain that he would pass on any important information to Inspector Emerson. More and more I began to fear that the Doctor's seeming frankness was a mask.

Nervously I glanced about the library for any evidence of her presence the night before that Barbara might have left—though I knew that was impossible. She had departed in the early morning, escorted, at Larry's suggestion, by Cuddy. There had been some discussion about a rear exit, but Larry had frowned it down. If the police were watching the house that would only increase their suspicion, for they would have every exit covered.

Doctor Millbrook sat in his favourite position, low in his chair, his legs in their baggy trousers stretched before him, his hands clasped over his stomach. Cuddy left the moment I appeared.

The Doctor smiled after him.

"Faithful fellow, Fullerton—and so discreet. Not many of his kind left since the war."

"Cuddy's a product of the war," I said. "There never was anyone like Cuddy, and my father thought the same. Cuddy would die for me."

"And lie for you?" the Doctor asked, his eyes twinkling.

"I haven't had to ask him to," I replied, a little coldly.

The Doctor laughed. "You needn't worry, Fullerton." He pulled himself up and examined his watch. "What I dropped in for was to ask if you and Rockford could spare a lonely man a few more moments to-night. You see," roguishly, "what you got yourselves in for."

I inquired if anything more had developed, and he rubbed his nose apologetically.

"Naturally. Lots—and yet, perhaps, little." Suddenly he pushed himself forward to the edge of his chair and whispered: "I've been reading more of that young man's diary. . . . And—I'm divulging no official secret —I think they've called in Scotland Yard."

I am not sure that I concealed the start it gave me. Indirectly I had come in contact with Scotland Yard several times, and I had a real respect for its capacity. Considering where I stood in the list of suspects, and with a vivid picture of Barbara's mysterious position, no wonder I was uneasy. I had the prevailing idea that a detective's first duty was to find a victim.

"I think I can promise for Larry," I said.

It was late afternoon, however, before I succeeded in getting in touch with my friend, and when he replied I knew by the extravagant drawl of his voice that he had been active since I saw him last. Indeed, he cut me short at the first word:

"Busy, Dill?"

"Not where I should be," I grumbled. "Since this thing happened I haven't been able to think of anything else."

"Then jump in your car and come over."

I fancied another voice somewhere in his room, a protesting voice. But Larry must have covered the mouthpiece, for the line went suddenly dead. When he spoke again it was to repeat the invitation.

Something about it sent me hurrying to the garage, and in eight minutes I was running up the stairs to his quarters. I knocked.

Larry opened the door so quickly that I knew he was waiting for me, and with some anxiety. My eyes, flying beyond him, understood.

Across the room, his arms resting on the table, a sullen, belligerent scowl on his dark face, sat Lee Moshier.

If I had disliked Vance Horton, I had little but contempt for his satellite. From the first time I knew him he was Vance's toady, his tale-bearer, his companion and prompter in his worst excesses. Brought up in genteel poverty, he had been driven to desperate sycophancy. Inheriting a world of false pride, and encouraged in it by the wrong kind of companions, he had attached himself to the spendthrift Vance, thereby smothering any decent instincts he may have had.

In him Vance found his complement. Insolence and

obsequiousness, the lord and his henchman, arrogance and flattery. And with it went the disgusting dignity of one who tried to save his face. A burly fellow, as Vance's bodyguard he had attempted vengeance on me for the spanking I gave his overlord. It had ended in a draw, but only because I managed to conceal to the end of the term, ten days away, the two broken ribs resulting from Lee's heavy boot when he got me down.

He glared at me now, then smiled sneeringly, endeavouring in his usual way to mask his discomfort. And in the smile I saw the break in his discoloured teeth that was the substitute for the one I had knocked out in our fight. It alone had stood up against its owner's dissipations.

"Hello, Lee!"

"'Lo!" he snarled. And his eyes fell away to his clenched fists on the table.

Larry pointed to a chair and seated himself. He had his most careless manner working magnificently.

"Lee," he drawled, "has a brain-wave. He's become a detective. It's the most besotted guzzlers who make the most flaming evangelists for temperance. And Lee's initial efforts show signs of budding genius. Eh, Lee?" Lee had listened with such a look of insulting contempt on his face that I could scarcely restrain myself from hurling a book in his teeth. Long practice had made him an adept in that sort of expression; it was his one refuge from the trials of a sycophant.

"Very clever, Larry, very. Unfortunately your friends are unimpressed. Your rôle always was a shallow smartness. Pity you didn't take to literature."

Larry didn't alter his manner an iota. "Who knows? I may start now. This murder of your friend promises a real plot—if you'll only let me in on the inside with you." I thought Lee's eyes sharpened a little, but he managed to keep his lip curled.

Larry continued evenly:

"Mutual admiration society, eh? But you've made such a brilliant start, Lee, I fail to see why you should waste your genius on Dill."

"On me?" I looked from Larry to Lee.

And Lee shifted uneasily, then his insolence and defiance swept back.

"You were there that night, Dill Fullerton," he jerked.

It caught me unawares. "There? Where?"

Lee shook his head wearily. "You were outside Vance's house that night."

"Where were you that you saw me?" I countered.

"And that," laughed Larry, "is the crux of the situation. Lee didn't think of that."

I caught a flash of uneasiness through Lee's defiance, and I knew how thin was the mask, a crust too thin to insist Larry's blows.

"Who said *I* saw you?" Lee demanded.

"I specialized in dead languages, Lee," said Larry, and whistled a bar. "I'm letting you in to a private view of Sherlock Holmes at work."

Lee Moshier could control himself no longer. His eyes flashed angrily.

"All right. I did see him. I saw his car. I recognized it."

"You should be in the navy," said Larry. "They're looking for men who can see in the dark. But you always had a flair for seeing things, even back at Cortwright. I hope you've told the police."

I said, half angry, half contemptuous: "Probably he did. That anonymous letter the police received—"

Lee started forward. "What's that? Did someone else—see?" He had gripped the edge of the table with his large hands and was staring at me.

Larry, under cover of the table, shook his foot at me to let him reply.

"See what?" he inquired carelessly.

"Why—why—see Dill."

"Evidently someone else had as good eyes as yours, Lee. They saw Dill drive past Vance's house—"

But Lee had himself under control. "'Drive past.'" he laughed derisively. "Dill drove past—yes, when it was all over. He was there inside the grounds, beside the billiard-room."

"Ah! So you saw him yourself. You were there. And you were there before Dill was. And Vance Horton was shot before Dill entered the grounds—when you were there. You, who had the best reason of them all for getting Vance out of the way, you whom Vance was about to kick out—and to cut from his will. I wonder if the police will hear of that, too—anonymously."

Lee Moshier had half risen from his chair, his wide eyes fixed on Larry's face. With a groan he dropped back.

"My God, Larry, you wouldn't tell that!" His hands writhed over the table.

Larry's face was set and merciless. "You were there, Lee, when Vance was shot—murdered in cold blood."

"I was not," Lee cried. "I was not. I was standing at the front door. I'd just come out when I heard the shot—or I thought I did. There was so much noise—the windows were open—that I can't be sure. It frightened me. I didn't know what to do. You see, boys, I was a little drunk—and upset. But—but it isn't true that Vance was going to kick me out. He couldn't—he wouldn't. I was his best friend, the only one he could trust, the one who stuck to him through everything— and you don't know what that meant. I didn't want his money—only Vance, the one real friend I ever had. Vance was—"

"You were saying," said Larry, and his quiet, deadly voice was like a threat, "that you heard the shot and didn't know what to do. What *did* you do?"

"I stood there. I—"

"Did you hear a woman scream?"

"They were all shouting and screaming there in the room beside me. . . . Perhaps I didn't hear the shot. Perhaps I was just nervous, perhaps—"

"You heard the shot," Larry insisted mercilessly. "Go on."

"I—I thought it was a shot," said Lee. He seemed to be hypnotized by Larry's cold voice and colder eye. "I stood there by the door ever so long. Then—then I crept out toward the billiard-room. I heard a rustle in the bushes, and then—and then—" He stopped, and a cunning leer made his wet face more repulsive. "And then I saw Dill—and you too, Larry Rockford. Perhaps now you won't be so eager to tell the police."

Larry's face widened slowly to an easy smile as he rolled his eyes toward me. "Hadn't we better duck, Dill? You keep him engaged till I get away. That settles us. Phew!"

"You're right, it does," Lee replied furiously, whipping himself to a rage. "I saw you running away. You climbed into your car and cut along."

Larry nodded thoughtfully. "Yes . . . you heard your patron shot . . . and you saw two men run away. And then," suddenly straightening, "as Vance's best friend, his henchman, you hurried on to see what the two strangers were running from. And, of course, you found your patron murdered. And equally, of course, you went right in to telephone and get help—called the police and all that. . . . No, that doesn't seem to fit into what the police know. It doesn't fit, Lee, what I know. Instead of doing what you should have done—if all this is true—what you won't be able to explain away for not having done, you fled back into the house through the front door—and when the police arrived you feigned drunkenness to Inspector Emerson."

Lee's thick lips had fallen apart, and the lump in his throat rose and fell.

"You—saw me?"

"I left Dill's car just around the corner and went back. You saw me there with the police. And when the police find out, I'll be able to say only that I saw you bolting back into the house after you saw Vance was murdered. And the French window was still open."

"I didn't do it, Larry, 'fore God I didn't." The big hands on the table shook and trembled. "I wouldn't do a thing like that. Can't you tell the police you saw me just look in and run away—if you must tell them anything? I did run away, just as soon as I saw. I was frightened, because—because I'd heard—what you said— that Vance was through with me." He stopped with a gasp, panic-stricken.

But Larry was not through with him yet,

"And you thought, to save yourself, you'd fasten the crime on Dill. Well, Lee, it won't work. For Dill and I are a jump ahead of you. We have evidence the police must know some time, because we're going to find who fired that shot—the proof of it, I mean. In the list of those who might wish Vance Horton dead Dill and I are near the bottom. Where do you stand? Shall we leave it to the police to decide—take our stories together to Inspector Emerson here and now . . . and to Scotland Yard?"

Lee gasped. "Is—have they—called in—"

"Scotland Yard," Larry filled in.

All the belligerency, all the caution, seemed to evaporate from Lee Moshier's mind. He fell back limply in the chair.

"You won't tell them, boys, please. I swear I've told the truth. But Scotland Yard—it wouldn't believe."

"Can you blame it?"

"But it's the truth, Larry."

"The whole truth?"

"The whole—yes, everything."

"You looked in and saw the dead body, you say?"

"Yes."

"Where was it?"

"Why—there—where it was when Inspector Emerson called me in—on the floor, I mean, between the billiard-tables."

Larry lifted his eyebrows at me. I shook my head stubbornly.

"How long was that after you saw us run away?" he asked.

"Two or three minutes, perhaps a bit more. I was frightened. I waited to see—to see if anything had happened. I just looked and ran back to the house—like you saw me."

"By the way, who was it called the police?" I asked.

"Effie Shannon." It was Larry who answered.

Lee's jaw squared. "Effie called them, did she? I didn't know that. I thought someone outside must have heard the shot and telephoned." He lowered his eyes to the edge of the table, his head nodding thoughtfully. Suddenly he pushed the chair back and got up. "I didn't really think you boys had done it," he said ingratiatingly, "but, just the same—"

"We were there," explained Larry, "because as we passed we heard the shot."

Lee was almost at the door. "All right. It wasn't any of us. I'm not going to say a word about what I saw."

He paused at the door, eyeing Larry anxiously. But Larry did not even look at him, and then the door slammed and we were alone.

Larry heaved a troubled sigh. "And still they accuse themselves."

"And us," I added. "The world was in Vance's garden or house that night."

"*Your* world," Larry corrected, with a laugh. "And now, to sum the interview up: Lee Moshier's afraid of us. . . . Don't forget he was afraid of Vance, too."

I am not sure that Larry looked forward as eagerly as I to our second visit to Doctor Millbrook. He said little, but I imagined the day was planned with the visit in view.

The Doctor interested me, even while he left me uncertain that we could trust him. He was a curious mixture of official conscientiousness and unofficial sentimentality. It was more or less well known, even apart from his confession to us, that much of his duty was repugnant to him; but there had never before been, so far as Larry and I knew, the slightest evidence that he was anything but punctilious in the performance of that duty. His defence of his treatment of the diary was the casuistry of one whose uneasiness demanded justification, weak as it might be.

I liked him, and I opposed my doubt of the propriety of his action with his innate sentimentality that had at last forced itself to the surface. I convinced myself that, should the diary reveal anything that might assist the police, he would find some way of getting it into their hands.

Larry's one comment on the invitation, on our acceptance, was:

"Unorthodox, but damned promising!"

"And now," I said—we were nearing the house—"we must keep before us that we're *after* information, not giving it."

"Passed with honours," Larry applauded. "D'you feel, Dill, we've accomplished anything in these two days?"

I was flattered that he asked. But I was forced to admit that I was more confused than ever.

"If only," he chuckled, "we weren't such damned gentlemen, we might get the whole story from Willo and Barbara, eh?"

"Aw, shut up!" I snapped.

"Fini. And now," as we left the car parked before Ihe house, "remember the warning of a famous detective: 'We're *after* information, not giving it.'"

This time Mrs. Jaggers received us affably enough. Indeed, by the speed with which the door was opened, she must have been parked inside, waiting for us.

Again the soft strains of the piano reached us along the hall—a sonata by Scarlatti—and Mrs. Jaggers, with surprising understanding, placed a warning finger to her lips and softly closed the door behind us. For half a minute we stood, Mrs. Jaggers with the door-knob still in her hand, listening.

And then, in the middle of a bar, the music ceased, and next instant the Doctor stood in the doorway, smiling awkwardly at us.

"I saw you," he confessed bashfully, "the moment you came in. I tried to go on, but I couldn't. I'm no good at that sort of thing."

He was clad in a worn velvet jacket, his long hair awry at the crown, his baggy trousers caught up on the heels of red morocco slippers.

"You don't know," he beamed, rubbing his hands together, "what all this means to me. I've looked forward to it all the afternoon. Usually—unless I'm called out— I sit here alone all the evening. All right, Mrs. Jaggers," waving her away.

He closed the sitting-room door.

"Did I speak sharply to her? You know, she's getting on my nerves. I advertised to-day for that pretty girl I told you about. Then I'll keep Mrs. Jaggers in the kitchen. I can't see that her sourness affects the food she cooks, at any rate. Her other good trait is that she plays the bodyguard to perfection. Indeed, sometimes the police themselves have a devil of a time getting to me. I'm thankful she doesn't complain about my music."

"'Complain?'" I cried. "Doctor, you could make a living at the piano."

"I put myself through college on it." He waved us to chairs. "But I had other—ambitions."

His tone had grown dreamy, and his thick hands, planted firmly on his knees, seemed to grasp at a never-to-be-forgotten past.

"Post-mortems, for instance," I laughed.

"No." He lifted his head abruptly and fixed his eyes gravely on mine. "No—that's why I'm resigning." He saw our surprise and smiled. "Yes, resigning."

But there seemed little pleasure in the prospect, for he rose and walked to the piano and leaned on it, his back to us.

"Is it this Vance Horton case?" Larry inquired.

"It's the last straw. . . . His diary." Again that dreamy tone, as if communing with himself.

"But you're finishing the case?"

"Of course." He came and stood before us, legs spread, hands in the pockets of the velvet jacket. "I'm giving to the police all I've collected about it to this time. But hereafter—well, I'm only a witness for what has already happened. But there can't be anything more for me to do."

"The diary?" asked Larry.

The Doctor nodded. "As a matter of duty I've kept myself from reading much of the diary. When my resignation's accepted I'm free to go right through that red book. I want to."

He surged about and hurried into the laboratory. We heard the twirl of the combination of the safe, and in a few moments he was back with a thick red-backed book that he held almost reverently before him.

"This is it. I'm not happy about it. I wasn't happy reading it; I'm not happy not finishing it. So unhappy that I won't be able— What's that?"

It was the hollow rattle of the knocker through the passage. In four long strides the Doctor had the door open, then he hurried back to the piano, to stand looking up into the mirror above it.

Mrs. Jaggers trotted along the passage, the front door opened. Larry rose and took his stand behind the Doctor, his eyes fixed on the mirror. Men's voices reached us. The Doctor stepped quickly aside to the bookshelves and thrust the diary among the other books.

"I had nothing to do with this, boys," he whispered unhappily. "Please believe me." Then he hurried to the door. "Ah, hello, Inspector! Come right in."

"Good night, Doctor." Heavy steps sounded along the hall, and Inspector Emerson and a strange man appeared in the doorway.

The Doctor had stepped back into the room while the two men were out of sight in the hall, and had made a motion toward the laboratory. But Larry shook his head.

Inspector Emerson was plainly annoyed, as well as surprised, at seeing us, but he contrived a cold smile.

"Good evening, Rockford—Fullerton. This, Doctor, is James Rountree, an old London friend. Doctor Millbrook, James."

We were introduced. Rountree was a large man with straight shoulders and the neck of a wrestler, but there was an air of refinement about him and his clothes that made one almost unconscious of his size and obvious strength. He greeted us affably. A man of wide experience I decided.

The Doctor hurried away, to return in a surprisingly short time with five glasses and a bottle on a tray. One was filled with water. This he removed and set on the desk before passing the tray. There was a sly twinkle in his eye.

"I hope you like this," he said. "It used to be my favourite wine. I've been on the water-wagon for three years. I found patients didn't like the smell of liquor on my breath."

Rountree passed his glass under his nose, and his eye lit up. "Cassis!" he murmured. "I haven't tasted it since a holiday around Marseilles two years ago. Am I right, Doctor?"

The Doctor's eyes widened. "How surprising! Of course you're right. I don't need, then, to tell you it's the real thing."

Inspector Emerson was sampling his glass gingerly. "They're all much alike to me—just sweet and sour. I'm no connoisseur. All I know is that if all the Chianti I meet over the world were raised in Chianti, then Chianti must be several stories high."

"Chianti," said Rountree, "is the King of Italy's speciality. And the Chianti you buy even in Siena isn't the same as you're given to drink in the houses of the peasants who raise the grapes. I don't know the explanation. I tried to buy from their private stores, but, while they'd serve it liberally, they always refused to sell."

We talked wines for a time. Rountree was an encyclopaedia on the subject, with a delightful facility of expression. The Doctor, too, though confining himself to water as a drink, knew only little less.

All the time he kept shooting us apologetic, unhappy glances. I felt for him.

And then Inspector Emerson struck at the purpose of their visit.

"I hope," he said, turning to Larry and me, "you won't mind if we talk shop for a few minutes." But as Larry and I rose to go he stopped us. "Nothing private. It's shop only to the Doctor and me. Rountree, Doctor, is as informed on fire-arms as on wines; he's made a hobby of them. I wish you'd let him see that bullet you extracted from young Horton's body."

The Doctor jumped to his feet. "Certainly. If he can help us it may save me a lot of guessing. It's here in the laboratory. Will you excuse us?" he asked, bowing to Larry and me.

They disappeared into the laboratory, and the door closed.

I looked inquiringly at Larry. But Larry was not thinking of me. The moment the door closed he was on his feet, making for the bookshelves. Without a moment's hesitation he drew the red-backed diary from its concealment with one hand, while with the other he took another book at random, glanced at the title, and set it on the desk. The diary he opened.

"Speaking of wines," he drawled, in a conversational tone, at the same time pointing to the closed laboratory door, "did you ever notice the difference between those of, say, Genoa, and those of Sicily? I've spent weeks in Northern Italy—and drunk vinegar. Except the vermouth of Turin, of course. I'm speaking of the *vins du pays*. But that's French."

He had the red-backed book open, his eyes devouring the pages.

"I'm afraid," I said, "I'm more like the Inspector—my taste is not fine enough to distinguish more than those I like and those I don't like . . ." I talked on, making the sound of conversation, but scarcely aware of what I was saying. My eyes were fixed on Larry's amazed and excited face. He would read a sentence and skip on for several pages. And as he read such a conflicting play of emotions passed over his face that I often forgot my rôle.

So absorbed were we both that when the laboratory door opened he had just time to shove the diary back and turn to the other book on the desk before him.

I suppose the state of my nerves made me more observant than usual, for I saw Rountree's attention fly straight to Larry's face; and the Doctor, even as he drew the door shut behind him, was turned toward my friend, now smiling sheepishly up from the big green book he held.

"Getting a line, Doctor, on the tools you use. I may want some day to commit a murder myself, and I should know how to circumvent you. How, for instance," pressing a finger against the open page, "could I poison my pet enemy and get away with it? Here's hyoscin. Isn't that what Dr. Crippen used?"

Doctor Millbrook sank into a chair and steepled his hands before him.

"D'you know, I've often wondered if Crippen really intended to kill his wife. Hyoscin has a medicinal value, you know—for nymphomaniacs. Do we know exactly what sort of a girl his wife was—in that way, I mean? And Crippen had his secretary. Let's see,

Rockford." He rose and lunged across the desk to take the book from Larry's hand. But Larry, as he handed it over, withdrew his finger, and the book closed.

Whether the Doctor noticed anything or not I do not know. He ran his eye along the shelf and withdrew a newer book. "This is later." Turning, he held it out toward Inspector Emerson. "The tool I used in the Dillingham case. By the time Sir George Mullet had me in the witness stand to stampede me I was letter-perfect against his client."

The Inspector laughed. "Lucky for you. We have to be letter-perfect in the cases he handles. What he doesn't know about poisons all the poisoners of the last ten years can't teach him."

"Nor," added the Doctor, "all the books of the last hundred years. It did me good to have to brush up."

Inspector Emerson had not sat down. "Well, we're much obliged, Doctor. Hope we haven't spoiled your evening."

"Not at all, not at all. That's my job—yet."

Rountree had said nothing since returning to the room. Now he said:

"I think you're right about the bullet, Doctor. Some time when you're in London I'd be glad to have you call and see my collection of fire-arms and cartridges."

Doctor Millbrook saw them to the door. He returned and, leaning weakly against the wall, let out a noisy sigh of relief.

"Did I look like the murderer myself?" he smiled. "Coming in just at that moment, when I had something in my hand I was keeping from the police, I wasn't what you might call at ease. I suppose you noticed it. I hope we looked to them more innocent than we are."

Larry slowly lighted a cigarette. "We managed it pretty well—for novices," he said. "The one who failed is the adept—Rountree. I've a good memory for faces. Of course, it's your duty to tell us nothing, but I'm telling you I saw Rountree at the inquest. I saw him at lunch with Inspector Emerson. Enter Scotland Yard, eh?"

XIX A TRAIL

NEXT day I could no longer afford to neglect the office. But the hours I spent there were largely wasted, for I found it almost impossible even to sign my own name. Larry and I had not been in touch all day, and Larry out of my sight meant missing some new excitement. For Larry, I felt, was not taking me entirely into his confidence.

For instance, he refused to be drawn concerning what the had read in Vance Horton's diary.

"Oh," he replied vaguely to my questions, "I hadn't time—just a line here and there. Did you notice the thickness of the book? A regular saga, Dill. It would take a week to read."

"Nothing," I declared, "in Vance Horton's life could resemble a saga. He would write only of himself, and Vance was generations from being a hero. Did you see any reason for Doctor Millbrook's secrecy about it?"

"I'm no diviner, Dill. With about four minutes to shuffle the pages—Just the same," thoughtfully, "I must have that diary."

"How about a touch of Rafflesing?" I suggested, "We might break in some night. We made such a success of it night before last."

"Luck, Dill, sheer luck."

"And all bad," I declared.

"No . . . no, not all of it. Indeed, quite a success. . . . But I've never learned the gentle art of safecracking. Vance's diary is kept in the Doctor's safe—with the bullet. I could do with both."

I could get nothing more from him. But as we ate a late supper in "The Mars" on our way home he was silent and thoughtful, and, I thought, none too easy in his mind.

All these things kept pressing against my work as I laboured in the office to crowd three days into one. Finally I gave up.

As I crossed the corridor to the lift a door at the end opened and Effie Shannon came out.

Effie is a beautiful girl. Ever since we played together as kids, and I was her champion, I have thought so, though I was always a little fearful of her temper. There had, indeed, been a time when I pictured her as something more than a friend, but Effie had put an end to that in a few laughing but frank phrases. And then Vance Horton had intervened. I have often wondered if my interest in Effie was not the cause of his sudden conquering attack on her defences. I had no chance with him. Few had.

Perhaps it was jealousy that had convinced me that with the advent of Vance Effie's beauty hardened, her femininity underwent a repellent change. Still, as she came along the corridor I saw no reason for changing my mind about the fact of her beauty and carriage, especially as now all her hardness had vanished. Her eyes were wet, her under-lip was caught between her teeth. Silently, without the relief of sobs, Effie Shannon was crying.

She was within three steps of me before she noticed me. Then she stopped, and one hand jerked upward to press a crushed handkerchief to her face. For a long moment she stood, her eyes fixed on mine, frightened, uncertain—the old Effie at her best. I knew she longed to turn and flee, but she dare not.

And then a movement beyond her, at the angle in the corridor, sent my eyes flying past her shoulder. It was only a fleeting glance, but enough to recognize Lee Moshier.

At that moment the lift arrived, and, bowing to Effie, I stepped aside and let her pass. She went with a rush.

"All right," I called to the liftman, waving him away. "I forgot something. Go on."

And in the moment the door slid shut, separating Effie and me, she threw a wondering but grateful look at me.

It was that glimpse of Lee Moshier's face that had altered my plans, not Effie's uneasiness. As the door of the lift closed Lee, thinking I too had gone down, shot out into the corridor. At sight of me he jerked to a stop, and his face reddened.

"Yes," I sneered, walking straight up to him, "you're sneaking after Effie now. Trying for another victim, eh?"

An almost uncontrollable impulse to crash my fist into his sombre face set my teeth together. Had I done so I would probably have landed in the hospital—or the mortuary—for Lee was a bruiser. Vance, I had heard, had had him take boxing lessons.

"Mind your own damned business!" he snarled, and I saw his fists clench at his sides.

Oddly enough, the very intensity of his fury calmed my own. "Not so fast, Lee," I warned. "Perhaps if Effie knew she might—take steps. Or perhaps you'd prefer that I tell the police."

He planted himself challengingly before me. He was a

different Lee Moshier with me from what he was with Larry. For Larry was his master, mentally and physically. He advanced his face until we were looking cross-eyed at each other.

"If you and Larry aren't damned fools, you'll keep out of this," he threatened.

"At any rate," I returned, not giving an inch, "we're not apt to get our necks stretched."

He stepped back at that, and once again there came into his face the look of dread I had seen there the afternoon before in Larry's quarters. I followed it up quickly:

"What have you in mind about Effie?"

"Same as you'd have, if you were me," he replied.

"What has she done to you?"

He glared toward the lift shaft. "She always hated me. She tried to turn Vance against me. . . . It didn't work," he ended, with a leer.

"You mean you turned the tables—turned Vance against her."

"Well, he threw her out, didn't he?" he jeered triumphantly.

"As he planned to do with you—if someone hadn't stopped it."

His face darkened. "It's a lie. You'd have to prove that. And you couldn't."

"Except that Vance is dead—and you were where you might have killed him. But what have you to do with Effie?"

"She's trying to save herself by fastening the murder on me."

"How do you know?"

"She accused me to my face. She's been at the police station, and Inspector Emerson was at her rooms this morning. And," whirling about and pointing, "what do you think she was doing in there."

I followed his pointing finger. On the glass door of the office Effie had just left was the inscription: "Mullet, Clarkson & Staples."

"What of it?" I asked, though I had the answer before I asked it.

"You know what of it. She's been putting Sir George Mullet on my tracks."

I laughed scornfully. "Sir George is a criminal lawyer, not a detective. He's always for the defence."

Lee stood with his eyes fixed on the glass door. A smile, a nasty smile, crept slowly over his face.

"Yes . . . that's so. . . . For the defence. And," furiously, "she's going to need him, because I can send her to the gallows."

With another nasty laugh he passed on toward the lift, while I followed the corridor around the corner. I could not bring myself to use the lift with him.

XX UNEASY COMPANIONS

OUT of sight of the lift I waited. And my eye fell on the office door at the end of the corridor:

"MULLET, CLARKSON & STAPLES."

Nothing else. The legal firm of Mullet, Clarkson & Staples required nothing more, for the name of Sir George Mullet was connected with all the famous criminal trials of the past decade.

In my profession I knew Sir George, of course. I had, indeed, called him in on two or three important cases I had the good fortune to direct. And Sir George had reciprocated by turning over to me work that was not in his line.

Mullet, Clarkson & Staples—and Effie Shannon—and Lee Moshier's leering suggestion!

Without anything very definite in mind I advanced and opened the office door.

Half a dozen clerks sat in the large, formal office I entered, two of them elderly men seated on old-fashioned high stools. No one looked up as I entered, and their industry struck me as rather overdone. Then I understood.

In the doorway of an inner room stood a group that made me doubt my eyes—Larry, Willo Venell, and Sir George Mullet.

Larry saw me and grinned, a little sheepishly I thought. And Willo, standing with her back to me, must have seen the expression on his face, for she turned quickly. At sight of me she took a quick step as if to return to the room they had evidently just left, but Sir George's hand fell on her arm.

"Good afternoon, Fullerton! Want to see me? I'll be free in a moment." He glanced at Willo, and a sly smile creased his face. "Ah, yes, I see—of course. Perhaps you'd all like to come into my office." His eyes were fixed keenly on Willo's face.

But the girl only frowned and stiffened.

"All right." The big lawyer shrugged indifferently. "The story is yours, not mine." And then the sly amusement in the lines about his eyes changed to something like pity.

Willo must have noticed that, too, for without a word she wheeled about and stalked stiffly past me to the door. She did not so much as recognize me with a nod; but under the cold grimness of her pretty face I sensed a trepidation she could not entirely conceal.

Larry lounged up to me, still smiling. But before he could speak Sir George beckoned.

"I can give you a few minutes now, Fullerton."

"Thank you," I replied. "I don't need to see you now."

And Sir George only nodded. "Quite in character—A run of them." Suddenly he laughed. "Everything left at loose ends. Well, it's your problem, all of you, not mine." With a bow he backed into the room and closed the door.

Larry took my arm and led me into the corridor. And there he, too, burst out laughing.

"'Quite in character,' eh? Great man, Sir George. 'Everything left at loose ends.' He's right. And you look as if you see yourself one of the loosest ends, Dill. Strange you should pop up just then. A little birdie must have—"

"I'm waiting for something more than the little birdie told me," I interrupted grimly.

"What more can you wish?" he asked. "You saw dear little Effie leave."

"And Effie's one of the loose ends. Particularly because, leaving you and those others there, she passed me without so much as speaking."

"H'm! And Willo did the same. What's the matter with you, Dill? Aren't you bathing enough?" I opened my lips to make an angry protest, but he would not wait. "Trouble is, Dill, you carry the most accusing face. You should be a policeman. Why, Effie knows you think she murdered Vance . . . and so does Willo Venell. And before Lee, and Jack, and Jordan, and goodness knows how many more—including myself—you look precisely the same. If accusation were conviction, old thing, we'd all be skipping the country."

Larry rippled with restrained laughter—and I had nothing of importance to say.

"Don't be an ass!" was what I did say.

"We're all asses, Dill . . . and in nothing so much as in thinking everyone but ourselves an ass. Take Willo, for instance. I wonder if she thinks Sir George Mullet an ass? She didn't tell him the whole story, and he knows it."

"So you've all been consulting Sir George," I scoffed. "If the police knew that—"

"In multitude of numbers," laughed Larry, "is safety . . . of a kind. I'm afraid I, too, insulted the great man by thinking I could fool him."

He leaned against the lift shaft and laughed till he shook.

"You don't know how funny it was, Dill. As luck would have it, we trooped into that office one after another. And Sir George, who seems to have been keeping his ear to the ground, sensed what we wanted as soon as each was announced. I was in his office when the other two arrived. It seems they don't know each other, and they waited their turns to see Sir George. And then Sir George, in a puckish humour, brought us all together. You see how funny it was. Fact is, Sir George doesn't seem to want the case of any of us. He saw us first separately for a few minutes. I caught the spirit of the thing and mentioned your part."

"You damned fool!" I protested.

"Well, it made it so much funnier. And, since it had gone so far, it seemed best to make it a scream. Now don't burst an artery, because—because I've been a good friend of yours. I have the Venell sisters' address. You see how a cool detective works. They've moved out from the parental—the paternal roof, for their mother is dead. It's the revolt of light-headed youth—though Barbara's dark head is in it too. I'm considering it as kindly as I can. See what you owe me."

I was never quite sure of Larry. His habit of teasing, his imagination, his reckless, care-free ways, sometimes left me uneasy, not only as to the truth behind his laughing remarks, but as to the consequences of what, in his thoughtlessness, he had effected. All I knew was that three of the suspects in the murder of Vance Horton had, by some coincidence, happened to seek to retain Sir George Mullet's services—certainly to consult him regarding the case. What had really happened in that inner office I could not be sure. In consequence I was something more than annoyed.

Larry saw it and thought to soothe me by suggesting "The Scotch Thistle" for tea. He knew how I liked the toasted scones there. But over the scones and the tea he was silent. All his chuckling had vanished, and he drank in a thoughtful silence that convinced me more surely than ever that he was not telling me everything. He even toyed with the cinnamon toast he preferred— and that was momentous.

Out on the street, he refused even to permit me to drive him home. And that, too, was momentous.

Weighed down with the muddle of deductions and fears that flooded through my mind, I suddenly decided to seek the relaxation of the golf club. Without going home, I drove straight there. And all my hopes were killed by the first couple I saw—Jordan Fleming and Nora. They were returning from a round. Nora has held the ladies' club championship for two years, so that she was no mean opponent even for Jordan. Their faces beamed with happiness and health. The wind had whipped a lock of golden hair loose from the white beret Nora wore, and as she flung it back with a gay lift of her head she saw me.

"Hello, Dill!" she called, waving her hand.

Jordan, who had not noticed me before, looked around and waved. Just then he noticed that stray lock and, turning, caught it playfully between his fingers and twisted it. Then he thrust it under the beret and kissed Nora squarely on the lips.

"My lucky day, Dill," he shouted. "I gave her seven and—"

Nora struck his hand playfully away. "You see how he's played all the afternoon, Dill—just like that. How could you expect me to play my game?"

"He doesn't," said Jordan. He trotted nearer. "I say, Dill, break away from the old desk and come for a holiday. Nora and I are going across to Brittany for a couple of weeks—or so."

The joy had vanished from his tone as he added the last two words.

"But—but," I stammered, "you can't—"

Jordan's face set in a cold stare. "We can do what we damn well please, can't we? Why not?" And he spun about on his heel and climbed the steps to the dressing-room door. At the top he stopped.

"Come and have dinner with us, Dill," he called. "Larry'll be here."

Larry'll be here! It held me speechless. Larry here, and he had not mentioned it! What wasn't he concealing from me?

My silence was consent, for Nora called, "Seven sharp. You can look after Effie till Larry comes—then you can fight it out between you."

I remained in the car, staring stupidly at the door through which they had disappeared.

Larry—the two Flemings—Effie Shannon! Arranged—and, but for a stroke of luck, I would never have known of it. Of course, but for the fact that we were all concerned in the murder of Vance Horton there was no reason why I should know. But everything that happened now bore a new importance, a real significance. Who, I asked myself, had arranged it?

Finding an empty corner of the club verandah, I sat down with my pipe. Out before me a steep bank dropped away for thirty feet to the wide expanse of one of the most beautiful courses in England. Golfers dotted the landscape, spots of white and grey against the vivid green of the grass. Now and then a group, concealed heretofore by the bank, would swing up the steps toward the club-house, laughing and chatting, to disappear around the verandah to the dressing-room entrance.

Most of them I knew, but with my pipe sucking absent-mindedly, I paid no attention, and the railing of the verandah concealed me. And then my pipe dropped from my limp lips. Climbing sturdily into view came a pair I could not ignore.

Effie Shannon and Lee Moshier!

The succession of unexpected associations, the confusion of impression, that had crowded one another all the afternoon left me gasping. I thrust my pipe into my pocket without knowing what I did. The pair passed on. Not a word had they spoken since coming into sight. Effie Shannon and Lee Moshier.

How long I sat there, seeing nothing, hearing nothing of the gabble of the crowd now swarming up to the verandahs from the dressing-rooms, I do not know. Not a knot in the tangle loosened, try as I would to straighten the simplest one out.

It was Nora Fleming's voice at my elbow that roused me:

"Lonely, Dill—or just thinking?" Her voice had that sweet, pouty tone that had made her so lovable in the early days of her marriage to Jordan. "It isn't healthy for a bachelor to isolate himself."

I scrambled to my feet and blinked at her. Her voice had sent my mind speeding back to those earlier days, and for a moment I wondered if all the horror and tragedy of the last three days was more than a bad dream.

Something of it must have carried to her—something in my eyes—for she turned abruptly away and fussed with the chair I had placed for her. And I knew instantly that this new-found happiness of hers and Jordan's overlay thinly a great fear.

"I've been comfortable here, Nora," I said. "Beautiful view. I was just—"

She was not listening. "Larry shown up yet?"

"I haven't seen him . . . Effie came in some time ago."

"Yes, she's in the lounge." She leaned forward on the railing without looking at me. "I hope you don't mind another in the party, Dill. Lee Moshier was on the course with Effie; we couldn't omit him."

"It's not my party," I said, and fell silent.

She turned her head and looked steadily into my eyes.

"I'm sorry, Dill. . . . Now let's talk of the view—or the weather."

"Or of Jordan," I suggested boldly.

Her eyes lit up at the name—and the shell of their happiness seemed more substantial than I had thought.

"'Of Jordan?'" she repeated dreamily. But before she could say more Effie and Lee joined us. Close behind came Jordan. Lee caught my eye and glanced at Effie. He was, I knew, begging me to forget the afternoon, and there was nothing else, of course, for me to do.

Lee bent over Nora's hand. "So sweet of you, Nora. Please don't let me be an intruder. A fifth is always—well, a fifth."

"Larry's coming, too," said Jordan.

"Oh, Larry!" Lee walked to the railing where I could not see his face.

Jordan looked at his watch. "It's seven now. What the devil's keeping him? As a matter of fact I mentioned a quarter to. Larry's never late. And out here he knows the penalty for missing the first service."

The verandah had almost emptied, for every club member knew the penalty. We were running the club short-handed for the sake of economy.

Jordan kept examining his watch fretfully. The light-hearted happiness so conspicuous in his face and manner when I saw him and Nora first had given place to a strange nervousness and irritability as he paced up and down.

Lee had turned back to Nora and was making himself agreeable. But Effie, beyond a cold nod to me, had shown no sign that she was more than a stranger to us all. So silent was she, so lifeless, that I wondered if she had been doping. There had been rumours—as there were always rumours where Vance Horton was concerned. She caught my glance and commenced to talk to Nora and Lee. But in a few moments she was silent again, her hands limp in her lap, her eyes unfocused. And all the time she chained her cigarettes.

At seven-thirty Jordan had worked himself up to muffled oaths. So that I went inside and called up Larry's rooms. But there was no response. And so we sat down without him.

The dinner was spotty in a social way, though the food was better than usual. Larry's unexplained absence, and a restraint that seemed to affect us all, made it anything but a success. Jordan's eyes flickered about the table, landing often on Effie and me; and when either of us caught his eye—as Effie certainly did—he would clear his throat in an embarrassed way and gibber something foolish. Nora was disturbed by it, as I could see. Lee tried to keep the conversation going, but it faltered badly.

Not one of us, I knew, but realized that at that table sat five whose connection with Vance Horton's murder was unknown to the others, whose innocence could only be established by one of them who might be guilty. And whoever killed Vance Horton was certainly not establishing anyone's innocence but his own.

I was curious about Lee. But on one point I was decided—that Effie should be warned. But I was not the one to warn her. Any warning I should give would be to two other girls whose position was much more precarious than Effie's.

Uncomfortable, constrained, the dinner broke up early. Whatever its origin, Larry must have played an integral part.

I was more than a little disturbed about Larry s absence. He was a stickler on appointments, punctilious in his observance of social amenities. And my anxiety grew as I drove at a reckless speed homeward. The whole affair—the arranged dinner, his secrecy about it, the constraint on the companions he would have had—assumed a sinister mystery. The one obvious fact was that Larry had planned that I should know nothing about it.

As I closed the garage door Cuddy came hurrying out to me. A new Cuddy—upset, excited, frightened.

My heart beat fast as he ran along the drive toward me.

"What is it, Cuddy?"

"Mr. Rockford, sir. He's been hurt."

CUDDY'S tense announcement had not for me the shock of surprise. Even as his lips opened I found myself anticipating his words. Larry was hurt. Nothing else would have kept him from the club. I spun about to return to the car, drawing on my gloves.

"He's here, sir, in his own room."

The north room had always been Larry's room.

"Here?" I puzzled.

"Yes, sir. Doctor Fleury brought him here."

Good old David! Good old Larry! I rushed into the house, Cuddy at my heels.

"Is he—bad, Cuddy?"

"Knocked up a bit, sir, but he doesn't seem too uncomfortable. The Doctor has him all bandaged up."

Doctor David Fleury was another of the old Cortwright boys, one of "The Clan," as eight of us called ourselves. Only three were in the city. The other five scattered over the world, only one a disgrace to our code: "Bigger Blows for Bigger Bullies." David had done well in his profession.

Shocked, no, but that did not lessen my anxiety. Three steps at a time I leaped up the stairs, straining to a comforting sound from the north room. But the house was silent as a tomb.

Was it worse than Cuddy had said? Was he trying to ease the blow?

My steps lagged, and at the door I paused and softly pushed it open.

David Fleury sat beside the bed in his best bedside manner. On the bed, turned slightly toward the door—they had heard me coming—lay Larry, a mass of bandages, while the bedclothes bulged sickeningly where his legs must be. Of his face only an eye, his nose and his lips were visible.

I flopped limply into a chair.

"Can he—speak, David?" I whispered.

"Yes, and hear too," said Larry, and the familiar chuckle brought tears of relief to my eyes. "They didn't get my diaphragm, thank Heaven—or my epiglottis, or whatever it is a chap speaks with. I'm not dead yet, Dill. A bit cracked up, but able to take nourishment."

It seemed too good to be true, and I appealed with my eyes to David for confirmation.

"In a couple of weeks or so," said David pompously—still the physician—"he'll be sitting up. Of course, the broken leg will keep him off his feet."

I inquired what had happened.

David rose and closed the door. It was Larry who answered:

"They got me, Dill. They put a stick of dynamite in the engine of my car—connected the fuse with a sparking-plug. Horatio"—his pet name for his Austin—"is going to have a funeral with flowers when I get up. There isn't enough left of the garage to have a funeral for it."

It required no special intelligence to fill in what he had omitted.

"The devil! It's lucky you weren't blown to bits. It means, Larry, we've got someone on the run."

Larry winced. "He's lucky to be able to run. Oh, well, I'll have a few scars to show my grandchildren—or yours. That'll be the reward for keeping me for a few weeks, old thing. Between you and David, it doesn't look so gloomy."

I turned inquiring eyes on David.

"Fortunately I happened to be passing," said David, "when the explosion occurred. I put him in my car and took him to my office to piece him together. He made me bring him here."

"But the police—what about the police?"

"A dynamite explosion, Dill," said Larry primly, "makes a certain amount of noise. Even the police heard of it. But they've come and gone. Pumped us all so dry Cuddy had to bring two bottles." He pointed to the table, beneath which a pair of bottles that had contained my choicest wine rested against the wall. "Naturally David, too, was upset and had to have stimulant. In fact, he looks a bit pale now—and I think I'm going to have a fit—or something. Will you ring?"

His bantering tone and words irritated me. "Stop it, Larry. This is too serious to joke about. Who did it?"

He opened his one eye in exaggerated surprise. "How do I know? I haven't an enemy in the world—except you, at this moment. I haven't even received a threatening letter. That's why the police went away with a flea in their collected ear."

I said through my teeth: "You know damned well who it was!"

"Do I?"

"Of course you do. It was Vance Horton's murderer. He knew we were—"

"But I thought you knew all about the murderer, Dill. Surely you don't suggest she—Here, now, I'm an invalid,"

I plunged to my feet and went to the window. "Oh, stop it!"

"All right. Anyway, the police didn't seem satisfied with my story. I suppose they're out digging among your neighbours. I hope you don't live in a gossipy neighbourhood. They might tell tales out of school. Fact is, Dill, someone doesn't like our ways. Someone fears we may dig up too much in this little excavation we're attempting into the Horton murder."

"At any rate," I groaned, "you're through."

"Me? Not a bit of it. The wisest generals plan their campaigns from a desk—and send their assistants to execute them. I have David and Cuddy to nurse me—and you to make the attack. Because, Dill," he ended more gravely, "you and I have just begun to dig."

David went, promising to return in the morning. Cuddy, I saw, had attended to everything, even leaving a box of my best cigarettes on the table beside the bed. He had, too, found a bed table that had been left in the attic by the previous owner. It stood now upended against the wall; and the bed had been moved so that Larry, from where he lay, could look through the window to the garden.

I had forgotten all about the club, but Larry reminded me:

"Where have you been all this time, Dill?"

"At the club—with Jordan and Nora. We waited till half-past seven for you."

He smiled a little sheepishly. "So you got in on it, did you?"

"Yes—no thanks to anyone but Nora. And Effie Shannon—and Lee Moshier, too."

"Lee?" he questioned eagerly. "H'm—tell me about it."

I told what I could remember. He listened without a word, now and then shaking or nodding his head. It was, I saw, the flaming happiness of the Jordans that interested him most.

"It was real all right, Larry, a rapturous pair, bubbling over, as if they were on their honeymoon again. But it wasn't hard to burst the bubble."

Larry nodded thoughtfully. "A bubble, you say. . . . Yes, perhaps. There are a lot of bubbles, Dill, in this affair that you and I must burst."

"I'm afraid," I declared gloomily, "you're too hopeful. I can't do much without you. The fiend who put that dynamite in your car knew it. . . . Surely it could not be—one of them. Not Jack Ponting, or the Flemings, or Effie, or Peter Davenport. Or even Lee Moshier."

"Someone murdered Vance," Larry reminded me. "Another little murder would be but a passing emotion. You see, Dill, we advertised ourselves. I did it with a purpose. But I guess I talk too damned much. Look at me . . .

"And, Dill," he called after me as I left the room, "this second little experiment in the realm of crime may merely have cultivated a taste for it. Look out for yourself."

"I'll examine my car each time before I use it," I promised carelessly.

I promised too much.

Not until I had seen Larry comfortable for the night did I realize the strain I had been through that afternoon. But as I stumbled back along the hall I felt weak, physically and mentally. Things had happened too quickly, too surprisingly, to give me time to arrange them even in their sequence of time, to say nothing of their relative importance as bearing on the murder of Vance Horton.

In a dim way I was conscious that Cuddy had passed along the hall downstairs, that he had opened the front door. A mumble of conversation reached me, then the door closed and, after a slight pause, Cuddy retreated toward the kitchen.

But he did not go through the door at the end of the passage. I knew it because that door always creaked a little. And then I heard him returning toward the stairs. I leaned over the balustrade. Cuddy saw me, but he came on without speaking. And as he rose to my level I saw him swallow again and again before he could bring himself to speak. It brought me sharply from my stupor of fatigue.

"A lady downstairs to see you, sir."

"A—lady?"

"Yes, sir, I—believe so." He stood now, straight and uncompromising, his eyes focused over my shoulder. "She's in the library, sir. The—the curtains are drawn, sir."

I had no time for the implication. "Who is it, Cuddy?"

"Miss—ahem!—one of the two young ladies who didn't leave their names, sir."

"Barbara!" I exclaimed, starting past him.

"I would say, sir, it was the other one."

I continued down the stairs at a slower pace. Willo Venell stood in the centre of the room, her eyes, wide and frightened, fixed on the doorway. So youthful she looked, so appealing and beautiful, that I hurried to her, my hands outstretched.

"I'm—alone," she murmured.

Unconsciously my eyes flew to the grandfather clock in the corner. She noticed it, and her manner altered.

"Yes, I know the time, Mr. Fullerton. It's after midnight, and—and a girl wandering about like this! But I daren't come any other time."

"If I can do anything for you, Miss Venell," I offered

formally, and suddenly felt weary again.

She dropped into a chair. "You can do everything—everything. And I don't know anyone else to go to."

"Your sister—"

She cut me short with a fierce movement that made me flinch, and a flash of pain contorted her face.

"Barbara—she's the last one can help me." It was the cry of stricken love, and I had sense enough not to try to understand.

"Please tell me what I can do."

I suppose it was cold and formal, repelling, for the fear returned to her eyes, and her lip quivered. My heart went out to her.

"I think, Miss Venell, you know you can trust me. I've kept a secret that was hard to keep. I'll always keep it. Shouldn't you have brought your sister?"

"Barbara?" Again that cry of protest, of distrust. And then her eyes filled with tears. "I just *have* to trust you, Mr. Fullerton."

The sound of Cuddy moving about in the pantry steadied us both.

"You must let me stay here, Mr. Fullerton," she begged. "I must hide—for a time."

"But—but, Miss Venell, how can I?" For I remembered Larry upstairs, and the visits of the police.

"It was Sir George Mullet sent me to you," she said. She hurried on, speaking to the surprise in my face: "You saw me there this afternoon. I had to have help—and I wasn't even sure what kind of help I needed. He said—he said—"

She lifted her hands to her face and broke into heartrending sobs.

Until three nights before I had never seen a woman cry, and there, alone with my second experience, I felt helpless. Doubly uncomfortable because, with such a tiny, pretty little creature, my impulse was to take her in my arms. Perhaps it was Cuddy, audible again, that forestalled it.

"I wish you wouldn't do that," I heard myself saying.

She made a brave effort. "I'm so—so alone."

That stiffened me. "If you don't know your sister better than that—" I began indignantly.

"I know her so much better than you," she replied coldly, "so much better after—after the other night." Her face softened again, and once more she turned those appealing eyes on me. "Mr. Fullerton, I lied. It wasn't Sir George Mullet who sent me."

I said: "You scarcely deceived me. Why should Sir George send you to me? If you felt it necessary to consult him, there's nothing I can do."

"But there is. It's—a friend I need. Sir George did advise me to hide. He didn't say where, because he doesn't wish to know. I could think of no one but you."

"Why must you hide?"

"Because the police are looking for me."

"And this house," I told her, "is where they'll find you sooner than anywhere else. They know you were there at Vance Horton's house that night. They know you came here afterwards. They came the next morning, searching for you. Someone saw you and your sister fleeing from Vance's garden, running to my car."

She raised herself wearily to her feet. "Then I must go—somewhere else." Suddenly she was alert. "I must hurry—hurry!"

"But," I tried to calm her, "the police have been here to-night and have gone. You're safe—"

"I must warn Barbara."

I'm not certain that the relief I felt showed in my face. They were still sisters, though something I did not understand had come between them.

"I might let her know—warn her myself," I suggested. "Larry Rockford tells me you've moved."

"Yes. We couldn't stand it at home with our stepmother. If any of this reaches her ears!" She shivered. "Barbara and I have our own money. We're at 'The Elms,' in Orland Street."

She stood for a time, her eyes half closed.

"You remember Mr. Rockford?" I questioned. "You met him in Sir George Mullet's office this afternoon."

"Yes . . . yes," dreamily. "And I liked him. I think I could trust him."

"He's upstairs now—in bed. He was badly injured this afternoon."

"How is he?" she inquired dully.

Something clicked painfully inside my head. "You knew of it?"

My tone must have carried something of my suspicion, for she started and examined me sharply. "Yes, you just said so. How was he injured?"

"Ran his head against a problem," I said, trying to keep myself in hand. "He's sworn to find the murderer of Vance Horton. Perhaps you expected—everything."

The blood rushed to her cheeks. "I—knew. I knew he was injured. I saw him carried in. You see, I've been walking up and down most of the evening, trying to muster courage to—to come to you. What happened to him?"

"An automobile accident. Someone put dynamite in the engine of his car."

"But—but why?"

"Ask Vance Horton's murderer."

Willo caught hold of the back of a chair to steady herself. Her face was white as chalk.

"It—can't be. It isn't true, it isn't true." It burst from her in a gush of protest, then the colour returned to her cheeks, and she looked away. "Surely—not another—murder! The one who murdered Vance would never—"

"'Vance?'" I repeated wonderingly. "Then you knew him well?" For the moment I had forgotten Barbara's story after we had come on her in the shrubbery behind the billiard-room.

"Would Barbara and I have been there if we didn't?" Suddenly she faced me. "I must talk, Mr. Fullerton, I must tell someone. It's eating my very heart out—all this secrecy—keeping things tight in here." She clenched her small fists and pressed them to her bosom. "Yes, I knew Vance Horton well—too well. I thought I loved him. . . . Is there any difference between loving and thinking you do?"

"The whole world," I replied. "Love, true love, never dies—I believe."

"Then I must have just thought I loved him. . . . But it was all the same while it lasted: I was almost helpless before him, worshipping him. I thought for a time that he loved me in return. I didn't mind helping him out—I was glad to."

"'Helping him out?'" I repeated vaguely.

"I gave him money. He—"

"But surely Vance had no need of money."

"He always said he needed it. Everyone thought him rich, but he told me he was really hard up. . . . I know what a wastrel he was. I know now what a liar he was. I'd heard stories, of course, but I didn't believe them. Barbara, too, heard them; but she never liked him, and I didn't believe her. I almost hated her for repeating them. . . . Then I found out the truth. I'd seen Vance with other women—just fleeting glimpses—and I questioned him about them."

"But I never heard of you, Miss Venell, I never saw you before," I said.

"We lived in London. Vance used to come to the city often. . . . It was only when we moved here two months ago that I began to find out what he was. . . . I threw it in his face." She stopped, and her lips tightened. "He laughed at me. . . . I hadn't seen him for weeks until—until the night he was—killed."

I felt as if I were dreaming it all. It was too terrible, too impossible. Yet Barbara had told me something the same story only a couple of nights before.

"You were—there—with him?" I stammered.

Her eyes fell before mine. "Please let me tell the story in my own way. I had found him out. I knew I meant nothing to him but conquest and my money—that he toyed with me as he toyed with so many women. It was fools like me who paid the cost of those orgies of his—like the one that night.

"When I heard of it I must have gone a little mad. There would be women there, women he was dragging to destruction as he had almost dragged me. And my money—and theirs—paying for it all. Can you blame me if—if I lost my head?"

"Go on," I said weakly.

"It was Mrs. Fleming opened my eyes to the scoundrel he was."

"You mean Nora Fleming, Jordan Fleming's wife?"

"Yes. I saw her one day in Lloyds hand him a bundle of banknotes she had just drawn. He caught me looking, and as he passed on his way out he grinned into my face and flipped the roll triumphantly. I knew then that Barbara was right, that the stories I had heard were short of the truth.

"That was why I couldn't keep away that night. So when the party was at its height I crept through the gate to a window where I could see without being seen. I saw—Vance making love to Miss Shannon. I saw him afterwards make love to Mrs. Fleming. I saw, too, what no one else saw—that Jordan Fleming was watching it all. And in his face was something that, had they seen, would have made them more cautious. Then Lee Moshier came to Vance and said something, and after a few minutes Vance left the room."

"And Effie Shannon gave evidence at the inquest that it was a woman told Vance of the telephone call—she couldn't remember who it was."

"I know nothing of a telephone message. I only know I saw no one else speaking to Vance while I was there, except the three. Well, right away after he left the room Mrs. Fleming followed. And after her went her husband. I didn't see where they went."

"And then?" I asked, for she seemed to be thinking of something else.

"Then—I waited for a few minutes. The noise they were making was deafening where I stood beyond the open window. They were drinking; I've heard there was absinthe at some of Vance's affairs. I don't know why I waited, unless it was for Vance's return. . . . I don't know now even why I was there."

"Did you see him come back?" I asked. I was a little impatient at the slowness of her story, but I knew to disturb it might seal her lips. Yet I must know, I must know about that scream—that shot.

"No, I did not see him come back. . . . It was Jordan Fleming and his wife who returned. And I noticed—even then I noticed—how excited they were . . . and nervous. He had her by the arm. They appeared only for a moment, then they ran across the passage, and I saw them climbing the stairs. Even then it looked like flight."

I was forced once more to urge her on.

"I began to wonder where Vance was, and I wandered past the other windows. But he wasn't in either of the downstair rooms. Then I noticed that the billiard-room had a light, though it hadn't been there when I arrived. I went on toward it."

Her lips closed tightly, and a shiver ran through her.

"Your sister?" I asked. I had to ask it, though I trembled for the answer.

"She must have followed me. I hadn't deceived her. She must have seen how desperate I was that day. She seems to know everything."

"Perhaps," I said gently, "I know the rest. You found one of the French windows open—or Vance opened it for you. You went in.

And there in the billiard-room—"

The look in her eyes stopped me. "No, no, Vance didn't open the window for me. He didn't know—"

"You went in," I repeated relentlessly. "And you and your sister—"

"He was dead!" she screamed. "Dead, I tell you!"

"He was not dead, Miss Venell. I heard the shot that killed him. I heard you scream."

And Willo Venell slid to the floor in a dead faint.

XXIII An Official Visit

NEXT day was Sunday. I was thankful for that, since it seemed to offer leisure to piece things together, to rid my mind of the racing, unorganized thoughts that rustled through like the leaves on a wind-blown street. Even as I stooped to pick Willo up Cuddy rushed in and took charge. And the look he gave me sent me slinking to my room.

But Sunday was not to be a day of rest.

I was still in my morning bath when Cuddy came tip-toeing to the door to announce that Inspector Emerson and a strange man were waiting to see me. I leaped from the tub and seized a towel.

"Cuddy!" I called. "Cuddy, for God's sake—"

But all I heard in reply was Cuddy's swift feet on the stairs, and I dare not call more loudly.

And then, as I dressed, I heard more footsteps on the stairs, and they passed on toward the room where Larry lay. I hurried. I trembled to leave them long with Larry, for he and I had not thought to arrange the story we should tell.

They were there in Larry's room, Inspector Emerson at the side of the bed, James Rountree at the foot, where he looked straight into my friend's bandaged face. It was no surprise that the stranger was Rountree.

Inspector Emerson smiled. "You know Mr. Rountree, Fullerton. You'd better know him as—Inspector Rountree, of Scotland Yard."

I think I managed a suitable amount of surprise and interest.

"Did Doctor Millbrook know last night?" I asked.

"Of course. But I ask you not to mention it outside. For the present we consider it best to say nothing about Scotland Yard—though it can't be kept long from the public. We're working on the Horton murder."

"And on this near one too, I hope," I said, pointing at Larry.

"It's the same thing," said Inspector Rountree.

"It's quick work, Inspector."

"And calls for quick work from us, you mean?"

"Exactly—if the list of murders isn't to be extended." A cloud had lifted from my mind. Surely the police could not now suspect us of any connection with the murder! But a moment's reflection warned me not to guess at the cards in a detective's pack.

Rountree was speaking: "I'm afraid you brought it on yourself, Mr. Rockford. It seems to be pretty well known that you and your friend are out to convict someone of young Horton's murder." (I noticed the wording of it, and so did Larry, I knew, by the glance he threw me.) "You must have stumbled on a clue—"

"The amateur, Dill, you understand," said Larry, laughing, "*stumbles* on clues. The professional digs them from solid rock—or something like that."

The two Inspectors laughed.

"My wording was unfortunate," said Rountree frankly. "The fact is, even detectives stumble on most of their clues. By keeping their eyes open, of course."

"I hope," said Larry, "no one, detective or other, stumbles on a clue that tells against us, Inspector. Because, you see, Dill must be among the suspects."

Inspector Rountree's face did not alter its expression. "All Horton's friends—his so-called friends—are suspects." And then, with the atmosphere of the room untainted by anything but the most conventional suspicion, the Inspector struck terror into me by saying: "You might help to wipe your names from the list, boys, if you were frank."

He was looking at me, not at Larry. In another moment I might have blurted it out. But Larry intervened.

"Someone," he drawled, "seems to know more about Dill than he does about himself. As for this clue we've stumbled on—I wish I knew what it is."

"I see," said Inspector Rountree, and Larry and I knew the Inspector saw more than we wished anyone to see.

But Larry was not giving up. "If it's any use to you—I can tell you that something like half a dozen have almost succeeded in convincing themselves they killed Vance Horton—and they're all doing their best to look like murderers."

"Including Mr. Fullerton," said the Inspector.

"Sorry, Inspector," I declared, in my most dignified manner, "but I fail to see how I qualify."

"You qualify more fully than anyone on the list. Look at it reasonably, Mr. Fullerton. You were there at the time of the murder, we might say at the moment. You ran away. Why? A jury would ask that question—and probably answer it in a way that would end the case—or drive us to more frantic effort to save you. . . . Then there are the two young ladies—h'm—an event, a twist, that must conceal a very interesting story. I can tell you that if it were not for the two girls we'd have had to arrest you long ago."

"But—but," I stammered, "how could they—what have they done to—to—"

The Inspector stopped me with a laugh. "You *all* can't have murdered the fellow."

My mind flew to Willo Venell, there in the yellow room. If they found her! I knew she would tell everything; she was in no mood to face the police and remain quiet. That they might not read the dread in my face I rose and went to the window.

Off in a corner of the garden Hodges bent over a rose-bush he was nursing back to production after an obscure blight for which he had a term that staggered my memory. Hodges loved nothing better than to put me in my place as a mere employer.

And then, as I looked, from the thickest part of the garden, in another corner, Cuddy came hurrying, dodging from shrub to shrub.

Larry was talking at my back:

"And still the list is incomplete, Inspector. Beside Dill's name you should enter mine. For I, too, was there that night. Indeed, I was nearer the billiard-room than was Dill."

If he expected to surprise them he must have been disappointed.

"We knew that," said Inspector Emerson. "You were at the Olympia with Mr. Fullerton. He purchased the tickets. You left together in his car, almost the last of the crowd. We know the time almost to the minute. Unless he threw you out you were with him when he drove along Figmore Street. But—this other you said—'nearer the billiard-room'?"

"You see," said Larry, "I'm doing my best to make it easy for you. I was in Vance Horton's garden, close to the billiard-room—and it must have been almost at the moment he was shot. I heard the row as we drove along. I was curious and climbed out. You may leave Dill out, for I went alone. Dill came later. And so it's foolish for us to say we didn't kill Vance. Every suspect would say that. But it may explain why we're so anxious to find the one who did kill him. It's common sense, selfpreservation."

I have no idea what Larry hoped for from his confession. I

only know it appalled me. Inspector Rountree asked:

"And the two girls?"

Larry stopped me as I started to reply. "Look at it reasonably, Inspector," imitating the Inspector's voice. "Isn't it enough to make us clear ourselves, without expecting us to make out a case for the other suspects?"

But that was far from satisfying me. "The girls," I insisted emphatically, "are as innocent as we are."

"The proof?"

"I—I haven't any. But I know, I just know."

The two officers smiled. "Then, perhaps," said Inspector Rountree, "you can explain why you ran away, why the two girls ran away—with you."

I told as much as I considered safe, not looking at Larry, for I was not sure of myself—except that I knew Larry couldn't hope to side-track these men.

"Who are they?"

"They wouldn't tell us," I declared in a half truth.

"Don't make him feel more badly," Larry laughed. "He's inconsolable. We never saw them before, never even heard of them. Probably part of the London crowd. Why don't you do some sleuthing there?"

"London isn't being neglected," replied the Inspector. . . . "We've discovered that those two girls were not guests of Horton's that night."

"How can you be sure of that?"

"Lee Moshier knew all the guests. He said they were all there when we called them down."

"Oh, Lee!" Larry and I said it in unison, but Larry's bandaged face handicapped its expression of contempt.

"Do you suggest he may have some reason for protecting the girls?"

"God forbid!" I exclaimed fervently. "He'd be more likely to try to inculpate them—to save his own skin."

"Moshier didn't know what we were talking about when we mentioned the girls. I don't think he was acting. But it's your part we're interested in just now. The girls fled in your car. What did you do with them?"

"Since when," I asked scornfully, "did the police lay such

store on anonymous letters?"

"How did you know it was an anonymous letter?"

"Because," Larry broke in, "whoever saw us wouldn't dare admit in person he was there to see. But there's nothing to hide. Dill had two guests that night in this house. And you were properly fooled next day when you tried to find them."

Inspector Emerson smiled. "Not quite, Rockford. They slept in that room at the end of the passage. Your servant did his best, but we all make mistakes. I saw him crush that bit of paper and throw it in the basket. It was clever. I took the liberty of reading it when I had the room to myself. I could repeat it word for word."

"Thanks," I said. "I'll take your word for it."

Larry was whistling quietly. He stopped to say: "The part that interests me—and, as a novice detective, I imagine it should interest you more than anything else—is who wrote that letter. Suppose all it said was true. What then? How were we seen?"

"By someone there to see, of course. . . . And that someone is trying to do the same as the rest of you are trying—to throw the blame on someone, else. Let it pass. Tell me what you did all the next day."

Larry's lip curled. "Let me commend the police. It must have taken a large part of the force to keep us all in sight."

"We'd devote the whole force," said Inspector Emerson, "to anything that promised to find the murderer."

Inspector Rountree seemed more inclined to discuss our part in a friendly way. "I've a feeling," he said, throwing a meaning glance at his companion, "that your efforts haven't been entirely wasted."

"And I," said Larry, "am flattered. If we've learned anything of value, we don't know it. We talked with several of the suspects, as you seem to know, but all it did was to muddy the water. Speaking of juries, I could send half a dozen to the gallows for that murder, yes, before almost any jury. And I believe you could, too. For instance, Peter Davenport was there. And he was not invited."

He chuckled at the look of surprise on the faces of the two detectives.

"Clue number one—that you didn't have. All right. Then, Lee Moshier was about to be cut off, kicked out to make a living he has never been able to make for himself."

Inspector Emerson grunted. "He comes out rather well in the will."

"Of course," said Larry. "But let's go on. Jordan Fleming and his wife have been brought together by Vance's—death.—It couldn't have happened more opportunely. Effie Shannon's case you probably know—and all that about a woman scorned. Continuing: Jack Ponting's narrow escape from a second toss into a cold market is due entirely to a murder timed to the very minute. I might go on. But that gives you some idea how muddy the water looks to a pair of amateur detectives."

"You've given us nothing new about those two amateurs, the pair who, always enemies of Horton's, were seen to run away right after the murder." Inspector Rountree laughed as he said it, but there was nothing casual about it. "Also the two young ladies."

"Did you expect me to do all the detective work for you?" asked Larry. "You asked about the following day. You probably know, but we worked hard that day among the suspects, and the evening we spent with Doctor Millbrook."

"What happened there," said Inspector Emerson, "we can get from the Doctor himself, I suppose."

"Keep on supposing," replied Larry impudently. "But you must know we were never intimate with him. Fact is—just to give you a starting-point—we met him outside the mortuary as he left the autopsy. He saw we were interested, and asked us to come around and see him. He showed us the bullet. . . . H'm—I think that's about all."

He lay back, his solitary eye fixed on the ceiling.

"All you wish to tell, you mean," said Rountree. "Well, you've the last word in that." He rose.

"We've *said* the last word, at any rate—for the present," said Larry. "But we're keeping on at the job, Inspector."

"And I've respect enough for you, boys, to feel sure that our paths will cross." He had almost reached the door when he stopped. "Just another word: We'd better warn you not to get in the way."

It was not a threat. Inspector Rountree was too clever for that.

"You can't put me in jail with a broken leg," laughed Larry.

"To come through that with only a broken leg and a few scratches," said Inspector Rountree, as I saw them out, "would seem to point to hanging as his ultimate end." He laughed. "I hope he has a good doctor."

Cuddy met me in the hall as I closed the door. I drew a long breath of relief.

"Phew, Cuddy! I thought they had us that time. I warned her."

"You mean the lady that was in the yellow room?"

"*Was* in?"

"Yes, sir. I hid her in the garden."

AND still, though it was Sunday, the day's excitement was by no means ended.

The afternoon promised well. David Fleury spent much of it in Larry's room, excluding even me. So that I might have lounged with my book and forgotten my worries. But I resented David's stiff formality, his professional ponderousness. I resented it more that Cuddy should be now and then admitted. But, of course, I could not protest.

Mrs. Beaton, who did not arrive until eight on weekdays, and not at all on Sunday, knew nothing of the use made of the yellow room on the two occasions. If ever she did learn of it, Cuddy would find some explanation.

It was not until the evening that I was permitted to see Larry. He seemed comfortable enough, but he did not seem disposed to talk. So I read to him. But I am not sure he heard much of what I read. Neither, for that matter, did I, for I had made the mistake of selecting a story that canonized Scotland Yard and its unfailing success. David had warned me that what Larry needed most was rest. And so, with the stroke of nine, I closed the book.

"It's the devil," I grumbled, "you being laid up just now. It upsets all our plans. This is your game more than mine. But I'm willing to be Doctor Watson—"

Larry groaned. "It's worse than you think."

I laughed. "Getting jealous? Well, I take my oath I've seen the little blonde only a few minutes. That was last night. To-day Cuddy has been my liaison officer."

He raised his head quickly and frowned. "You mean—she's here—Willo's here?"

I imitated his whistle. "'Willo' already, is it?"

"You said nothing about it to me," he complained.

"I hadn't her permission. She's hiding from the police."

"Are they that close—do they know her name?"

"I don't know. But Sir George Mullet advised her to get out of sight."

"Ask her to come up."

I shook my head gravely. "Doctor's orders. What you need is rest. If you can't see me you certainly mustn't face the excitement of seeing her. In Doctor Fleury's absence I'm your doctor."

"David'll let me see her," he growled. "Don't be smart."

"David may have the say in this room, Larry, but outside it I'm still boss. Shall I close the windows a little before I tuck you in for the night?"

I left the room, laughing to drown his curses. It was more than childish revenge that I carried no message to Willo. She had, indeed, not even yet given me permission to tell Larry that she was in the house. And I thought it safer to keep her confined to her room, since I had no idea when the police might revisit the house, or how clever they were at sensing the presence of a woman. For both Willo and Barbara seemed to breathe something new and thrilling into the old house.

In the library I was restless. It was a breathless summer night, and every window and the door to the garden were wide open. I tried to read, but I could not fix my mind on it, and for a time I wandered about the room—fighting the desire to have Willo down to talk to. But her presence had always meant added discomfort and misgiving, and I could not face her spasms of terror, or her strange, intermittent antagonism to her sister. I feared that those flashes of resentment might induce me to say more than was wise.

After a time I turned out the lights and lay down on a chaise-longue where a draught from the open door blew soothingly over me, for a slight breeze had sprung up.

I must have fallen asleep. But it was not a restful sleep. I seemed not so much to lose consciousness as the power to move or speak. It was a sort of stupor of muscle that overcame me, but eye and ear seemed to remain active, and my mind functioned dully.

I heard David Fleury come and go, but I did not move.

In that condition presently I thought something was in the room. How or whence it had come I did not know. I saw no definite shape, heard no noise, yet eye and ear seemed involved in the feeling I had. It was, as it seemed, a matter of little importance at the most. It was a shape, a presence, and nothing more.

It flitted about the room, and I followed its every move. At first it paid no attention to me—it was not, I knew, aware of me there on the chaise-longue. Then, opposite me, it saw. It had been at my desk for a time. Now it stood before me, not three paces away. And then it commenced to creep slowly nearer—nearer.

I was not alarmed, and only slightly interested. It seemed part of my condition, rather than an actuality. . . . Then it stood over me. Stooped. So real was it now that I fancied I heard it breathing. A hand moved—vanished into some garment—reappeared.

And in the hand now gleamed a long stiletto. That was the one real thing about the whole affair—that glint of light, picked up from some vagrant beam that must have entered the open garden door from the street. And still I was not alarmed,

But I waited, my curiosity roused, for what was to happen. My eyes were fixed on that bright line of steel.

What did happen—in the waking dream—was that the stiletto, after hovering over me for several moments, faded away—back into the garment from which it had come. I heard a heavy sigh. Then the form was gone.

How long it was before I really wakened I do not know. But with my senses and returning bodily control came a great fear. The dream remained, every move, every breath—that slinking shape, the stiletto, the sigh from a hand that could not bring itself to strike.

I was terror-stricken. The dark room seemed to be peopled with threatening shapes, leering faces, hovering peril. But because of the very intensity of my terror I would not let myself turn on the lights. The luminous face of my watch revealed half-past twelve. So that I had slept a couple of hours—long enough for everything I had fancied to have really happened. That and more.

How much more? For a time I sat with my gaze fixed on the outline of the doorway to the garden, angry and surprised that the terror continued. I shivered.

Suddenly into my consciousness worked the sound of stealthy movement over my head. My bedroom! Then, with an abruptness that brought me to my feet with bated breath, the clamour of a short, sharp struggle. And after that, as I stood shaking, wondering if it was still a dream, silence.

I raced into the passage. Excited as I was, I noticed that the door I had left closed was now open. I thought of calling to Cuddy, but I remembered Willo and Larry asleep upstairs. I hesitated. And down the stairs someone came creeping—creeping—creeping.

Crossing to the wall, I waited, struggling in vain to stifle my frightened breathing.

A weight crashed against my temple, and I staggered into the library, shouting to Cuddy. Dazed by the blow, I heard Cuddy come pounding down the stairs, calling to me. I heard the library switch click, but no light came on. Cuddy continued to call my name, more frantically now. But I still floundered dizzily against the wall. And I realized that all the time I had hold of something that fought to get free.

And then Cuddy groaned.

The sound cleared my head a little—and my eyes. Against the garden door I saw Cuddy stagger away. And then two other shapes were locked together for a moment.

"Cuddy! Cuddy!" I called. "A match, for God's sake!"

One of the struggling pair broke free at that moment and vanished. Indeed, they seemed to part by mutual consent. And Cuddy, feeling about for me on the floor, calling in heart-stricken tones, touched my leg. I fainted.

The blazing light and enamelled cupboards of the butler's pantry surrounded me when my senses returned. I lay on the floor, with Cuddy bending anxiously over me. His lip quivered as I opened my eyes.

"You're all right, sir?" he almost sobbed.

A pain shot through my temple, and I raised my hand to it.

"If that's all, sir, you'll be all right."

And then I saw the great red stain on his shirt-sleeve. "Look, Cuddy, you're hurt."

"Just a little jab, sir. I'm all right."

I jumped to my feet. "Here, get that sleeve up. I must see that wound."

I helped him roll back the sleeve. On his arm, just above the elbow, a narrow blade had caught the flesh and passed through. And then I noticed that, save for his coat, he was fully dressed.

"How's this?" I demanded. "Weren't you in bed?"

"Yes, sir—lying down I was. It seems best, with so much going on, and—strangers in the house."

"Cuddy," I reproved, as I bandaged the wound, "you're a fool."

"Yes, sir, my mother always said so."

Then all my dream must have actually happened. "What—who was it, Cuddy?"

Cuddy shook his head.

"There were two of them," I said.

Cuddy looked surprised. "I only saw one, sir."

"Two," I insisted. "And the two fought together. You were on the floor, trying to find me."

I led him into the library. The floor lamps had been turned on, but the wire that wound down through the chain to the centre light had been cut. An upset table and a ruffled rug were the only signs of the struggle. The door to the garden still stood open, and Cuddy hurried to close it.

"I think," he said, "I'd better go upstairs, sir, and see if Mr. Rockford's all right."

"He's sure to have heard it," I agreed. "We'll hurry."

"If you wouldn't mind, sir, it would be better if I went alone, so as not to frighten him."

"Bosh! I'm tired of all this formality. Come on." As I reached the passage I chanced to raise my eyes. Something moved swiftly back from the balustrade over my head. Calling to Cuddy, I leaped up the stairs. At the landing I glanced back. Cuddy was racing after me, a heavy brass poker in his hand.

The passage was empty, but a slight noise sent me running toward the turn. And as I reached it a door closed softly. I did not hesitate. In half a dozen long strides I had the door of the yellow room open. I switched on the light.

Willo Venell stood at the foot of the bed. She was dressed in a man's outfit, and a flashing review of the incidents of the last few minutes made my head reel. Speechless, I sent my eyes racing about the room. What I thought to find I do not know. Perhaps it was the stiletto.

Cuddy entered behind me. Without a word I pointed to the boyish figure of the girl. But Cuddy only grinned.

"Yes, sir. I had a time getting something to fit. She ain't what you'd call normal—not for a man."

I resented his flippancy. "Miss Venell," I demanded icily, "what's the reason for this—this masquerade?" Willo only edged farther beyond the foot of the bed. It was Cuddy who replied:

"You see, sir, with the police about the house so much, you might say, it wasn't safe to have a woman here."

"And do you think for one moment," I asked scornfully, "that that would deceive them?"

"It was the best I could think of, sir."

And as Willo crowded farther to the concealment of the bed, her face crimson, Cuddy coughed and stalked noisily to the door.

"It ain't quite what she's used to, sir, as you can see. I think I hear Mr. Rockford calling, sir."

There was nothing for me to do but follow, though I was anything but satisfied. As I reached the hall I could hear Larry calling Cuddy, and I hurried to his room.

"Don't turn on the light," he ordered peevishly. "My head's aching fit to split. What's all the noise? Why are you all about?"

"There's been someone in the house," I explained.

"A burglar?"

"I suppose so. We fought him off. Cuddy was stabbed."

"Stabbed? Is it bad?"

"Just a jab in the arm," Cuddy answered for himself. "I'm all right."

I heard the bed creak as Larry rolled on his side. "Tell me about it in the morning," he said sleepily. "What's that?"

It was the thunder of the knocker, and it rattled through the house like a battery of guns. No one spoke for a moment.

"Call David, quick, Dill!" Larry's voice rang with excitement. "Tell him he must come at once."

I went to the bed, my heart beating fast with a new dread. "What's the matter, Larry?"

"Go away!" he screamed. "Do what I say."

Cuddy was waiting. "Shall I answer the door, sir?"

"If you don't someone is going to knock the house down. Don't hurry till I get David."

I ran to the telephone in my room, while Cuddy took his time to the front door. David had just come in from a night call and had not yet undressed.

"I'll come right away," he promised excitedly. "Don't let anyone to Larry till I see him. Doctor's orders, remember." And the telephone rattled as he hung up.

As I turned away Inspector Emerson stood beside me.

"Who was that you were speaking to?" he demanded.

"Doctor Fleury. Larry's had a bad turn, and Fleury's coming right away. We've had some excitement here."

"That's why I'm here."

I looked him up and down. "How the devil—"

He interrupted with a crisp question: "What was happening?"

"Oh, nothing." I laughed mirthlessly. "Only the usual run of surprises. Someone got into the house through the garden door in the library. Perhaps you may find him. Go to it."

He shook me impatiently. "Give me the story."

"Someone came in, got upstairs here, and Cuddy and I had a fight with him before he got away. The police seem to have a flair for arriving just too late." His eyes bored into me, as if he scarcely believed me. "There's a lump here on my forehead to prove it, and you can look at Cuddy's arm," I said.

He hurried to the hall, issued a short order, and returned.

"Do you think it was a burglar? Did he take anything."

"I don't think he had time. Cuddy was on the job. But I haven't had time to look around. Larry heard the noise and got all worked up. I've been with him ever since. But how the devil did you happen to drop in at this moment?"

Instead of replying he led me to the hall and down the stairs. Rankin and another policeman were stationed there.

"Stay here, Fullerton. I'll look about. Come with me, Rankin."

They ascended the stairs, the large, heavy feet of the policeman keeping stolid pace with Inspector Emerson's lighter passage. Cuddy and I stood in the hall with the other policeman.

I was bewildered. The events of the day had moved with the swiftness of a story read in the same space of time. In some inexplicable way the police seemed to know everything in which I was concerned. Yet it could not be that they had seen or heard what I had passed through in the last forty minutes, or they would have come sooner. The uncanny timeliness of their appearance awed me a little.

Upstairs I heard the two policemen moving about the passage, then they turned into my room. I sighed.

This time they would be certain to discover my guest of the yellow room. After all my care and Cuddy's schemes it was to end like this. I glanced appealingly at my servant. But Cuddy stood straight and stiff, his face expressionless. He, too, had given up.

After all, I asked myself, why should I care? Why should I protect the girls and expose myself? It was no affair of mine—and it certainly was an affair of the police.

With another hopeless sigh I seated myself on one of the three chairs in the hall, determined to let things take their course. From where I sat I could see a narrow line of the upper hall, and with my head resting against the wall my eyes turned idly up to it.

Somewhere upstairs a door closed—not stealthily but naturally. Then light footsteps sounded along the hall, and before my eyes Willo Venell passed on toward the back stairs.

My heart missed a beat. Surely she was unaware of the presence of the police—right there in my room beside her!

Rankin appeared from the room, but after a careless glance in the direction Willo had taken turned back and disappeared. And as I directed at Cuddy a look of frightened inquiry the knocker sounded again.

It was David Fleury.

With a quick glance from me to the policeman he dashed up the stairs and back to Larry's room.

A few minutes later Inspector Emerson appeared at the head of the stairs. His face was set more grimly than I had ever seen it before. His right hand was extended before him, but what it contained I could not see until he had come down to my level. Then, without a word, he thrust the hand under my nose.

In it lay an automatic—a .25!

"Not a very clever hiding-place, Fullerton," he said. "I'm afraid it soiled your shirts."

AGAINST circumstances the most complete innocence is unconvincing. To believe that you have only to face Inspector Emerson when he finds in one of your drawers a gun that might have committed a murder he is investigating.

I had nothing to say. I could only stare from the gun to his cold face. Even my thoughts were chaotic—except that I was almost prepared to question my own innocence.

"A .25, you see," he declared shortly.

"But—but I never saw it before."

A cold, contemptuous smile creased his strong face. "Of course not. It just walked away from Vance Horton's billiard-room to play you a dirty trick."

David Fleury's calm voice dropped to us over the balustrade:

"What s the matter, Dill? Larry wants to know."

I pointed to the gun in the Inspector's hand. "He says he says he—he found it in my room."

Without another word David vanished, and I heard the door of Larry's room close behind him. I sat staring with parted lips at the automatic. Inspector Emerson waited, coldly professional and accusing.

Cuddy stepped forward.

It's mine, sir. I thought—nobody would find it there."

And so my unbelieving eyes shifted to the face of my servant. Cuddy a murderer! Cuddy a murderer! But why—why?

Inspector Emerson was little less surprised than I. But the silence that followed Cuddy's confession was broken by David's quiet voice over our heads:

"Mr. Rockford would like you to come up, Inspector."

Inspector Emerson hesitated. Then, herding us before him, he stalked up the stairs and back to Larry's room. Larry received us chuckling. All his excitement, his headache, his peevishness were gone. Something David had done or given him had killed all that and left him the composed, insolent, care-free Larry I knew so well.

The Inspector walked straight to the bed and stood scowling down on him.

"Fullerton isn't laughing," he said through closed teeth.

"Oh, Dill!" Larry expelled a contemptuous breath. "Dill never had a sense of humour. Oh, la-la! And you call yourself a detective! I'm only the rawest of amateurs, but I see through it. The gun's a plant, the crudest kind of a plant."

I thought the Inspector's face relaxed a little. "They all say that," he growled.

"Did Dill? I'll wager he never thought of it. He'd just gape and swallow—and wonder if he didn't shoot Vance Horton after all. And so the faithful servant—quick-witted fellow—came to the rescue. Cuddy would hang for his master." He chuckled again. "What do you think that chap was doing in the house an hour ago? He was no burglar. Rather a bungler. Cuddy found him in the very room where you discovered the gun."

Cuddy rubbed his nose, not looking at me—actually blushing. Inspector Emerson seemed for a moment uncertain what to do.

"This burglar," he murmured. "Opportune fellow—for Fullerton."

"Not with that bean on his forehead. And look at Cuddy. Cuddy, show the gentleman your wound. But perhaps he thinks you did it to yourselves. Only it happens that I heard the racket myself. Did Dill give you the whole fanciful story? Go on, Dill, tell it in your inimitable style with all the frills about suspended animation and mental stupor, and all that. David, here, might add the technical comments that would make it more bewildering. It might even be that the handle of the gun fails to show Dill's finger-prints."

Inspector Emerson's fingers slid to a more gingerly hold on the gun, and a slight flush coloured his cheeks. He had been so confident, perhaps, that he had not thought of finger-prints.

"At least," he said, "the gun will tell a story of its own."

Larry twisted his face wryly, what face was uncovered by bandages. "And even a gun may lie."

"Not to Doctor Millbrook, my boy. And now," preparing to go, "I must ask you all to keep yourselves available to the police. By the way," as he reached the door, "who was that passed along the hall while I was in that room?"

Cuddy was equal to the occasion. "It must have been Hodges, sir. He's the gardener. We brought him in from his rooms over the garage after the burglar got away."

David hurried them out. "I must ask you to go now. Larry has had more than he should be asked to stand in his condition." He had taken Larry's wrist in his hand, and he looked very solemn. "Please go."

Inspector Emerson bowed himself out. But I knew by his tight lips that he was anything but satisfied. Still, he must have been relieved that there was sufficient excuse for arresting no one.

I stood in the doorway, watching the policemen file down the walk to the gate. As I turned to close the door Inspector Emerson pulled up sharply and peered to one side into the shrubbery. Then, like a runner at the crack of a gun, he leaped off across the lawn, drawing his gun as he ran. The two policemen, after a moment's wondering immobility, dashed after him.

With tingling veins I followed.

At the end of the garden I came up to them.

"Did you—find anyone?"

"No." The solitary word snapped into the darkness.

"He's certainly bound to see it through," I declared with a short laugh. And then I remembered Willo Venell. "Did you hear something?"

"Did you think I was taking exercise?" he replied scornfully.

"It was probably just the wind," I suggested.

"I don't think you can be of any help, Fullerton," he said, and slid off into the darkness. "We'll search about a little."

I found my way back to the house. To my surprise the door was locked, though I had left it wide open. Irritated, I rattled the knocker, for I had no key with me. But it was not till I had hammered several times that Cuddy, easing it back a few inches, peeped through at me.

"What the hell, Cuddy "

Cuddy's fingers went up warningly to his lips, and opening the door quickly, he drew me in and closed it behind me.

Standing back against the wall were the two sisters— Barbara and Willo!

THERE is a limit to the capacity of the mind to receive impressions, and I suppose mine had reached that limit for a single day. At any rate, I turned, after a single glance, and reached for the door-knob.

I have no idea what was in my mind, unless it was to escape a succession of disturbing events that had me floundering in helpless mental confusion. There were too many things happening, too many people in the house. Even the outdoors, with a horde of policemen searching the grounds, appeared less confusing.

Whether Cuddy knew how I felt or was simply following his rule of anticipating me, he sprang before me and drew the door open a few inches. His action, and the cool night air, steadied me.

To cover my embarrassment I peered stealthily out into the garden before closing and bolting the door. Then I faced the two girls.

"The police are all about the place," I warned.

It was Barbara who replied: "That's why we came in. We saw the door open. It seemed the only safe place to be."

They had me there, and they knew it. Of course, I could not turn them out to a police-ridden garden. Yet I did not see how it was possible to keep them.

"You may go to bed, Cuddy," I ordered.

Cuddy bowed. "Yes, sir." He cleared his throat.

"The curtains are drawn tight in the library, sir. If the police should come, the ladies would be safe in the kitchen, perhaps. Tea and sandwiches as usual, sir?"

"Nothing to-night." All I wanted was to see the end of the day, to get everyone out of my sight—and sleep myself into oblivion. But Cuddy lingered, fussing with the disturbed chairs in the hall.

"So you followed her again," I said to Barbara. "You might have been in at another murder."

She shrank from me, her lip caught between her teeth. So that I felt like a cad. In defence of my unprovoked outburst I pointed to Cuddy's bandaged arm.

"He was stabbed. I don't understand how I escaped. There was a man in this house a couple of hours ago who had no right to be here. Two of them." And without realizing what I did my eyes ran deliberately over Willo's masculine attire.

Barbara turned to her sister, and a look of horror, of incredulity, came slowly into her eyes.

"I—I came to take her home," she stammered.

But Willo, straightening to her full height, moved away. "I'm not going with her."

It was to me another of those inexplicable, embarrassing moments of recurrent disdain and repugnance that marked the younger sister's manner.

"Hadn't we better go to the library?" I suggested. "It's more comfortable there—and safer."

Cuddy scurried ahead of us, reached in through the doorway without looking, and snapped on the lights. Somehow he had found time to mend the cut in the wire.

I had stepped back to let the two girls precede me. Cuddy had vanished toward the kitchen. They reached the door. Halted. And such a look of terrified surprise spread over the two pretty faces that I hastened before them.

In a chair beside the centre table sat Inspector Rountree. He was busy filling his pipe, paying no attention to us. I took two quick, angry steps toward him, and he rose, bowed, smiled, and continued to pack the tobacco with expert thumb.

"Surely an unexpected and not unpleasant meeting," he cooed. "Will you be good enough, Fullerton, to introduce me to your friends?" As I continued to glare in speechless anger, he introduced himself: "I'm Inspector Rountree, of Scotland Yard. I've wished to meet you for several days, but Mr. Fullerton didn't take kindly to the idea. And yet, you know, I'm almost old enough to be your father." He smiled more broadly.

Of the two girls it was Willo who reacted most noticeably to the introduction. She shrank backward and caught hold of Barbara's arm in both her hands. And suddenly her arms wrapped themselves about her older sister, as if to protect her.

"Oh, Barby, dear! We should have gone away, far, far away. I knew it all the time, but—but—My darling, can you ever forgive me? I knew all the time what you did was for the best."

Inspector Rountree's hand closed spasmodically over his pipe and he stepped swiftly toward them.

"Please, please!" he begged, and a look of real distress on his face made me wonder more than ever what it was all about. "Please restrain yourselves. I hate to do it—here, but I must warn you that I'm a police officer, and anything you say may be used against you. It's my duty to find the murderer of Vance Horton, but I hope—I hope—" He turned away. "There's another duty," he continued, working once more absent-mindedly at the pipe, "and I'm desperately keen on it just now—to intercept misleading evidence. I can make mistakes enough without it. . . . I don't wish to make a mistake in this case."

Barbara had turned coldly-accusing eyes on me.

"I had nothing—I didn't know—" I began.

The Inspector helped me out. "No, he didn't know. He's even more surprised than you to see me here. I, too, found the door open and came in . . . just before you did. Of us all Mr. Fullerton is the only one with nothing to explain. In fact," glancing slyly at me under his brows, "it's all quite plain."

With no sign of relenting in her face Barbara faced the Inspector.

"What are you going to do, Inspector?"

"To sit down—with your permission—and talk things over."

He swept his hand about, and involuntarily we sat down.

"I owe Mr. Fullerton an explanation. Everything of the last ten minutes was arranged in cold blood. There was no one in the garden. I wished to get into the house without being seen, so Inspector Emerson was to attract your attention, Fullerton, by appearing to hear someone in the shrubbery. I was hiding behind one of the pillars within two feet of you in the doorway. It was simpler than we could have hoped, when you set off in pursuit.

"I confess the entrance of the two young ladies was not part of the plan. But here we are. Would you mind telling me the result of Inspector Emerson's visit, Fullerton?"

"He found a gun planted in a drawer in my room—among my shirts, I believe. Someone entered the house by the open door there, while I was asleep down here, and went upstairs to plant it." I narrated the story in some detail. "I'm not worried about the gun the Inspector found. What I'd like to know is what brought the police at this hour of the morning."

"I suppose you do. Odd coincidence, wasn't it?"

"These are not coincidences," I protested angrily. "This sort of thing has happened from the moment Vance Horton was shot."

Inspector Rountree lit his pipe with leisurely match.

"And did you think the police were so stupid not to see—something of what you see? The gun might have given you a few uncomfortable hours, had you not caught the marauder at it. H'm—there can be no doubt of that?" He eyed me gravely, demanding the truth.

"Here's a lump to prove it, and Cuddy will show you his arm. Besides, Larry heard it—"

"So did I!" Willo broke in.

Inspector Rountree's eyes shifted slowly to the girl's. "Then you must have been somewhere nearer the fight than the garden out there."

"I was. I was here in the house." Willo stood with her shoulders thrown back, looking boldly into the Inspector's eyes. "That, too, you may easily prove. I was in the yellow room upstairs. I walked along the hall and left the house by way of the back stairs. Inspector Emerson and his men must have heard me. I've been hiding here since last night."

The Inspector nodded. "Because you knew we were anxious to meet you. Not a bad idea of yours. It's a wonder you didn't take refuge in the police station. I suppose those clothes were part of the scheme to keep out of our way." A kindly smile suffused his keen face. "My dear girl, did you think for one moment we suspected you of murdering young Horton?"

"I know you did," said Willo defiantly. "I know you do still. You know I was there when he was murdered. You know I ran away—"

"Willo! Willo!" cried her sister.

But Willo, for once the stronger, raised a silencing hand. "I was there. I saw—"

"Inspector Rountree"—Barbara stepped before her sister—"Willo had nothing to do with it. It was—"

"Your sister is at least a brave girl," the Inspector interrupted, so eagerly that I stared with amazement, marvelling at a detective who refused a clue when it was offered. "You have no more reason to hide than have half a dozen others. I never yet found a murderer by a voluntary confession. It's the one kind of story I'd refuse to consider seriously. . . . I've met many a mother, or son, or daughter, or brother, or sister, or lover, who'd willingly assume a murder to save the one who really did it. Please let it rest there."

"There's one thing," I declared stubbornly, "that I don't propose to let rest without an answer: How did the police happen to come to-night?"

"How," countered the detective with a smile, "did we discover you were in Figmore Street at the time of the murder? How did we learn of the presence of the two young ladies?"

"By an anonymous letter. But you couldn't have heard—"

"The telephone works at all hours of the night," said the Inspector dryly, tapping his pipe on the tray at his side. "But, no, that's hardly fair. I'm trying to be frank—as frank as my duty permits. We did not learn by telephone—not that way. By telephone, yes. We've had this house under our eye all day. Our man happened to see a strange face at an upstairs window. Then he heard something of the disturbance of your fight with the intruder, and he telephoned Inspector Emerson."

"But the automatic?" I puzzled. "Inspector Emerson found it within a few minutes."

"Better ask him about that," said the Inspector. "It may have been an accident. It was the strange face at the window we were interested in. Oh, well," as he read my incredulity, "you can't expect the police to take you completely into their confidence."

"I expect nothing," I said brusquely.

Barbara stepped forward. "I must speak, Inspector. It's not fair to Mr. Fullerton to leave it like this. Surely there's no reason for him to be made uncomfortable by your suspicions. I—"

"You must tell me nothing, young lady," said the Inspector firmly.

"But—but I could tell you—everything."

The Inspector smiled enigmatically. "You *think* you can. Will you take my word for it that there's much more in this than even you're aware of? In fact, what you might tell me scarcely interests me—it's irrelevant to what we wish to know, to be certain of. We're on the trail of the murderer. Doctor Millbrook has the key almost in his hand—if you'll forgive the mixed metaphor. It's the Doctor will solve it."

He rose and stood before Barbara, smiling on her in a fatherly way.

"You've had to endure all this for four or five days, my dear young lady, and to endure it almost alone. I don't wonder you scarcely know what you're saying. Your worries have played havoc with your sense of values. I'd say that before any jury. And yet—and yet, I'm going to find young Horton's murderer and see that he's punished—or she. To show you how foolish a guilty conscience may make its owner: This morning Jordan Fleming and his wife attempted to escape to France. We managed to stop them at Dover. He's—under restraint."

"But they were only going to Brittany for a holiday," I protested.

"A holiday? Perhaps. A holiday this side of the Channel, but what beyond? And now," moving to the door, "with your permission I'll have a word with your ailing friend upstairs."

"But Doctor Fleury turned us out not half an hour ago."

"I think," he replied with a confident smile, "Doctor Fleury will admit me. And alone, if you please," as I started to follow.

He had taken a step or two along the passage, but he came hastily back, a look on his face that I did not understand until he spoke.

"My advice—as a friend—is that the young ladies have told their whole story. I even plead with them to consider it so. It may be that I failed to hear some of what they said—or that my memory is bad. Inspector Emerson? I don't know. He had remarkably good ears and a wonderful memory."

His face reddened, and he hurried away.

I turned back to find the sisters with their arms about each other. Willo sobbed softly, while Barbara crooned over her like a mother. Then, over Willo's fair hair, she murmured:

"Mr. Fullerton, I apologize—if it's worth anything to you—now."

I sighed happily. "It's the difference between torture and peace, Barbara."

David Fleury came down the stairs. I intercepted him.

"Damn it, David, you should have kept him out! You shouldn't let—"

David raised his eyebrows in his most superior professional manner. "I believe I'm Larry's physician, Dill."

Far into the night I lay awake—rather until daybreak. At intervals I tip-toed to the passage. From Larry's room came the rumble of voices, and at the other end of the passage Cuddy's door stood wide open, revealing him lying across the bed fully clothed. Cuddy's was no eight-hour day when the house was not at peace.

At five o'clock Cuddy wakened me to say that Barbara and Willo insisted on leaving. I had followed Inspector Rountree's advice to the letter and had refused to let them talk. Cuddy had seen them to the yellow room.

But had they told their whole story? I knew they had not. I knew, too, that some time I must hear it for my own peace of mind. Peace? If only I might ask one question and be answered! On the answer hung my very life itself, or so it seemed. And yet—and yet, in that strange half hour with Inspector Rountree in the curtained library had the question not been answered? Answered in Willo's defence of her sister, in Barbara's refusal to accept that defence, in their very reconciliation?

But as, in my dressing-gown, I let them out of the house, only one question came to my lips:

"Will you call me, Miss Venell, when you need me?"

And Barbara, her hand touching my arm for a fleeting moment of ecstasy, murmured: "You've done so much for us now, Mr. Fullerton."

And then the maze of uncertainty overwhelmed me once more. For as Barbara transferred her hand lovingly to her sister's shoulder Willo shivered and shrank from the touch.

That night I was to understand—and the understanding was to be the greatest shock of all.

LARRY slept late that morning, but I waited with more or less patience. Inspector Rountree's extended visit worried me. Cuddy had told me he did not leave until shortly before he wakened me. I was annoyed, too, that so much was taking place that I was not permitted to share.

David did not come again. But Cuddy brought Larry's message that he wished to see me. He received me without his usual teasing welcome.

"I wish," he growled, "you'd be more of a doorman and less publicity. What do you think I came here for? That damned cop!"

I explained that I was helpless to prevent the visit. Besides, David, "your personal physician," was there.

"Judging by the time you kept him—"

"*I* kept him? Damn it! did you expect me to leap on him with this cracked leg and kick him out?"

"You seemed to have much to talk about," I declared irritably.

He fixed me with his one unbandaged eye. "Dill, you weren't eavesdropping?"

"Only because I didn't think of it."

Larry grinned. "I didn't know a Scotland Yard detective had such a line of parlour tricks. But don't imagine I wasn't on my guard. Now and then he tried to pry things from me, pumped and pumped; but if he brought up anything but bilge I don't know it. At the last I yawned in his face."

"Did he tell you about Barbara and Willo? How he sneaked in by the front door on a mean ruse?"

"Ahem! Barbara and Willo didn't sneak, of course. No, he didn't seem interested in the girls."

"That," I said, "is what makes me more alarmed. . . . Larry, those girls have something to hide—and Inspector Rountree knows it."

Larry widened his one eye in exaggerated surprise. "You don't say! Imagine a girl with a secret! . . . I suppose, as usual, it had no value unless they could speak of it."

"Inspector Rountree wouldn't let them speak. I've been asking myself why all night."

I crossed the room and took my stand before a window. It was a dull but warm day, with promise of rain. Through the open window came the flurried rustle of leaves whipped by the gusts that raised dust from every bare spot in the garden.

"Larry, it's the very devil!"

"Don't be so pessimistic, old chap. It may only be Hodges with a new jaw-splitter to puzzle you."

His flippancy annoyed me. "It's you," I said, "you being laid up at a time like this. More than ever we must do something."

"For our two fair friends, you mean? Oh, well," as I swung on him angrily, "have it your own way—for your own reason. Fact is, Dill, you don't notice that I'm downhearted, do you? I can plan better here in bed. I think I was intended to be an invalid. I have a schedule for you to follow. I'm going to be that fictional hero, the arm-chair sleuth."

"I see nothing else for it," I sighed. "What's first on the list?"

"You might have a game of golf with Jordan Fleming."

"I forgot. Jordan's in jail. He and Nora tried to skip out. The police caught them at Dover."

Larry whistled with surprise and consternation. "You'll bail them out, of course?"

"I'm afraid they won't give me the chance. They're probably holding him as a material witness. At least that's what they'll say."

Larry looked disturbed. "Sort of complicates things," he muttered. "Next on the list—let me see—" He lay for some time with closed eyes. "I wonder what would come of another visit to Peter Davenport. He may have another story by this time. We haven't half exhausted that source. He's our most difficult nut to crack . . . and when you visit him keep one hand on the door and your other fist clenched. Quick-tempered lad, Peter; but you always had the quarter-mile at Cortwright. . . . I'd like to know what Peter has in mind. Ten o'clock, isn't it? All right, you'll catch him at his desk now. Last night still owes me some sleep. Send Cuddy to me, please."

* * * *

I was, I suppose, peculiarly sensitive to impressions that morning, for as I closed the gate behind me my eyes followed the street in both directions. Not casually, either. A new peril seemed to be crowding in on me.

Both sides of the street were lined with plane trees, their leprous trunks a distracting medley of greys. The foliage was at its densest, and shadows lay thickly mottled across the pavement, for the sun had burst through the clouds.

A confusing scene. But it failed to confuse me that morning.

And so, far up the street near the corner, I detected movement in the heart of the shadows, its very stealthiness focusing my attention. Closing the gate, I started slowly toward it. It was not on my way to the city, and I tried to cover the change of route by exhibiting a profound interest in my own garden as I passed along the fence. But from the corner of my eye I saw someone flit round the corner and vanish.

Nothing more than a glimpse, but enough to satisfy me that it was the very man I was going to interview—Peter Davenport.

It gave me an odd feeling, even a shock—the tiger stalking its hunter. I remembered what Larry had said, "I'd like to know what Peter has in mind." And forthwith I decided that I, too, must know.

I looked about for the police, knowing well, however, that, with Peter keeping the house so frankly under observation, the police must have withdrawn. Continuing my way to the corner, still apparently absorbed in my garden, as I turned I saw that Peter was not in sight. And so I retraced my steps past the house and on to the lower corner, as if on my way to the city.

Peter, I knew, would be watching me.

The moment I rounded the corner I set off on the run, sped around the block, and in less than a couple of minutes was peering carefully along the street past my house.

Sure enough, there was Peter, having followed me to the corner below, standing in the shadow of a tree, staring along the street below into which I had vanished.

Convinced—as I planned he should—that I had entered one of the houses there, he remained on watch for more than an hour, his impatience and anxiety growing with each passing minute. At last, with a final lingering glance along the street and another toward my house, he set off at a rapid pace toward the city.

I followed.

What was in my mind I scarcely know, except that it seemed more important than ever to know what was in Peter's mind. Any move of any of the several suspects seemed pregnant with a new significance since Jordan Fleming's foolish attempt to escape. I was prepared to believe, with Inspector Rountree, that there was much more in the murder of Vance Horton than appeared on the surface. Indeed, I had reason to hope with all my heart that it was so.

Peter continued on his way at a rapid pace. He seemed to have forgotten me, for he never once looked back; and the rate at which he went convinced me that he had a definite goal before him. Since, judging by my own feelings, none of the suspects could have anything in mind but the murder, until it was solved and the murderer punished that goal was important to me.

I was more convinced of that when Peter did not turn in to the store but continued his way, even increasing his pace.

And then, with a real shock, I found myself in Figmore Street.

Peter had slackened his pace. He still moved with bent head, as if unconscious of the route he followed, but I knew by sundry signs that he was keenly alive to everything about him. Except myself, I hoped. And then, with a start, I asked myself if it was another case of the murderer returning to the scene of his crime. In spite of that scream at the moment Vance Horton was shot, I found it the easiest thing in the world, at times like this, to dissociate the two girls from the crime, even from any knowledge of the murderer. Larry, and even Inspector Rountree, had encouraged that unwarranted lapse of common sense.

Dropping farther behind, I watched Peter's every move.

As he passed the Horton house he raised his head and ran a swift eye over the place, from end to end of the garden. Peter's presence there was all the more puzzling because everyone knew the police were still in possession of the house, with the servants dismissed and everyone refused admittance. Taking a stand at the corner above the house, I waited to see what Peter had in mind.

He did not stop, but passed on and around the corner to the street below. It carried him along the end of the garden. I hurried to keep him in sight. Once beyond the gate I moved more cautiously, for the hedge was low. If Peter looked around he would see me over the hedge from the other street. And so I crouched a little as I advanced.

I had reason to, for at that moment the hedge at the bottom of the garden toward the far side shook violently, and a moment later Peter's head appeared inside. I bent out of sight. But through the hedge I saw him crawl into the lawn and disappear into a thicket of ornamental shrubbery. Cautiously I continued, under cover of the hedge, to the corner. And then Peter reappeared, making his way along the far side of the lawn toward the house.

What was he after? What could he hope to do there, with the police everywhere? What a desperate risk to take! What could make it worth taking?

I straightened, screened by the trees and shrubbery that grew thickly over the lawn. Peter had vanished behind the billiard-room. The thought came to me that perhaps he was hand and glove with the police, that he had told them a story and was working to prove it—to convict someone else. Perhaps to turn suspicion from himself. But the police were more readily available elsewhere than at Vance Horton's home.

A heavy hand fell on my shoulder and a stern voice demanded to know my business.

I looked up into the face of Policeman Rankin.

"Oh, hello, Rankin!" I tried to cover my confusion and fright with a friendliness I did not feel.

"We've 'ad 'em swarmin' about 'ere ever since the murder, Mr. Fullerton, but I didn't expect *you.*"

"Neither did I, Rankin. But I was trying to place exactly where I was the night of the murder when I heard certain sounds. It seems to me I should have heard a shot if there was one. I drove around that corner. I wasn't going fast, either."

Rankin made a sound of disgust. "From what I 'ear they was makin' noise enough to drown an eighteen pounder. I don't know, Mr. Fullerton, but I think you better leave your investigations till you can make them with the Inspector."

I thanked him. "Perhaps you're right. Well, good day."

I set off briskly along the end of the garden. Across the corner I saw Rankin stalk back to the house and disappear. Crossing the street, I took my stand in the angle of a stone fence, just such a fence as Vance Horton had torn down to make way for the hedge that had figured so often since the murder. Peter Davenport could not leave without my seeing him, for both streets lay under my eyes.

I had been there only a few minutes when Peter came into sight, creeping back as he had come, dodging from thicket to thicket. And then I lost sight of him beyond the hedge.

In a moment his face appeared through the hedge, looking up and down the street. I stood absolutely still, and he failed to notice me. Apparently satisfied that the way was clear, he came out on the street and hurried away.

I set out after him. Even then I had no real plan in mind, but I made no effort to keep out of sight. Peter must have heard me behind him, for, without looking around, he lengthened his stride. But unless he broke into a run, he could not escape.

Realizing that at length, he looked back over his shoulder.

"Hello, Peter!"

His face had paled a little at sight of me. But the next moment it reddened with anger and he faced me squarely, his legs set wide.

"Damn you, Dill Fullerton! Poking your nose in again, are you?"

"Again and always, Peter, until Vance Horton's murderer is found. Larry and I warned you."

"And I'm going to warn you," he returned furiously. "If I find you again on my heels—"

I laughed easily. I was well beyond his reach. "First catch your hare, Peter. And, speaking of poking one's nose, you tried some of it yourself this morning, didn't you? You made a mess of it."

"You—you saw me? You followed me all morning?"

"I beat you to it, Peter."

He snarled: "And you're beating me to end it. If I find you following me again—" His face was almost purple with fury.

"Fie, Peter!" I smiled. "If Inspector Emerson saw you now he'd know you quite capable of murder."

He took a stride toward me, but I evaded him. At the same time I had an unhappy feeling that I had not gone the right way with Peter. It was only by soothing him off his guard that I could hope to take anything back to Larry worth repeating. As he was now he had no thought but to crush me with those powerful hands.

"I might condone the murder committed in that billiard-room, Peter," I laughed, "but not my own. And if you lost your head enough to murder me, you'd have something more on your conscience than you have now."

"Go to hell!" he blustered, and turned away.

Like a cat I was on him, running my hands over his body. For I had seen a bulge in his pocket that I was certain had not been there as I followed him across the city.

"So you found it!" I exulted.

Then he had me by the throat. I did not resist. It would have been useless. For a moment a stab of cold fear shot through me, then with a fling he sent me rolling into the roadway.

"So you knew—what I was after?" he muttered, standing over me.

I picked myself up, brushing my clothes. "I've an idea now and then, Peter. Better look out for Scotland Yard. Doctor Millbrook has the bullet."

"Scotland—Yard!" he sputtered, his eyes wide with dread.

Too late I recalled Inspector Emerson's request not to speak of Rountree.

"They're sure to get Scotland Yard in."

"It'll be too late—for this," he said, clapping the pocket where the automatic lay.

"Not too late for Larry and me," I replied. "We're just amateurs, but Larry has a way with him."

"Perhaps," eyeing me keenly, "Larry isn't so impressed with his way now. Things happen to those who interfere."

"Larry never changes, Peter. Vance's murderer may learn that too late. He was less successful with Larry than with Vance."

Peter's fury had changed to a heavy thoughtfulness. He stood for several seconds frowning at me.

"Did it ever strike you and Larry that the one who tried to put him out of the way may not be Vance's murderer?"

"What do you mean?"

"Don't you think it might pay me—and half a dozen more—to put you both out of the way? Yet only one fired that shot in there. And don't you think there may be others quite as anxious as you, if only for their own safety, to find the murderer? You've found it wise—"

"'Wise?' What do you mean?"

It was his turn to smile. "The evidence is more convincing against you and Larry than against anyone else. Yes, even than against me, gun and all. And I might add to that evidence."

"Who told you—that?"

Our rôles had altered in a sentence, and Peter took advantage of it. He shrugged contemptuously and started away. Before I could speak he turned.

"My warning holds, Dill Fullerton. I don't propose to hang for a while yet."

But I had one question to put: "A .25, wasn't it? And the one in your pocket, too? I recognize it."

He made a rush for me, but I was prepared.

"Remember," he boomed. "Larry escaped *that* time."

I COULD hear Larry whistling as I hurried down the hall to his room.

"Larry! Larry—"

He held up his hand to silence me and gravely attacked a fresh bar.

"Larry, I've just seen—"

"D'you remember that fourth bar in that two-hearts-in-three-quarter-time melody? I can't get it." His forehead puckered to a worried frown as he started again.

I strode to the bed and glowered on him.

"To hell with hearts and time! I've just seen Peter Davenport."

"He's not hard to see, is he?"

"He carried a .25 to Vance's that night. I've just watched him—"

Larry had been looking me over. "Looks as if he was rude about it, Dill."

"He was. I'm lucky to have got off with my life."

"How dramatic!" Larry grinned teasingly up at me. "That was a crude bit of sleuthing you performed out there on the street a while ago, Dill."

"You saw me?" I leaned forward toward the window. "But you can't see from here."

"Oh, the faithful Cuddy is eyes and ears to me."

"God, Larry, I wish you'd been along."

"You look as if you needed me. I'm only temporarily disabled. Can I work up a fight later about it?"

I told him what had happened, and with the last word Cuddy knocked and entered with a letter for me. Stiffly he waited, chin outthrust. A glance at the handwriting, and I blushed like a schoolgirl.

"Cuddy," said Larry in a stage whisper, "how dare you look!"

And Cuddy, impertinent fellow, gravely turned his back.

I tore the letter open and read. When I had finished I read it aloud:

"'Last night haunts me—and all the days and nights since— you know when. I'm terrified. What is to come of it all? Won't you please come to us tonight, for I must talk with someone? You know the address—Flat 32. Ring the bell three times. Don't telephone or use a messenger. I must count on you.—*BARBARA.*'"

Larry held out his hand. "Let me see it." He eased the bandage
from his other eye and scanned the letter closely. "Do you recognize
the handwriting?"

I sniffed. "Do you think I wouldn't know?" And as the blood
rushed to my cheeks I hurried to add: "I can find the note she left in
the room that first night."

"What's the use? You'd go anyway."

"Of course."

He considered it for a time. "Then you'll take Cuddy."

"But that's foolish. What has Cuddy—"

"You'll take Cuddy," he repeated firmly. "My dear Dill, you
don't take this affair seriously enough. I don't wish to be buying
flowers for you. Now, send Cuddy to me, then lunch. I'm hungry as a
bear."

*****

Before Cuddy and I left the house that evening David Fleury,
summoned by telephone at Larry's request, arrived. Though I made
no mention of it, I wondered if Larry, concerned for my safety, was
equally concerned for his own, since he would have been left alone in
the house.

David had got on my nerves. He annoyed me. Close as was
the friendship between Larry and myself, David insisted on seeing
Larry last at night and first in the morning. And David the physician
was vastly different from David the schoolmate.

Another source of annoyance that evening was Larry's
insistence on delivering his instructions to Cuddy direct. "You must
both carry guns," he decided.

I laughed scornfully. "It isn't a raid, Larry."

"Not on your side," he retorted.

"Well," I declared, "that's off. I haven't a gun—which turns
out to have been lucky."

Larry said: "Cuddy has one. And here," thrusting his hand
under his pillow, "is one for you."

"Where in the world" I began.

"Don't ask questions. I believe you know which is the trigger.
Better leave the fireworks to Cuddy—unless you're hard pressed. You
and Cuddy must keep your wits about you—and your hands on your

guns. You're playing a more desperate game than you know. We're not absolutely sure of that note, and it's a damned dark night. Get the feel of your guns and keep it."

"Even when," I scoffed, "we're seated comfortably in conversation with Barbara and Willo?"

"Even then."

Something in his tone nettled me. "You never did think they were straight."

Larry was undisturbed. "Did you ever think they've told their whole story, Dill? Listen, old man. No one can be trusted till this thing is over. . . . And in the street don't walk too close together."

"One thing I like about you, Larry," I said, "if it weren't so foolish sometimes, is that you never miss a chance to send tingles through my veins."

"If I can tingle you into a state that gets you back on your own feet that's all I care."

Half an hour of that, and no wonder the night seemed different, as Cuddy and I, five paces apart, set off for Ormond Street. Larry had thought it better that we should walk, both because we might leave by the back way and because there would be no tell-tale car to park.

It was a dismal night. Since six o'clock it had been raining, and the rain had settled to a thick mist. The trees dripped. In the street lights white branches started out like writhing ghosts. The streets were almost deserted. Even the lights failed to pierce the fog for more than a few steps, so that the tramp of unseen feet added to the ghostly, uncanny feeling that sent me hurrying along. Now and then a figure loomed suddenly from the fog, with just time to avoid colliding. The steady thud of Cuddy's feet behind me did nothing to soothe my jumping nerves. As we passed beneath each light I slowed my pace to satisfy myself that it was really Cuddy.

Everything was unsubstantial, ghoulish, a sort of nightmare— the muted wirelesses behind closed doors, the misty square of a lighted window, suddenly looming trees and fences, the muffled horns of passing cars, half-seen figures that hurried on secret missions of their own.

An ordinary damp night in England, you might say. But Vance Horton had been murdered—and his murderer was still at large.

By unfrequented streets we arrived at our destination.

"The Elms" was a large new building in a part of the city with which I was none too familiar. It was a hive of small flats that on completion almost two years before had been widely advertised. As we halted before the three-storied building I recalled the glowing account of its "American conveniences"—electric refrigeration, electric stoves, vacuum cleaning, disappearing furniture, and all the rest. It accounted for the high rent demanded, since servants were not what they used to be, and economy was a popular cry—to justify another form of extravagance and growing unemployment.

The structure had three wings, a great W, each entered by its own street door. Flat 32 was in the middle wing—the number in small figures above a brass frame intended to display the tenant's name. It did not surprise me that the frame was empty. Just below was the janitor's name. I pressed the bell of Number 32 three times, and something clicked in the lock. I pushed, and the door opened.

Cuddy and I found ourselves in a bare hall, with rough grey plaster walls that extended back into deep shadows. A single light burned dimly over our heads, for most of the flats in that wing were still untenanted. A stairway rose before us.

As we looked about, wondering where Number 32 was, a slight noise over our heads made me look up. Barbara Venell stood beside the balustrade, peering down on us. She beckoned, and Cuddy and I climbed. And as we reached the upper hall I realized that we had come on tip-toes.

A door at the rear of the hall stood open, letting out a flood of light. For this hall, too, was none too brightly lighted. Barbara stood in the doorway waiting for us. Softly she closed the door behind us.

The room we stood in was a small living-room, small enough for it, too, to be an American innovation. Though inadequately furnished, what there was showed care and expense. Yet, somehow, it had the appearance of impermanency. A fire-place much too large for the room almost filled the opposite wall. A soft, pleasing radiance bathed the room, flowing from indirect lights along the top of the walls.

A single almost unconscious moment of curiosity told me all this, and then I had eyes for nothing but the two girls in the room.

Barbara had taken her stand beyond a small table in the centre of the room. Her face was grey and gaunt, her eyes dark-rimmed and haunted. In the fifteen hours since I had last seen her she seemed to have aged as many years. Some crisis, something tragic, had happened or was about to happen.

To one side, in a large mahogany chair whose dark, glossy surface stood black against the cream wall, sat Willo. Her hands were gripped tightly together in her lap, so tightly that the knuckles were white. And her face too, was drawn and unhappy. But, in contrast to Barbara's, it bore a certain grimness and rebellion that warned me that the coming interview would not be happy for any of us.

She had eyes for no one but her sister, and in those eyes was angry antagonism. But I was able to convince myself there was no hatred. She was at the moment, as once before, the stronger of the pair.

Cuddy remained standing just inside the door, his eyes on the floor. His iron-grey hair was smooth as ever, but he fussed uneasily with it.

Not a word had been spoken, not so much as a greeting.

Suddenly Barbara opened her lips:

"I'm so glad," she murmured, her voice quavering.

"I'll always come when you need me, Miss Venell," I heard myself saying. "I hope you won't mind Cuddy. Larry made me bring him. I suppose," trying to laugh, "he thought I needed protection."

Barbara leaned forward on the table, her slim fingers gripped about its edge.

"Protection—yes. We all need it." With an effort she regained control of herself. "Please sit down." Suddenly Willo's tight lips parted:

"Barbara, I warned you. You mustn't—speak."

Barbara bit her lip, and a flash of pain crossed her face. "I can't help it, Willo. I must, I must. Can't you see how terrible it is for me, hiding it all, choking it back—smothering, haunted, terrified—too miserable to sleep or eat . . . and only you who knows? I can't go on. Besides, I must know—where I stand."

Willo sighed heavily. But she had not given up. Before Barbara could go on she was on her feet, standing before me, her eyes, wet with tears, pleading into mine.

"Don't let her tell, Mr. Fullerton, please don't. What she did she thought was for the best; it was for my sake."

In that moment Barbara was again the elder sister. "Willo, dear." She came round the table and gently led her sister back to her chair. "If we can't trust Mr. Fullerton now who is there to help us? Don't you see we can't fight through this alone? If you love me, Willo, don't stop me. Give me a chance to save myself, the one chance I have."

I sat, silent and distraught, feeling for the meaning of it all, yet challenging it. Cuddy's cap dropped to the floor with a clatter that made me jump.

"Shall I go outside, sir?" he whispered over my shoulder.

Barbara heard him. "If Mr. Fullerton trusts you, Cuddy, that's enough."

I made a sign for him to stay. My throat was too dry to speak.

With a pitiful whimper Willo covered her face with her hands. Barbara returned to the table. She raised herself to her full height, clenched her fists, and in a voice toneless as a machine said:

"Mr. Fullerton, I shot Vance Horton."

THERE are moments of such crowded emotions that the mind refuses to function, when the shock is so terrific that the power to think is numbed. The one outlet is hysteria.

As Barbara, the beautiful girl there beyond the table, the girl I knew now that I loved, made her confession, the one impulse I had was to break into foolish laughter. Barbara a murderess!

It was Willo brought me back to realities. With a low cry of agony that rang through the room, she dropped her face in her hands. A wave of vertigo seized me, so that I clutched the arms of my chair to steady myself.

"You said you—you—I don't believe it."

Barbara smiled wanly. "Thank you, Mr. Fullerton, but it's true."

"I—I don't believe it," I repeated vaguely.

But I did believe it. I had known it all the time, since the moment I saw that dark head at my back in the car as I fled from the scene of the murder.

Barbara's two hands reached falteringly toward me, and she breathed quickly. Next instant she stiffened and looked away. I drew a hand across my forehead.

"Why did you tell me this?" I was half angry, wholly miserable.

Barbara's answer was at first a wondering, softly questioning look straight into my eyes, then a beautiful flush crept slowly into her cheeks and she dropped her face. I too reddened, and a wave of sudden ecstasy swept through me.

I altered the form of the question: "Why did you tell anyone?"

"Willo knew. She—it's been such a shock to her. Besides, I need help."

"I warned her not to tell," Willo wailed through her hands. "And now it's all over."

"'All over?'" I repeated indignantly. "Do you think she's in danger through telling me—*me?* Did you think I'd hand her over to the police?"

"Willo knows," said Barbara, "that you and Mr. Rockford are trying to find the murderer."

"We—*were,*" I said. "I think you know I'd protect you with

my life, Barbara. I knew Vance Horton too well to think he deserved less. You said, Willo, that you'd found out what he was. But you don't know half. Almost every guest there that night had cause to wish him dead—and many of us who weren't his guests. Every friend he ever had hated him—with good reason. Your sister, Willo, was the only one with courage to rid the world of him. Had someone done it years ago many an innocent girl would have been saved."

The words poured from me, a declaration I was powerless to restrain. But at the end I blushed.

Cuddy stirred at my back, and I turned. He had risen noiselessly and opened the door to look into the hall. With one hand he motioned to us to be silent. We watched, spellbound. Presently he withdrew his head and closed the door.

"I thought I heard something," he muttered. "I must-a been wrong."

Of us all Barbara was the coolest. With the confession off her mind she seemed to have dismissed the weightiest of her troubles.

"Yes," she said, "you must be wrong. No one can get into the corridors unless a tenant presses a button that connects with the lock of the front door. In this wing there are only four or five tenants."

"I wish you hadn't told me," I sighed.

"I had to," she replied simply.

"Yes. . . . yes. It was too awful a secret to bear alone."

She smiled. "Only partly that. I wished you to know." Her eyes were fixed on one hand rubbing back and forward along the edge of the table. "And, as I said, I must know where I stand. With the police, I mean. I don't wish to pay the penalty for what I did. I thought maybe you might know what the police think. I nearly confessed last night to the Inspector. I'm so glad now that I didn't. And now you and your friend—it's safer for you. He was so nearly killed."

"But I don't understand that," I said. "If you—did it, why should anyone try to kill Larry?"

"I've thought of that. I suppose it's because so many feel guilty, and the slightest evidence might convict them. So many have no real alibi. Don't you see how desperate they must feel? If Willo had done it I'd do anything to save her—or even if I thought she had done it. You know," she added, "what desperate things I can bring myself to do. The night after—after he was killed, I went alone into the dark garden. I was searching for the revolver I had thrown away after—it happened."

"It was Willo who screamed," I said.

"Yes. I'd followed her. But you know—I told you. I fired before she could speak to him, before he could move."

A shiver ran through her, and her lips tightened.

"What do you propose to do—that we do?" I asked.

"To save myself—with your help."

"You know I'll do anything. First of all, you mustn't even hint at it again, not to anyone."

"But Inspector Rountree must know. He wouldn't let me speak last night. But—Scotland Yard must find a victim. I couldn't let anyone else suffer for it."

At my back Cuddy cleared his throat. "If I may suggest, sir, hadn't you better talk it over with Mr. Rockford?"

It lifted from my shoulders a responsibility I felt unfitted to bear. Larry would be calmer about it. I was in love.

"That's it," I declared. "Larry will know—"

Willo was on her feet. "Mr. Rockford mustn't know, he mustn't. He mustn't know my sister is—is—" She could not finish the sentence.

"You can trust Larry as myself," I assured her, puzzled nevertheless by the outcry. "Larry is wiser than I, more ingenious, more experienced in this sort of thing. Besides, he stands in well with the police. If anyone can save you it's Larry Rockford. Please leave it to us."

"But," said Barbara, "I'm not going to sit down and do nothing."

"What can you do?" I asked.

She made no answer, and I rose to go.

Cuddy opened the door and looked into the hall. Everything was quiet. Barbara went with us to the head of the stairs.

"Why—why, the light's out down there," she whispered, looking over the balustrade.

"Burnt out, I suppose," I said. "All the better for us. We can slip out without being seen."

"Hadn't I better ring the janitor?" she inquired nervously.

"And have him for a witness, perhaps, if—if things go wrong? No, this is just what we want."

Half-way down the stairs, where she could still see us in the light from the upper passage, I stopped.

"Go on back," I ordered. "We'll wait till your door closes."

With a smile she vanished. The door of her flat slammed gently.

CUDDY was waiting for me at the foot of the stairs. He let me pass, and I set out for the door, feeling my way along the wall. Suddenly a blinding light flashed in our faces.

In that moment I recalled Larry's instructions that Cuddy and I should not walk together. And now, at our first failure to observe his warning, we were caught. At the same time I was conscious that the street door was ajar, for a slight draught blew in our faces and the city noises were more audible.

All this must have flashed through me with the first glint of light, for my eyes had scarcely closed to the ray when Cuddy sent me staggering to one side, and I heard him leap like a cat to the other. A pistol shot deafened us, and Cuddy called out, not with pain but with anxiety.

In the doorway two men struggled. But as I rushed toward them I collided with Cuddy, who was searching for me. And then the two figures vanished into the street. Cuddy still held me, though I fought to free myself, to get out there on the street and take up the chase. And then I saw how dark it was outside. The light over the door, too, was out.

Doors along the corridor were opening, and faces appeared. I thought of Barbara and looked toward the upper floor. She was half-way down the stairs, peering into the darkness. I hurried toward her.

"Go back," I whispered. "Quick, quick! We're not hurt."

She turned without a word and flitted lightly up and out of sight.

The lights from the open doors dispelled the darkness in the passage. A man came forward.

"What happened? Anyone hurt?"

I explained that we had been attacked as we left the building, probably by a burglar.

"Who turned off the lights?"

"I suppose it's the burglar's idea," I replied.

"But the switch is in the janitor's flat there." He pointed to a door at the foot of the stairs. Passing out to the street, he pressed the janitor's bell. But there was no response.

"That's strange. There's always someone in."

Another tenant pounded on the janitor's door, but still no

answer.

"Better call the—" I began, to be stopped by a nudge from Cuddy. "Isn't there some way to get into his flat?" I asked.

"There's a rear door. We might try there."

He led along the corridor to a grass-covered court at the rear and turned to the right. At a door there he knocked, and when there was still no response he turned the knob. The door opened.

The room we entered was dark, but a line of light showed beneath a door straight before us. We found our way to it through what must, by the odours, have been the kitchen, and at the end of a long passage we entered the office.

There we came on the explanation. On the floor lay a small man, hands and feet bound fast, and a handkerchief thrust tightly in his mouth. Freed, he staggered to his feet and slumped into a chair, feeling at his temple where a red lump showed. A little whisky brought him to his senses.

His story was that someone had entered the unlocked rear door, and when he went to investigate he had been struck down. He could give no description of his assailant.

The police, of course, had to be called in. But Cuddy and I managed to get away, leaving our address, before they arrived. My first thought was to leave a false name and address, but I saw in time what a mistake it would be. What I wished most was to talk it over with Larry before I was forced to tell the story to the police.

Free of the building, Cuddy and I hastened homeward. Everything seemed to depend on Larry. What was fixed in my mind was that, at all cost, the presence of Barbara and Willo in "The Elms" must be concealed.

We had gone no more than a couple of hundred yards when a car, whirling around a corner before us, skidded in against the curb, and a man leaped out and blocked our way. It was Inspector Rountree.

"What are you running from?" he demanded.

I replied: "There's been trouble back there at 'The Elms.' They're waiting for you." I was breathless with excitement and dismay, for the one man of them all I had hoped not to see until Larry had decided on what to say stood before me.

"Take your time, Fullerton," advised the Inspector. "We know we're wanted there. Just now we seem to be wanted more here. . . . So you managed once more to get mixed up in a disturbance, eh? You seem to have a flair for it. Come along."

"We were at the wrong end of this disturbance," I said. "Someone shot at us in the passage. Someone had got in, trussed up the janitor, and turned off the lights."

He took hold of my arm and directed me close to the car. Inside were Inspector Emerson and, at the wheel, Doctor Millbrook. The Doctor exclaimed when he recognized us.

"By jove, Fullerton, I hope you weren't in that. I happened to be passing, and I heard a shot. I hurried off for the police."

"Did you see those men run away?" I asked.

"I didn't wait to see anything. At first I thought the shot was at me."

"Well," I said, addressing myself to the officials, "they'll tell you back there all they know. You'll find us at home to give you the rest of the story."

"You'll come—" Inspector Emerson began.

But Inspector Rountree cut him short. "All right, boys. We'll see you later. Don't go to bed."

They drove away, leaving Cuddy and me staring after the red tail light. I was troubled, for we had been let off more easily than conditions warranted. Inspector Rountree was too deep for me.

The rain had ceased, but water still dripped dismally from the trees. I looked about for a taxi, but none was in sight, and scarcely any other sign of life. Cuddy and I set off at our best pace for home.

I made straight for Larry's room. In the upper hall Cuddy, still at my heels, said:

"The doctor said, sir, we mustn't waken Mr. Rockford, ever. He was very particular about that."

"To hell with the doctor! This is life or death."

"Perhaps to Mr. Rockford too, sir. If you'll let me go in quietly first, sir."

"Certainly not. If I can't—" I stopped. From Larry's room came the sound of voices. "Someone's in there now."

I threw the door open. David Fleury was bent over the bed, a roll of bandages in his hand. With an angry look he waved us from the room.

"Didn't I say you weren't to do this? Get out!"

I slunk to the door, and Cuddy closed it after us. In no more than a couple of minutes David called us in.

"And please to remember, Dill," he threatened, "my orders must be obeyed, or I'll be forced to take Larry elsewhere."

"But, David," I objected, "this is different. Larry must see me now, right now, and," growing angrier, "to hell with the professional palaver! Larry won't die of a little talk at half-past ten. One would think Larry was a woman, to have her face-pack last thing at night and her rouge first thing in the morning before she can see her friends."

"I'm Larry's physician," said David stiffly, looking to Larry for support.

Larry lay quietly laughing. "One of my daily entertainments. Life would be dull without it. Poor Dill! Have a heart, David. Probably the brunette has turned him down—or confessed that she shot Vance Horton."

"Why—why—how did you know?" I looked wildly from Larry to David.

"Anyone less in love than you must have seen it long ago."

I dropped into a chair and felt nervously for my cigarettes. "What are we going to do, Larry? We must decide right away. Inspector Rountree is coming."

I had commenced the story of the evening's adventure when I noticed David and stopped. He saw my embarrassment and prepared to leave.

"Such secrets!" he jeered. "If I told all I know about you all!" And with a smile and a bow he left the room.

Larry heard me through with no visible excitement. "Well," he drawled, "you came through without a scratch, didn't you?"

"That isn't important," I objected impatiently. "It's the two girls. And who was it?"

"Who was what?"

"The man who tried to shoot me. But even that doesn't bewilder me as much as the other—the man who fought with him in the doorway. It was just like Sunday night here in the house."

"Your special Providence, you mean? Why worry? So long as he stays on the job all you need do is return thanks. What you have to worry about is the unknown who shot at you. Of course, he's the one who tried to blow me up."

"You really think someone is trying to kill us both—the one who murdered—" I stumbled to my feet and paced about the room.

"Larry, you make me forget. We *know* who—shot Vance Horton. For some reason someone else is trying to get us out of the way. . . . But perhaps it was a burglar."

Larry shook his head hopelessly. "Use your head, Dill A burglar would get nowhere simply by tying up the janitor. He couldn't get into any of the other flats. Had he had that in mind he'd have let you pass on to the street. You'd never have known he was there in the darkness.

"But if he was after me how did he know I was there? Barbara sent her note through the mail. If he followed Cuddy and me he had a better chance to shoot me on the way."

"'Barbara'?" he teased. "Has it gone that far?"

But the time had passed when I could be teased about Barbara. A thought struck me. "Could it have been Peter, Larry?"

"It could have been . . . but it wasn't. Never mind how I work that out; just accept it. Your trouble is—may I call her Barbara? What a terrible shock to hear it from her own lips! But, Dill, if Willo should tell me that *she* fired that bullet I'd—I'd go whistling on my way and forget all about it."

"'Willo?'" I teased.

"'Willo,'" he repeated firmly. "I wouldn't believe her."

"That's what I told Barbara."

Larry laughed till his one eye misted over. "What a nice scrappy evening you've had! But you *did* believe her, you see. And, believing it possible that she shot Vance Horton, why couldn't it be that she shot at you for calling her a liar? Ah," as the knocker rattled through the house, "that'll be the police. And bear in mind, Dill, that they haven't knotted the noose for you or Barbara Venell yet."

EVERY word, every look, even the things that might have been said but weren't—and there were many of them of the next couple of hours are stamped on my memory more indelibly than anything else that marked the search for Vance Horton's murderer, except the final astonishing scene that explained everything.

In the first place Inspector Rountree came alone. That in itself introduced into Larry's room an atmosphere of mystery.

And it was an Inspector Rountree who had dropped his idle of Scotland Yard investigator and become a friend—considerate, only slightly curious, protecting us from ourselves, eager to be helpful. I see now that it was part of his cleverness, a manner that led us imperceptibly to frankness. But I see now, too, that Inspector Rountree knew so much more than I thought he knew, that all my fears were groundless.

With unwonted cheerfulness he tossed his hat carelessly toward a chair and sat down. And with a comfortable sigh he drew out his pipe and started to fill it.

"Eleven o clock," he sighed, "and I'm ready for bed. But I must smoke one last pipe. And while I'm at it there's a form to go through. Let's have your story Fullerton."

It struck me then, in a moment of panic, that the minutes Larry and I had been together had prepared me in no wise for the police. But I hope I managed to conceal my uneasiness, as without hesitation I started in where we found ourselves in the dark corridor on our way to the street. To my surprise he asked no questions about what had happened before, how we came to be there.

There was, in fact, little I could add to what the tenants of "The Elms" had already told him. I spoke of the blinding light and the shot. I said nothing of the struggle in the doorway.

But Larry, apparently as interested as I in that curious feature of the adventure, filled in the omission:

"There was someone else, too, it seems—a second stranger. And the pair struggled together. Dill saw them in the doorway, then they were gone."

Inspector Rountree blew a lazy ring of smoke over the bed. "Much the same as happened Sunday night, wasn't it?"

"Exactly. There seems to be someone who has it in for me—

and someone who is trying to protect me."

"Perhaps," said Larry, "Dill's so heavily insured the companies are guarding him. But he seems to resent being saved without an introduction to his saviour. I've tried to make him silently grateful—and look forward to the rope as the reward for his many crimes."

I was not sure whether Larry ridiculed my story or not.

"Cuddy saw him, too. I was wide awake this time."

"I'll talk to Cuddy on the way out," said the Inspector. He sat for a time smoking placidly, his eyes closed. Suddenly he lifted himself in his chair and removed the pipe from his lips.

"Fullerton, you'd better watch your step. If I were you I'd keep off the streets at night. And see that windows and doors are locked here. We've a reckless fiend to deal with . . . a clever one . . . an unscrupulous one. If anyone must go abroad after dark send Cuddy. He can look after himself."

I laughed recklessly. "I've managed so far, thanks. I'm not going to let any ghostly menace like that keep me in should I wish to go out. Larry and I have a job to do, and we're not going to be frightened off it."

"Can't you leave that job to the police?"

"We're not going to interfere with the police."

"But that's exactly what you're doing. It's our duty to protect you, quite as much as to find Horton's murderer, and the distraction of it is nothing short of interference. See what happened to your friend. Instead of a single task, now we have two."

"And," I persisted, "the more that happens to us the more clues you have—or the more likely to have. It's all connected with Vance Horton's murder. If his murderer were wise he'd avoid everything that would bring him again to the notice of the police. That's the way I look at it."

Inspector Rountree smiled indulgently. "It would be little satisfaction to us to lay our hands on the murderer as the result of a second murder."

I saw the point. "All I can promise is to take no rash risks. But, I warn you, the further these attacks go the more I'm determined to find who and what is at the back of them. And," looking to Larry for support, "if Larry doesn't feel the same, then a dynamite explosion must be as overwhelming as the Oxford Movement. You should try it in the prisons."

Larry and the Inspector regarded each other with amusement.

"You continue as a liability, then, Fullerton," said the Inspector.

"A debt," I said, "you'll never be called on to pay."

And all the time back in my mind was the spectre of Barbara's confession, a vague misery that somehow lost definite form when I was with Larry or Inspector Rountree.

The Inspector rapped out his pipe on the tray and thrust it in his pocket.

"Short of locking you up, Fullerton, we can't stop you. . . . But," rising, "I want to assure you that we're not going to force you to recklessness by keeping an eye on you. Still, I hope to God we're on hand when that Providence of yours fails you. And now for sleep."

He stretched his massive frame, yawned, and left.

I rose to see him to the door, but he stopped me.

"I want a word with Cuddy."

Larry and I sat with the door open. Neither spoke. From the hall came the intermittent rumble of voices, then the front door slammed. I sat on. Larry lay with his eyes closed.

The telephone rang distantly, and a few moments later Cuddy came to say I was wanted. "A woman, sir," and that disapproving cough.

I hurried to my room.

"Yes, Bar—" I stopped just in time.

"Is that you, Dill? I hope you weren't in bed."

It was Effie Shannon. In spite of the tremor in her voice, the tenseness of the whisper, I recognized her.

"Yes, Effie."

"Dill, I must talk to you."

"Certainly, Effie. I'll see you any time you say to-morrow."

"But it must be now, Dill, right away. It's very important. I daren't see you in the daytime. I'm being watched, I think."

"If you're being watched I can't come over there—"

"No, no. I thought—if it's all right—I'd come to you."

There could be no doubt of the urgency in her voice. Its anxious, frightened tone sent tingles through me But there were two objections to what she proposed. I had little faith in Inspector Rountree's promise not to keep an eye on me; and there was Larry.

But I could see no other way out, except to refuse. I could not do that.

"If you must come, Effie, you must. It's at your own risk. I'll send Cuddy for you. No one will notice him, But Larry must share what you have to tell me. He's here in bed, you know. He's worth a dozen of me."

"Larry there?" she questioned sharply.

"Larry had an accident on Saturday. He's staying with me."

"I'd like Larry to hear," she said after a pause. "I'll wait for Cuddy. Tell him the front door will be open. He can walk in. You know the flat."

Cuddy took instructions with no more expression than if I were sending him for a postage stamp.

"And before you start the car make sure the engine's not been tampered with."

Cuddy smiled. "If anyone gets into that garage when I've locked it he'll go away in a hearse."

I hurried back to Larry to prepare him. He whistled thoughtfully for a time, evidently puzzled.

"Sort of busy day, Dill. If only you could turn it into cash. I'm afraid when this is over there's nothing in life short of a private murder of our own, or a South American revolution, to keep our blood at a comfortable temperature."

"I wish you were up, Larry," I moaned.

"Why? What's to be done? You know who murdered Vance. That's all we had to do."

I groaned. "There's more than that to do now. Larry, we must save her."

"How?" He yawned in my face.

"You see a lot of Inspector Rountree. Can't you discover what the police think, what they plan to do?"

Larry considered that. "There's one more prolific source of information than that, Dill—Doctor Millbrook."

I had forgotten the Doctor. "By jove, Larry, that's right. I'll cultivate him. I'll pay him another visit."

"I was going to suggest it," he drawled.

"But, you know, it doesn't seem quite—quite sporting to take advantage of his trust in us, his friendly frankness."

"Not for Barbara's sake? It's for you to decide that. It's your move now, Dill."

And then we heard Cuddy coming along the hall.

XXXII A Frightened Woman

THE door opened and Effie Shannon slid into the room. That was the only way to describe it. Had we not been prepared we would not have recognized her. She wore a heavy veil, and no longer was she the self-reliant, almost defiant Effie we knew so well. Her ungloved hands were clutched together before her, and she breathed as if she had been running. She was, I saw, on the verge of hysteria.

Two days before, it was true, I had seen her eyes wet with tears, a strange Effie, but this was stranger still. Not grief, but an overwhelming terror. It breathed from her eyes, from her white face, from those tightly-clenched hands, from her bent shoulders and creeping steps. Of late years she had grown hard, I thought, reckless, aggressive in her flouting of the conventions. She and Vance, in their months of association, had made themselves conspicuous. Her beauty and recklessness and his flair for publicity had made them a striking pair.

Even after he threw her over she had carried herself with a high head. And into her eyes and lips had come a new hardness that made me sigh for the Effie I had once known and liked in something more than a friendly way. She had gone her reckless way as usual, but without Vance. I had avoided her, fearing her type and uncertain to what excesses she might endeavour to carry me.

But now all this was gone. With a quick glance about the room, as if to assure herself that we were alone, she threw back her veil and ran to the side of Larry's bed.

"Larry, I didn't know of this. What happened? Are you badly hurt?"

The tenderness in her voice, the shock, surprised me, as it did Larry. He squirmed.

"Stop holding my hand, Effie—in public." He grinned.

Effie stiffened. She turned to me, a spot of colour in either cheek.

"Is this a game?" she demanded.

I spread my hands. "Ask Larry. He's playing it."

Larry said: "Better ask David Fleury. Fact is, Effie, I'm lucky. Someone played a trick on me with a stick of dynamite, and beyond a broken leg and a few scratches I'm all right."

"The hell of it is, Effie," I added, "it put him out of the only game we know just now—finding the murderer of Vance Horton."

"You're very much in earnest about that, both of you, aren't you?" she murmured, moving to the foot of the bed.

"We can't afford *not* to be," Larry told her. It's sheer selfishness. Besides, a born detective like me can't keep from dabbling in these major crimes. I admit you people have managed to make a muddle of the trail."

She faced him. "Who do you mean by 'you people'?"

"Effie Shannon and the rest."

She drew a sharp breath, and her lips parted as if to speak, but she restrained herself, while I waited for a gush of the violent temper of which I knew she was capable. Instead, she seated herself slowly in the chair Inspector Rountree had so recently vacated.

"That," she said, in a tight voice, "is what I came to see you about. Lee Moshier has the same idea."

Larry asked what idea.

"That I killed Vance. . . . No, that's not quite what I mean. Lee has something much more serious on his mind. He's trying to fasten the murder on me, whether I did it or not."

"And," said Larry brutally, "he has such a good case against you that you're so frightened you scarcely know what you're doing—or saying."

Effie drew a sharp breath. I could see how hard she strove to keep herself under control. "If I did it do you think I'm fool enough to confess, even to you? Of course, I'm frightened. But so are others, and we can't all be guilty. We fear what a jury might decide."

No one spoke for a time. A motor horn sounded so suddenly at the corner that we all started, and a quick fear flashed across Effie's face.

"If it comes to that," said Larry, "there's something against Dill and me, but you don't see us trembling. You probably don't know that we were on the spot at the moment of the murder."

Effie's face went whiter than ever, I thought. "I—didn't know that. I thought it was just that everyone knows you didn't like Vance."

"That would only make us a pair of a long list. We simply have no sort of alibi—except for each other. . . . But I wonder if you appreciate what the police have against you? You were *inside* the house. You had access to the billiard-room. Everyone knows how Vance treated you. And, Effie, you managed to acquire a reputation.

Will any one of the guests swear to an alibi for you at the moment of the murder? H'm—if I were in your shoes I'd be in a panic."

Effie seemed to shrivel before it, and the foot I could see under the corner of the bed shifted restlessly. She was still struggling with herself, but suddenly her terror burst into words:

"It was Lee did it, Lee Moshier. I know it was Lee. He's trying to place the blame on me to save his own neck. If you knew what I know you'd see it. Lee and Vance hated each other. They always did, ever since I knew Vance."

"That scarcely seems possible," objected Larry.

"No because they had to endure each other. No one but myself knew. I was—close to Vance. Vance was afraid to turn him out. They'd done things even Vance daren't give Lee an excuse for talking about, they had terrible quarrels. I heard some of them—and Lee knows it. Vance kept sneering at him; he thought he might shame him away. But Lee couldn't afford to go. I think," she said, leaning forward and dropping her voice, "Lee knew Vance was living off fools like me—his women friends. Lee had his place in all that. He found the women for Vance, women with money. It was a hideous combination.

"The trouble started, I believe, when Vance discovered that Lee was taking some of the pickings for himself. I know I paid him well—Lee, I mean. Other women probably did the same. And Lee . . . Lee tried to work the game for himself before he passed us on to his patron. He tried it on me. I threw a glass in his face. . . . God, he's made me pay well for that!"

"And now," said Larry, "you think he made Vance pay."

Effie sprang to her feet, her face crimson. "And I'm glad, glad. It was time Vance paid. The shame of it is that a fiend like that had only one life to pay with. How many girls has he ruined—worse than murdered. I *could* have killed him. But I didn't. Lee had most to gain by it."

She walked up and down the room, wringing her hands.

"I lied at the inquest," she cried, "lied! It was I who took the telephone message for Vance. It was something in that message that took him to the billiard room. It was a man's voice. . . . I'm sure now it was Lee's."

I looked at Larry, to see what he made of it. As for myself, it only added to my confusion.

"But Lee was there in the house."

"Lee was not there all the time. I saw him leave the house."

Larry shook his head reprovingly. "This isn't the inquest, Effie. No need to lie here."

And Effie Shannon, after a frightened, startled glance into my friend's cold face, dropped back in her chair and covered her face with her hands.

"Effie," and Larry's voice had grown wonderfully gentle, "you're foolish, so very, very foolish. You think to take a leaf from Lee Moshier's book and fix the crime on another. But if you did not murder Vance yourself, how can you *know* who did? Don't be so blindly set on blaming it on Lee that everyone will know you're trying to save yourself. Don't play his game. You're not the sort to make a success of it. . . . As a matter of fact, Effie, I know who did murder Vance Horton."

She lifted her white face from her hands and stared across the foot of the bed at him.

"You—know?"

Larry nodded. "We're collecting the evidence——and it doesn't matter who it was. The murderer must pay the penalty. Now you'd better go. Cuddy will drive you home. . . . And put Lee Moshier out of your head. It's not your business to find the murderer. You've enough to do to think of your own safety."

THE moment Effie left the room Larry turned his back on me.

"Go to bed," he ordered as I commenced to speak.

"Go to bed, or I'll send for David again."

"But, Larry, she'll tell the police you know the murderer. I never thought—"

"You seldom do. And don't start now. I'm tired. But before you go to sleep bring any loose guns there are so I can hide them under the mattress. The police will never search there."

Infuriated at Larry's treachery, sullen and defeated, I left the room. Larry had betrayed a trust. Would Effie, terrified for herself, carry the story to the police? If she did, what would happen to Barbara?

Far into the morning hours I lay awake. I heard Cuddy creep along to Larry's room. And though I thought I lay awake long afterwards, I did not hear him return. In the morning, weary and distressed, I waited for David. But at ten o'clock, when he had not arrived, I went to Larry's room.

My friend's cheery whistle greeted me while I was still far down the passage. And when I opened the door I came on a surprising scene: Cuddy softly whistling an accompaniment and keeping time on a tea-cup with a spoon. He jerked about at my entrance and, picking up the tray, hurried from the room.

"What the devil, Larry—" I muttered, glowering after Cuddy.

Larry interrupted the music he had continued as Cuddy tip-toed away. "He's your servant, Dill; he's just my friend and nurse. Now don't interrupt till I'm through the chorus."

"Listen, Larry—"

"Listen, Dill," he mocked.

"I don't wonder you're ashamed of yourself," I reproved.

He countered laughingly: "What does it feel like to be ashamed? You should know. Here I am, sick and helpless, your guest, and you roar into my bedroom with a brickbat in your voice and a thunder-cloud in your face. I'll tell David. He'll have me moved to a hospital—or the mortuary, if you're not more considerate."

I rumbled an oath.

"It was a despicable thing to do, Larry. Barbara confided in me. I trusted you. Effie may go to the police with it."

"Oh, no, she won't. Effie's last thought is to attract the attention of the police. She's been through that twice or three times already, and she won't forget how it felt. But suppose she told? Do you think Inspector Rountree would be deceived? He'd think she was lying, or I was. If he came to me he'd *know* I was. All right. Now for to-day's assignment: First, a nice, friendly return of Effie's pleasant visit. You may take my card, too."

"Not me. I'm through with Effie."

"You'd like to be, you mean. What you're afraid of is that she might draw from you what she knew she couldn't make me tell. Such a pusillanimous lover!"

"I'm not such a liar as you, you mean."

"Perhaps," he agreed cheerfully. "Now, if Willo were involved—But let that pass. Listen to this, Dill." He raised his head and fixed his one uncovered eye on me.

"Effie is badly frightened. I want her more frightened still. Lee and I have accomplished a lot. You must do the rest. I want you to make such a job of it that she'll go into retirement till this thing is cleared up. She could muddle things terribly."

"But—but, Larry, it *is* cleared up. You and I know that."

"Dill Fullerton!" He sighed heavily. "Can't you forget anything, just for a few days? Can't you see that you must? If we stopped now what do you think Inspector Rountree would think? Besides, you're getting a thrill from it. Give yourself a good time. You take life much too seriously, my friend. What I want you to do is this: Effie thinks I know the murderer to be someone other than herself. What you must do is to make her think I know *she's* the murderer—that I was just trying to make her confess. It's for Barbara's sake."

It wasn't at all clear to me, but Larry knew best.

"I'll make a mess of it," I grumbled.

"Oh, no, you won't. Of course, if Effie is not the murderer—"

"We know she—Oh, all right, I've forgotten."

"If she's not the murderer we must face the danger that our suspicion may make her lose her head still more. . . . But in reality that will play your game. All the suspects seem gifted with that complex."

I groaned. "I couldn't let another suffer for a crime of which I knew her to be innocent. Neither would Barbara."

"All right." He remained maddeningly cheerful. "Go straight down to the police station and give them Barbara's address."

"I must do something, I suppose," I agreed helplessly. "I'll do my best with Effie. I'll call her up right now."

But Larry had it all thought out. "You'll do nothing of the sort. You must catch her unprepared—walk in on her and throw it in her teeth, as it were. Prepared, she'd be too much for you, Dill. . . . She was almost too much for us last night. She came here, the little actress, with something in her mind more pressing than the terror she wished us to think she felt. We were to think she knew Lee to be the murderer. Why? Well, perhaps you'll find out. Now, run along. It's early enough to find her at home."

"One moment," as I hurried from the room. "Here's the other assignment: You promised to cultivate Doctor Millbrook. Start in this very night. He'll receive you with open arms—his newest friend, one who understands him. He's had four days to learn to appreciate us. He'll probably have read Vance's diary by this time. Get him to talk—and to blazes with your scruples! Remember, it's for Barbara."

No part of the programme pleased me. I could not be sure of myself with Effie. If she was acting the night before, then I was much too easy for her. And there lingered still the memory of our earlier relations. As for Doctor Millbrook, even Barbara's danger failed to reconcile me to a breach of the trust he so evidently placed in us.

I was worrying over these things when, as I ran the car out on the street, a man stepped directly before me. It was Inspector Rountree.

"So," I cried angrily, "this is how you keep your word."

His forehead wrinkled. "I don't understand."

"You promised not to keep an eye on me. Please get out of the way. I'm in a hurry."

"So I noticed. And I've just one observation to make, one question to ask; Neither I nor anyone else of the police is keeping an eye on you. I'm on my way to see your injured friend. The question: Are you trying to give us the slip—with all this hurry?"

"Why should I? And I don't believe Jordan Fleming was trying it."

"Then perhaps you can explain why we cannot find Mr. Ponting."

"Ponting? Jack Ponting? Why—where—"

"That's what we ask ourselves. He has gone—and even his wife professes not to know where he is."

"But I didn't know you knew—about Jack."

"There are several things you don't know, Fullerton."

"Do you think I know where he is? I assure you I don't. And if my word is no better than yours you'll probably open my mail till this crime is cleared up."

A slight flush showed in Inspector Rountree's cheeks. "Fullerton, I kept my word. No one has been near this house since last night. Hereafter—I promise nothing. You wouldn't trust me if I did." He removed his hand from the window and stepped back. "On your way. I've much more serious things to do than bother about you." I threw in the lever with a jar of gears and plunged into the street. I felt ashamed of myself. And with my shame came a sudden disturbing thought: Was this Providence of Larry's, who had come to my rescue so opportunely on two occasions, none other than Inspector Rountree himself?

As I drove along I kept my eyes on the mirror to see that I was not followed; and, though I saw nothing suspicious, I parked my car around the corner from the building where Effie had her flat, and walked the circle of the block to the door.

I was in the most expensive part of the city, on the slope of the hill overlooking the river. The house, an old stone structure, repointed and repolished, had been made over into half a dozen high-priced flats whose tenancy carried with it a certain social distinction. I was admitted on ringing the bell by an elderly woman who, recognizing me, let me go upstairs alone. Larry had counted on that.

Nevertheless, I climbed with no stomach for the interview. This was more in Larry's line than mine. He had given me only a bare outline of what he wished me to do. But suppose Effie took things into her own capable hands and directed the interview. Conditions then might warrant some other course of action on my part, and I questioned my capacity for changing the plan I had before me.

For instance, suppose she laughed at me, sneered, toyed with me—played a part such as Larry suggested she had played the night before. In that case might it not be better—for Barbara's sake—to laugh with her and confess that Larry had lied, that he had merely meant to draw her on?

Effie could not be more unprepared than I felt myself to be at that moment.

As I raised the knocker, a fine old copper fist, Effie's voice reached me through the door. Effie's voice, yes, but a tone I had never heard her use before, no, not at her wildest, most defiant moments. I stooped shamelessly to the keyhole.

"Don't move, Lee Moshier! Stay where you are!" It came through clenched teeth. And then, in a low voice—I knew she was telephoning: "Is that you, Cuddy? Ask Mr. Fullerton to come right away—quickly. . . . Oh-h!" A faltering cry—and I knew what it meant: Cuddy had told her I was not in—and I had not informed him where I was going.

Then Effie's voice once more, grim and determined:

"Take one step nearer, Lee, and I'll shoot you like the dog you are!"

"As you did Vance," said Lee, a sneer in his voice, but a healthy fear as well.

"No one knows as well as you that I did *not* shoot Vance."

"No one," he retorted, "can prove as well as I that you did."

"You mean, no one would try so hard to prove it for his own skin."

Lee laughed nastily. "So the chivalrous Dill isn't available. Why don't you call the police? They know you too well to believe you."

I placed my lips to the keyhole. "Effie! Effie!"

A chair knocked against some other piece of furniture, and then the door opened.

I was not unprepared for what I saw: Lee Moshier's big frame in the middle of the room, and Effie, her eye never leaving him, and a capable finger on the trigger of a businesslike automatic, standing aside to let me in.

Lee's face was a study of conflicting emotions—fear, surprise, chagrin, and a vast amount of disturbing uncertainty. But in a moment he was his old contemptuous self—outwardly at least.

"So opportune!" he jeered. "Like a scene from a play."

I ignored him. "What has he been doing, Effie?" I stepped boldly toward him. Lee was forty pounds heavier, and though he had once been a bruiser and bully, dissipation had softened him. And certainly this was not his hour. That steady automatic had made him limp.

"Get him out," Effie cried through her teeth. "Get him out quickly or I won't be responsible for myself." Her voice rose to a scream. "I could justify, yes, even to the police, shooting him down."

Lee paled a little, but he made one more stand:

"Can you justify—"

Effie circled me, her face purple with rage. "Get out!"

We had left the door open. I pointed to it.

"I'll back her in anything she does," I warned.

And like a whipped dog he crawled away. As he reached the doorway he hissed back at us:

"Perhaps you were both in it."

It was too much for Effie. I saw the muscles of the hand that held the gun tighten, and I had just time to leap at her and knock the gun upward as the shot crashed through the room.

And then I laughed. For down the stairs, three steps at a time, tumbled Lee Moshier, and he whimpered with fright as he ran.

I closed the door.

The gun had dropped from Effie's hand, and she stood trembling, staring at the hole in the wall made by the bullet. Her eyes were wide with the glare of crowding hysteria. Gently I took her by the arm and led her to a couch.

"All over now, Effie. And you should have seen him run."

Then her arm was about my neck, her head pressed into my shoulder.

"Oh, Dill, Dill! If I'd—killed him! . . . And I never fired a gun before."

"I believe you, Effie."

She caught the significance of my assurance and raised her face to mine. "You—believe—that?"

I laid her on the couch. "Of course."

"But," she moaned, "he says—Lee says he can prove it. Perhaps he knows—he knows—"

She stopped there, but I had to hear more.

"Knows what?"

"That I did follow Vance to the billiard-room that night. But I didn't go in, I didn't. I watched where he went, and then I crept through a side door and around the house. But all the billiard-room curtains were drawn at the back, and I had to go round to the street side. There was one French window open there. I waited. And then I heard voices. No, I mean Vance was talking. I looked in. But he saw me right away, and he rose in a rage and ordered me away. He came at me as if he would strike me. I ran away. Before God I did, Dill. . . . Lee must have seen me."

I tried in my mind to piece all the stories together. Here were two of Vance's discarded flames at the billiard-room that night—and the sister of one had fired the fatal shot. Lee, too, was somewhere there.

"If he saw you, Effie," I soothed, "he daren't tell the police. He'd find it more difficult to clear himself than you would. The police know Lee Moshier."

It steadied her, and in a few moments she dried her eyes and sat up.

"What was Lee doing here?" I asked.

Her eyes flashed. "He thought I was too frightened to—to resist, that I was in his power. If I hadn't had that pistol!"

The automatic lay on the carpet where it had fallen. I picked it up. Only then did I realize that it was a .25.

THE report I carried back to Larry was somewhat confused. I had gone with a definite purpose in mind and had accomplished no part of it. And things had happened so swiftly, so surprisingly, that vision and hearing and thought got at times badly tangled. Larry was interested only in what I saw and heard.

Over it all hung the certainty that the murder of Vance Horton had moved from violence to violence.

Larry must have untangled my account, for he asked few questions even when I was finished. Indeed, he seemed inexplicably indifferent about it, and I wondered if he were in worse shape than I suspected. He had always been so keen, yet of late, since his injury, his curiosity had confined itself to such strange, unimportant things, and had passed by the more exciting.

"A .25, you say. H'm! I wish you'd brought it with you."

I took it proudly from my pocket. "I'm not always a fool."

Larry examined it closely. "Doctor Millbrook will be delighted to get this, Dill. He'll welcome you to-night with open arms."

"Doctor Millbrook will never see it. Look here, Larry, let's not forget some of the decencies. I'm not going to get Effie into trouble when I know she doesn't deserve it. And remember the conditions under which I got it. I'm not cad enough to whisper a word about that gun to Doctor Millbrook."

Larry listened wearily. "Don't you see? If this gun didn't fire that bullet how could it get Effie into trouble?"

"But the bullet the Doctor got from Vance's body was too badly mutilated to be identified."

"Don't you believe it, Dill. Doctor Millbrook's far too clever for that. No, you're taking this gun to him to-night. I've been troubled about your visit—it seemed to call for an excuse, if you can hope to get him to talk freely. This gun will give you the excuse."

"I won't—take—that gun," I declared.

"You'll take it, or I'll get up, game leg and all, and take it myself in an ambulance. Or I swear I'll tell the police about it. Take your choice."

I was helpless. "What the devil's got into you lately, Larry?"

"Just a splinter or two—and a few original ideas. David

captured the splinters. You and I are going to use the ideas. See here, Dill, the confession you heard last night by no means clears this thing up. I can't explain—partly because I know so little. But I assure you there are a dozen side issues with which the Venell sisters are not connected. Those are the mysteries we have to solve. I'm confident that if you take that gun to Doctor Millbrook there'll be no trouble for Effie Shannon. Take my word for it. . . . You've an interesting, a promising evening before you, Dill. I only wish I could be with you."

When I went to have a last word with Larry before setting out for the Doctor's David Fleury was there. It did not surprise me, therefore, when he refused to let me into the room. He was, he said, changing the bandages. It was no time for a visitor.

*　　　*　　　*　　　*　　　*

My hand had no more than left the knocker on Doctor Millbrook's door when the door was opened. A new maid, in neat service costume, stood to one side to admit me, her face partly concealed by the door. The Doctor, I decided, had lost no time in improving on Mrs. Jaggers. And, as I looked about the hall, I saw that the new maid had lost no time in improving on the Doctor's quarters.

The maid had closed the door, but she had not moved. I turned to her.

She stood back against the wall, finger to lips, nodding warningly toward the room, through the open doorway of which came the low strains of Chopin's "B Minor Sonata."

My lips fell apart, and I stood staring at her.

For the Doctor's new maid was Barbara Venell!

Instantly I remembered those revealing mirrors, and stepped close to the wall where I knew I was out of sight.

"The Doctor is in?" I inquired formally. "My name is Fullerton."

"Yes, sir." Barbara came out into the centre of the hall and pointed. "He's expecting you. You know where the sitting-room is."

I walked slowly back. Deep within me was a vast surprise that I was not more surprised, that my head seemed suddenly to have become so clear. It was not difficult to understand why Barbara was there, but only that she dare risk it.

The music ceased abruptly as I reached the door.

The Doctor sat at the piano, his hands resting on the keyboard, smiling up into the mirror before him. When I smiled back he lifted his feet and whirled about on the smooth bench like a child, to hold his hand toward me.

"This is kind of you, Fullerton. I had no idea what good friends I was making that day at the mortuary." His eyes beamed through his glasses. "I never knew before what a lonely codger I am. I only hope you've better luck than your friend had. How is he?"

I told him of Larry's regret that he was unable to share with me the evening's companionship, and the Doctor almost purred.

"Ah, well," he sighed, "I don't think I could stand being laid up as philosophically as he does. And he was always so strong and active, wasn't he? By the way, I never heard the complete story of what happened to him. Inspector Emerson spoke of someone dynamiting his car. They haven't given me anything to do on that yet."

I told him what I knew of it.

"I hope there'll be no permanent effects," he said.

"Doctor Fleury says he'll be all right by the time his leg mends. The rest seems to be superficial—and he isn't suffering, though one could never be sure of that with Larry. Another month and he'll be around as usual, I hope."

Doctor Millbrook ran a hand through his hair, standing it on end. "It's dastardly crimes like that, so unnecessary, so beastly, that make me sometimes regret my resignation. It's those rogues I like to help run down. And that strange attack on you last night at 'The Elms.' It's the same fellow, of course, who tried to kill Rockford."

"That's what Larry and I think. Do the police think the same?"

He smiled ruefully. "If Inspector Rountree hasn't told you what he thinks I'm afraid my lips are closed. But you know what *I* think." He sat with his hands hanging over his knees, his head shaking dolefully. "Who'd have thought the Horton murder would spread to all this?"

Suddenly he rose and crossed the room to the desk.

"You don't know it all either, Fullerton. It's a greater puzzle, a far wider problem, than you and your friend imagine. See this."

He had opened the drawer in the desk. Now he turned and held out to me a long, gleaming stiletto. As it moved a glint of light struck the steel blade. In a flash my mind flew back to Sunday night, as I lay on the couch in my library, and that same stiletto hung above my face.

"You see, they're after me, too, Fullerton. Half an inch, and

I'd have been less fortunate than your friend. But," smiling, "a miss is as good as a mile."

He told me what had happened, while I listened with amazement, my eyes fixed incredulously on that thin line of steel.

He had gone into the garden in the afternoon, as was his custom, for a smoke. That one pipe a day was his limit, a time of uninterrupted reflection on the more troublesome phases of his profession. His favourite seat was a bench in the shade of an old oak, one of the few large trees in his garden. The previous owner had cut down the older trees to make way for new growth, substituting saplings that were still too small to provide the shade the Doctor sought.

As he seated himself he noticed without interest that the bench had been moved a little, but it was heavy, and one end remained in shade.

He felt the bench give a little with his weight. Next instant something struck sharply close to his shoulder. The instinct that went with his police connection made him drop swiftly forward to the cover of the bench and remain there while he looked about. But nothing further happened.

On the edge of the top bar of the bench was a fresh scratch in the paint, and he knew it was not there when he sat down. Then he recalled a sharp, whistling sound immediately preceding the thud. Something, he decided, had been thrown at him with great force.

The trembling of a sapling ten feet or so behind the bench drew his attention, and he saw that a thin cord extended from it to the bench. The sapling had been stripped of its branches, leaving it a strong, supple pole. To the tip of it was tied the stiletto he held in his hand.

"An old East Indian trick," he explained. "I've read of it somewhere. The sapling was sprung back until the point of the stiletto could be inserted in something—in this case a tree, more often the ground—with sufficient resistance to withstand the weight of the bench that, tilted slightly backward, was attached to the bow of the sapling by a strong cord. The extra weight of my body on the bench jerked the stiletto free, and the spring of the sapling curved it over, swift as a bullet, to strike where I was accustomed to sit. Fortunately the position of the sapling made it necessary to move the bench a foot or so to one side, leaving the shade I sought only at one end, not in the centre where I always sat.

"At any rate," his round face creasing to a whimsical smile, "it gives me another souvenir to add to my collection, to remind me of my police work."

I reached for the stiletto. I had not spoken from the moment that revealing reflection struck my wondering eyes.

"Ah, I thought so. I've seen this before."

Instantly the Doctor became professional. "You mean—you know where it came from?"

I shook my head. "Not that, but Cuddy carries its mark on his arm to-day. Somehow I escaped."

I narrated the incident. He listened eagerly, for he had heard nothing of it from the police.

"You see?" he cried. "It's all part of the Horton murder. The murderer is trying to wipe out every threat. He knows, of course, where I stand. He must think you and Rockford have dangerous clues against him. I must—think this over."

He trotted to the piano and slid along the polished bench. And his fingers touched the keys lightly, dreamily. It was a Beethoven Sonata this time, but he played with little expression, the music only an accompaniment to his thoughts.

My own thoughts flew back to Barbara. Barbara here where she might watch the police at work, where she might hear their plans, perhaps, where the bullet she had fired into Vance Horton's body was locked in the safe of her employer! What a risk! Where was the automatic she had used? Someone must have picked it up. Was it the police? And were her fingerprints on it?

And then a startling suspicion sent a shiver through me: Was it all part of a police scheme, and was Barbara all the time in league with them, seeking the murderer—even trying to pin the crime on Larry and me?

I gritted my teeth against it, but the misery remained.

The Doctor had finished, but he still sat staring blankly into the mirror. I remembered Effie Shannon's automatic and my promise to Larry.

"You might be interested in this, Doctor," I said, taking the gun from my pocket.

He whirled about on the bench, saw the weapon in my hand, and pounced on it.

"A .25! My God, where did you get it?"

I shook my head. "All you need know, Doctor, is that before this morning I had never seen it."

He turned the gun over and over. "If it incriminated you or Rockford you wouldn't let me have it. I hope," he added, a sudden fear in the eyes he turned on me.

"I'm still a police official, you know, Fullerton. Er—do you wish to take it back? I might be able to forget."

"Larry made me bring it. I'm trusting you to say nothing about it—unless—unless you can prove it had anything to do with the murder." I was uncertain what I hoped he might be able to prove. "If the bullet you took from Vance Horton's body fits that gun, then— then I can't ask you to protect her."

"'Her?'"

I flushed hotly, angry at the slip. "Please forget the sex."

"A woman, eh? I've long had my suspicions. H'm—what do you wish me to do with it?"

"Can't you test it—with the bullet you have?"

His round eyes stared at me through his glasses. "By jove, Fullerton! I've had that bullet under the microscope, and it tells more than I thought possible in its condition." He made swiftly for the laboratory door. There he turned, his eyes half closed. "By the way, Inspector Rountree brought me a .25 to test yesterday. That must have been the one that fellow planted on you. He didn't explain where he got it. You may be relieved to know it wasn't difficult to prove that it hadn't fired the bullet that killed young Horton."

"Then why was it hidden in my room?"

"Perhaps—perhaps the murderer knows more than we think. He may know how mutilated the bullet was, and that we would be unable to trace it. In that case the police would be sure to jump to conclusions. I'll test this right now."

I started to follow, but he waved me back.

"No, I don't care to have anyone in a tight room when I'm using a gun. It makes me nervous—and the noise is frightful. I know the tricks the most careful handling of guns can play. I won't be five minutes,"

The door closed behind him.

Alone in the room my mind became disturbingly active. If only I could have a word with Barbara! My eyes fell on the bookcase, and I remembered Vance Horton's diary. From the laboratory came intermittent sounds of activity. Without much hope I glanced along the shelves where he had thrust the diary on my last visit when the two Inspectors walked in. But the red-backed book was not there.

I went nearer.

And there, on the top of the desk, lay the diary, open and face downwards! I picked it up, noting the page.

I knew Vance's handwriting, precise, sloping, neat, with odd, irregular lapses to carelessness. Vance himself, posing when he could put his mind on it, careless when he forgot. I was surprised at the size of the book, a voluminous record of the passing years, penned, I saw at a glance, with great deliberation.

I let my eyes flit through the pages. A shot from the laboratory made my heart leap into my throat, but I kept on. And then my attention was riveted by a name. I started at the beginning of the paragraph:

"This has been a miserable day—miserable to a miserable brute with a taint too strong to fight— or too weak or too insane to fight it. To-day the Managing Editor of *The Planet* has done what I ordered—no, what this irresistible something in me ordered—and Jack Ponting is on the street, damn him!

"I should be content, but I'm not. Instead I sit here to-night and shiver. What can be the end for me—"

A second shot from the laboratory broke so startlingly that the diary dropped to the floor. I stooped in a panic to retrieve it.

It happened that as I straightened I faced the door to the hall. And I saw the handle turn ever so slightly. Transfixed, the diary clutched in my hand, I watched. A crack appeared—widened inch by inch, and I saw with a start that the hall beyond was now dark.

Taking a long breath, I replaced the diary on the desk and crept slowly toward that opening door.

Suddenly Barbara's face appeared. I moved nearer, fixing my attention on an etching on the wall beside the piano, a snow scene, with just a touch of bare shrubs slashed across the white, and a glimpse of a half-submerged stream. Barbara was only two paces away.

"You know why I'm here," she whispered.

"I think I do," I said. "It's foolish—dangerous. Doctor Millbrook is no fool—and he's still a police official. This is what you had in mind last night when you said you were going to do something for yourself."

"Yes. What's he doing with that revolver?"

"I'm trying to help you," I replied. "Do you know Effie Shannon?"

She looked puzzled for a moment. "Yes, I think I've heard Willo speak of her."

"It's her automatic he's firing in there. I found it in her flat."

She shook her head. "Thank you, Dill, but it's no use."

My heart leaped at the sound of my name on her lips. "Anything may be useful, Barbara."

"He'll know it isn't the one. And even if he suspected it was—don't you see I couldn't let anyone else suffer for me?"

"Larry made me bring it," I said. "It may just mean more confusion for the police. By the way, you see that red-backed book on the desk?"

"Yes. He's been reading it all day."

"I want you to get that book for me. Steal it—get it any way you can. I must have it."

"What is it?"

"A book Larry and I want badly. Now, you'd better go."

I had returned no more than half-way to my chair when the Doctor burst into the room. His glasses had fallen down on his nose, and his eyes danced with excitement.

"Fullerton, Fullerton, you've found it! It's the gun that was used to kill young Horton!"

I had stopped in the middle of a stride. The Doctor trotted to me, hand outstretched. In it lay two bullets, one badly crushed, the other unmarked.

"But—but, Doctor, it can't be." I dropped limply into the nearest chair.

"I tell you it is. Look at them. If you can't see it come in and use the microscope. They've the same markings."

He cleared his throat, and his face clouded.

"Whose gun is it, Fullerton?" And as I gulped and stared he repeated the question. "You'll have to tell, you know." A twist of distress marked his face. "I'm sorry, Fullerton. Why did you bring it to me, if you feel that way? I know I've encouraged confidence, but I had a reason. That diary of Horton's had me all worked up." He nodded toward the desk. "I wanted to see if his friends could let a little light into what I read there."

He had turned to face the desk. I cannot be sure that he noticed the diary was not as he left it, but for a moment or two he was silent.

"It's been a revelation, that diary. It's made me a little uncomfortable about the things I've always believed. Men like Vance Horton were to me blots that should be removed for the good of mankind. . . . I believe now that, back of it all, was a professional curiosity based on an instinctive thought that certain unfortunate men were pathological problems rather than incorrigible criminals. I believe it now because of the readiness with which I succumbed in reading the diary. Vance Horton had another side, one even his best friends, I'm quite certain, did not suspect. A sort of Doctor Jekyll and Mr. Hyde. You saw the Hyde. In the diary he's Doctor Jekyll. It was Hyde who was murdered. . . . But our laws protect from murder the Hydes as well as the Jekylls. That's why Horton's murderer must be found."

He studied my face for a long moment, but I had nothing to say. Suddenly he turned to the desk and picked up the telephone.

"What are you doing?" I demanded.

"My duty." And I sat, helpless and ashamed—ashamed of what I had done to an innocent girl, ashamed that I had not had the courage to take a stand against Larry's commands—while Doctor Millbrook talked to Inspector Rountree.

He did not look at me when he had hung up, but went and sat before the piano. But he did not play.

"You know how I feel about this, Fullerton. The Inspector's coming right away. I must ask you to wait for him. This is no time for exaggerated chivalry—nor for me to neglect my duty. I don't believe you have it in you to protect one you know to be a murderer. It doesn't matter to me to whom that gun belongs. All I know, all that comes within my duty, is that the gun you brought to-night fired the bullet into young Horton.

"You have this to soften the blow to a chivalry that cannot be recognized—that there are few juries who'll exact the extreme penalty from the murderer of a wastrel like Horton, a young man who brought worse than death to many. Do you mind if I play?"

He ran his fingers lightly over the keys before breaking into a composition I did not recognize. From that he passed to something of Debussy's. I cannot be sure, for I was busy with my own thoughts, floundering in the new maze he had created. How could Effie Shannon's automatic have killed Vance Horton, when I knew Barbara had fired the shot? Had Willo somehow secured Effie's gun, and after Barbara pulled the trigger had she returned it to Effie?

Inspector Rountree must have come without delay, for the doorbell rang while I still lingered on that unanswerable question. At some time in the interval, though I had been unaware of it, Doctor Milibrook must have opened the door to the hall, for I saw him now, his fingers poised over the keys, staring intently into the mirror. And when the front door opened, and the firm footsteps of the Inspector came straight for the door of the room where we sat, the Doctor turned and threw me a last regretful, apologetic look. . Then he greeted the detective.

"Hope I didn't interrupt a game of bridge, Inspector."

Inspector Rountree had come to a stop in the doorway. Plainly he had not expected to see me, and his inquiring gaze passed from me to the Doctor. But Doctor Millbrook failed me. Instead of explaining, he shrugged and turned away. It's up to you two, the gesture said.

I was in a quandary. Aware that Effie was innocent, I dare not give my reason. And I knew what a small thing would swing a jury against her. Then, too, Effie was not the girl to conduct her own case with discretion. Should the police wring from her the story she had told me I could see only one end for her.

And where would I stand then?

For several tense moments the room was silent. Suddenly the Inspector's keen eyes fell on the automatic.

It lay on the bench beside the Doctor, and he strode swiftly to it and picked it up. Then he smiled at me.

The smile only confused me more. It expressed neither elation nor scorn. It was, I thought, a friendly smile.

"At least," he said, "you can't say I trailed you here, Fullerton." He held the gun carelessly in his hand. "Fact is, Doctor, you did break in on a game, and at a vital place. My partner and I had Emerson and the Chief where we wanted them to finish a rubber. To whom shall I send the bill?"

He sat down, the gun in his lap, and proceeded to fill his pipe.

When he was finished he pointed to the gun with the burnt match.

"Anything in this to start you talking? I'm in no hurry."

"Doctor Millbrook sent for you," I replied gloomily.

"Doctor?"

The Doctor, after a quick, appealing glance in my direction, was forced to speak:

"Yes, I sent for you. Inspector, the gun you have there fired the bullet that killed young Horton."

Slowly the Inspector removed the pipe between his teeth. For a moment he seemed too startled to speak, then, coolly, he reinserted the pipe and struck a second match.

"Where did you get it, Doctor?" He might have been asking the time, so casual was the tone—so casual that I felt for the undertones.

"Ask Fullerton." And the Doctor swung about on the bench and turned his back on us.

The Inspector had his pipe drawing nicely. He eased himself lower in his chair, resting his head against the back. His eyes were half closed.

"I'm listening, Fullerton."

"Yes," I said defiantly, "I brought it. I prefer not to tell where I got it."

"You'll find it easier to tell here," said the Inspector.

"If I told I'd feel like a cur."

"And if you don't you'll feel like a criminal. . . . Why won't you tell?"

"Because I know the owner of that gun did not shoot Vance Horton."

The Inspector looked at me in frank surprise. "You know that?"

"I'm certain of it."

"H'm—and I believe you really think so. . . . I can respect your silence, Fullerton, feeling as you do, but I daren't recognize it. You must tell. All I can do is to promise not to be hasty. Indeed, I promise not to accept this as complete proof of guilt. You probably know something that is hidden from me, and I can't force it from you. . . . I believe I can promise to make no arrest without further evidence. After all, Doctor," addressing himself to the stiff back on the piano bench, "you and I know how in murder cases guns have a deceiving habit of wandering—"

"As one wandered among my shirts," I put in.

"Exactly. Will you speak now?"

I considered. Plainly enough I could not hope to conceal for any length of time where I had got the gun.

"It was a woman, Inspector—Effie Shannon."

The smoke continued to curl lazily from the bowl of his pipe. Not a line of his face altered. But in a moment he took the gun in his hand and turned it over. Carelessly, I thought.

"The promise I gave was quite superfluous, Fullerton. Miss Shannon is already under our eyes."

"Since when?" I wished much to know. Had anyone seen me entering and leaving Effie's flat? Had the police heard the shot that sent Lee Moshier whimpering away?

Inspector Rountree ignored the question. "You're satisfied it's the gun, Doctor?"

"Absolutely. Here are the two bullets. If you'll come to the laboratory we can put them under the microscope."

"All right. I wouldn't know as well as you. By the way, you've the one Inspector Emerson found in Fullerton's house, the one I brought you yesterday. I'll take it with me, too."

The Doctor slid from the bench and trotted to the laboratory. I got up.

"May I go now, Inspector?"

"Certainly. We're not interested in you—not just now. I don't think you'll imitate Ponting."

"And," I said, as a parting shot, for I felt bitter and angry, "I'm sorry I made a mistake."

"Perhaps you didn't," smiled the Inspector. "Who knows?"

As I turned from the door a car started noisily not far up the street and whirled around the corner.

ON reaching home I was surprised to find David Fleury there. It was an hour or two later than his usual final visit of the day, and once again I was faced with his professional imperviousness to emergencies. I wanted to talk to Larry right away, but the door was locked against me.

As I raved up and down the hall Cuddy came into view. But he must have seen the mood I was in, for he turned and disappeared down the back stairs. He left me with another worry, for I felt certain that had I not been there my servant would have gone on to Larry's room—and he would have been admitted. A foolish source of annoyance, of course, for Cuddy was Larry's hospital orderly.

When at last David admitted me Larry received me with a disarming smile.

"I'm glad I have Cuddy to nurse me, Dill. You're bad for the pulse. All right, David. I'm settled for the night. I promise not to let Dill upset me."

But when we were alone his manner altered.

"Damn him and his pompous ways! The great surgeon deigning to direct his skill to a charity patient! For he won't let me pay, of course. And the worst of it is, if I protested he'd walk out on me."

"I'm damned if I'll stand it much longer!" I growled. "Very little more and I'll walk out myself. I've got so much to tell you, Larry."

I waited, with a full sense of the dramatic nature of what I had to tell. But Larry yawned—and waited too.

"It was Effie's gun that fired the shot that killed Vance Horton!"

Larry whistled one long rising and falling note. "The hell it was!" Then he chuckled. "Now, I call that damned clever!"

"Clever? I wish I was clever enough to see why. All it does to me is to make my head swim. I'm going daffy if something doesn't straighten out soon."

"David," said Larry, "could vouch for it right now. I could easily find a couple more doctors, so you could be put away. But don't worry, Dill. I'll stand by you. . . . And, old chap, there's hope in this: Things are straightening out right now. Tell me what happened."

I poured out the miserable story—all my chagrin, my shame, my dismay, my anger at him for urging me to what I had done. And at the end I added what I had thought to conceal from him:

"That's not all. Barbara is there."

He raised his head sharply. "There? Where?"

"She's taken a position in the Doctor's house—the maid he told us he was going to get."

This time Larry's whistle was expressive. "And that, too, is clever." He whistled a few unmusical bars. "Good! . . . Good!"

"All I can see about it is that it's brave—and rash."

Larry winked. "Dill, she's too clever for us. She's getting me all tangled up."

"What do you mean?"

"It would be Sanskrit to you if I tried to explain. . . . But—rash? I don't know. Barbara Venell can look after herself."

It did little to dispel my gloom, my foreboding. "I hope she's as clever as you think. I've asked her to try to get Vance's diary for us."

Larry gave me a look of approval. "You're getting clever yourself, Dill. I'd never have thought of that. . . . But," sighing, "how can she hope to get into the Doctor's vault?"

"It isn't in the vault all the time. It was lying on the desk to-night. Barbara says he's been reading it all day. I managed to read one paragraph myself. It was—funny—in a way."

Larry said nothing, just lay watching me.

"I know you want that diary, Larry. You read enough to see in it the other side of Vance, as the Doctor said. Dr. Jekyll and Mr. Hyde, he calls him. That's why he kept it from the police. It touched the sentimental side of him. Listen to this." I repeated word for word what I had read it had burned itself into my memory. "I believe you found something like that yourself in the moments you had it in your hand. Why did you keep it to yourself?"

"Because," said Larry, "you've a sentimental side of your own, Dill, and I wasn't sure how you'd react. You might even have been so sympathetic that you'd have felt it your duty to hand Barbara over to the police."

I scoffed. "But I didn't know then—about Barbara."

"You knew as much as you do now. . . . And so did I. Fact is, Dill, there's no sentiment whatever about that diary. There was certainly a Vance we did not suspect, but it was the Vance we all had to deal with, to suffer, who was shot. And the world is well rid of him. No," thoughtfully, "the diary I want is not what you read, but what you couldn't read . . . because it isn't there.

"You had no time to see what I saw, perhaps, but pages have been removed—cut out. That's what I want—those missing pages . . . I want them so badly that, if it would do any good, I'd go in an ambulance where they are."

"But, Larry, you don't think the Doctor—"

"If Doctor Millbrook did it it was because they contained something even more appealing to that sentimental side than what is left. He has to face the fact that the diary may have to be shown the police. Under certain conditions he warned us that was possible—and the pages he cut out are too sacred—in his opinion—to be exposed to callous official eyes. Or innocent people may be involved, and he can't bring himself to expose them to the ignominy of police suspicion. After all, a diary can scarcely be used as evidence. The Doctor may have half a dozen reasons for cutting them out. . . . Or Vance may have done it himself. I don't see how I can find out."

He fell into a reverie from which I had no wish to disturb him, for I too had much to think about.

"So it was Effie's gun," he murmured. "Dear me. That does mix things up. Are Barbara and Effie friends?"

"Barbara has only heard of her from Willo."

Larry winked at me. "What a lot of conversation you had with the girl! And all those mirrors!"

"Doctor Millbrook was in the laboratory with the door closed. That doesn't worry me. It's the gun."

Larry shrugged. "Go to bed, Dill. And console yourself to sleep with the thought that certain things are possible and others impossible. . . . And that a lot of extravagant, absurd, inexplicable—yes, and impossible—things are possible, after all. And that things are never as black as they seem. To-morrow is another day. I've a hunch that it's going to be an important one. And I haven't a care in the world, no, not even about Barbara. Don't you dare lay a hand on me, Dill Fullerton. I'm still an invalid."

THE following day I was forced to spend at the office. An accumulation of documents and of other work awaited me, much of which fortunately I could pass on.

As I expected, my mind was only half on my work. I was worried about Barbara. Kindly as was the Doctor, he would be ruthless if he discovered her purpose.

Now and then Larry popped into my head. I didn't understand him. No longer could I look with confidence to the old partnership. What interested, even excited me, seemed to pass over his head; and what I considered unimportant often brought that quick look of animation and that questioning whistle that revealed a lively mind. He was, I knew, not being frank with me. Was it because he feared my feelings for Barbara Venell might make me less cautious, less guarded as to what I revealed.

Yet, lying there in bed, what could he know beyond what I told him? Of course, there was David Fleury, and Cuddy, and once or twice Inspector Rountree.

Vance Horton's diary, too, kept intruding on my thoughts. What a strange revelation it was! But was it the real Vance speaking, as Doctor Millbrook considered it was? I decided not. To me it was nothing more than the faint-hearted acceptance of a condition any self-respecting man would have overcome. The missing pages meant nothing to me.

It struck five as I left the office and hurried home. I had gone without tea, and by the time Cuddy brought our meal to Larry's room I was famished. In the hour and more that prefaced the meal Larry and I had drifted back almost to the old frank friendship. Almost, but not quite—and the little that was lacking struck home more cruelly.

"And such an important day it was to be!" I scoffed as we ate. "When does it commence?"

For answer he asked what day it was.

"Wednesday."

"Exactly a week since the murder. . . . It's a goal for Scotland Yard—a week."

"It's a pity a broken leg takes more time to heal," I grumbled.

"Ah—yes—this damned leg! . . . If it were no more than the leg, Dill, but David tells me there's still danger of infection in the slight wounds I got. I suppose that's why he's so particular about keeping you from the room while he's changing the dressings."

It was his apology, and I felt like a cad. "It's because so much depends on you," I excused myself. "I seem to be able to do so little without you."

"You've done more than you think, old chap." David had removed the bandage from his other eye, and Larry, in consequence, looked more himself. "Ah, well, the day isn't over yet. Now, I think I'll have a snoozle. Send Cuddy to me, please."

I retired to the library and tried to read. But my brain refused to respond to my eyes, and I slammed the book on the table and leaned back to think. Thinking—thinking—thinking—always thinking—and seeing no way out for Barbara!

The knocker rattled, and when Cuddy opened the door I heard David run up the stairs. A few moments later someone else was at the front door, and presently Cuddy knocked and entered with a small parcel.

"A messenger boy left it, sir."

"A real one?" I took the parcel gingerly. I had heard of bombs by mail, or delivered at the door, and I remembered Larry's narrow escape.

"A real one, all right, sir. I'll take it out in the garden and open it, sir, if you wish."

It looked like a book, and a startling thought seized me.

"It's all right, Cuddy, you may go."

The moment the door closed behind him I ripped the paper off. Yes, it was Vance Horton's diary!

My hand shook as I blinked down on it. Barbara had done what I asked. Somehow she had managed to get the diary and dispatch it to me. But surprise and anticipation were dulled by another thought: Doctor Millbrook was certain to notice its disappearance, and whom could he blame but the new maid?

I was half-way to the door with it, to carry it to Larry, when I remembered David. And so I decided to wait— and while I waited I read.

Vance Horton's diary was, I suppose, such a diary as had never been written before—the picture of a losing struggle, the cry of an anguished conscience. But that was only at the first, back in the Cortwright days and earlier, for it was the record of his life from the age of eight. Even while he was at Cortwright the tenor of it altered. It became then the cry of a lost soul, a soul that knew it was lost and accepted it, an outpouring of helpless regret, a sighing capitulation to a diseased mind. Vance knew early in life of the strain of insanity that ran in his mother's family, and almost as early he sank beneath the cloud, surrendering with little resistance.

But all the time he knew, he realized, the brute he was. Page after page it continued, a record of shocking vices and misdeeds, flaunting them, throwing them in the teeth of God. Here and there the page was blistered with long-dried tears.

And all through the terrible story was merely the regret that he could not help being the fiend he was—not a sigh of regret for the misdeeds themselves. Right from the start there breathed from the pages a consuming hatred of his family—of the father who had probably seen the way Vance was going, of the older brother who had left home and lost his life somewhere in South American disturbances, even of the mother who had spoiled him. Of his sister he said little, but that little with disgust. She had early shown signs of insanity, but the mother had secluded her, striving to hide the shame of it. Vance's thought was only of the shame should the boys at Cortwright discover it.

It was toward the end that I came on the blank of the missing pages. They had been, as Larry said, cut so close to the binding that, without reading the diary, they might well not have been missed. . . .

The grandfather's clock striking behind me roused me. Nine o'clock! I couldn't believe it. But my watch told me the same surprising story.

And as I sat, scarcely crediting my eyes, I heard David leaving the house, after settling Larry for the night.

But Larry, settled or not, must know of the diary in my hand. I hurried into the hall. Cuddy was moving about somewhere at the back of the house, after letting David out. With a feeling of boyish delight at defying David's orders, I dashed up the stairs and made straight for Larry's room.

But David had not gone. As I opened the door he whirled about from the window, and, plunging toward me, thrust me fiercely into the passage. Closing the door behind him, he placed his fingers to his lips.

"He's had a bad turn," he whispered. "Something this evening has upset him. I've given him a draught." My lip curled. With a sweep of my arm I sent him staggering against the wall and pushed the door open. For in the moment it took for David to reach me from the window I had seen the bed.

Larry, who had lain there for four days, bandaged to his eyes, the bedclothes bulging with the splints about his broken leg, was no longer there.

The bed was empty!

I UNDERSTOOD. The evidence was clear. For on a chair beside the bed lay a pile of loose bandages, and against the chair leaned the splints that had bolstered his dismay at a broken leg.

David stood in the doorway, flushed, smiling foolishly. "Where is he?" I demanded.

David lifted his shoulders and let them fall. "Professional secrets, Dill."

"You were never his physician," I stormed. "There never was anything wrong with him—I see that now. You were nothing but a conspirator. It was a despicable thing to do—with me."

"I'm sorry it had to be in your house, of course, Dill."

"Then are you going to explain?"

"I've enough to answer to Larry for now." He sighed. "I should have kept the door locked."

"If you had I'd have kicked it down. It needed only that to make me smell a rat."

"Yes," David laughed. "Larry was afraid your olfactory organ might be more acute than your brain."

"A damned dirty trick—and on his best friend!" I complained.

"It was because you're his best friend that he played it. It was that, too, that made it possible."

"And *you* made it possible. You saw him last thing at night to remove the bandages, and first thing in the morning to replace them. It let him move about at night. Was the whole dynamite story a myth?"

"No, indeed. There's the wrecked car to prove it. Larry happened to discover the stick attached to the engine. He telephoned me to pass the house at a certain time. That was when he set the dynamite off, while he was safely hidden; and I rushed in and carried him to my surgery to bandage. You know the rest."

"But why all this?"

"So he could go about at nights—do the work it seemed impossible to do at any other time. And it gave him a chance, too, to keep out of the way of the fiend who tried to blow him up."

I saw it all then. "So he was my Providence. It was he came to my rescue in the library on Sunday night, and the next night at 'The Elms.' He must have followed me everywhere I went at night."

"I believe he did."

"But why couldn't he have taken me into his confidence?"

"It would have been a difficult role for you, Dill. It was safer as it was."

"And you, David, have been in this to the hilt. I saw your car last night outside Doctor Millbrook's when I came out. You had Larry there, and you rushed him home to replace the bandages before I arrived. . . . And, David, I know where he is now."

I made for the door. David called to me:

"Where are you going?"

"To see Larry doesn't make an ass of himself and spoil the game. To see he doesn't shame us both."

As I ran to the garage the sight of the open door brought me to an abrupt halt. Then I rushed forward. Cuddy was there. He had just lifted the hood of the car.

The garage was in darkness, but he heard me and, against the doorway, must have recognized me.

"What are you doing here, Cuddy?" I demanded. "Get out. I'll attend to you later."

Switching on the light, I gave the engine a quick glance, closed the hood and pressed the accelerator. Cuddy had slunk away into the darkness. Nothing happened, though, for a moment, my heart was in my mouth.

Only defiance of every speed regulation could have landed me, as it did, before Doctor Millbrook's house in something less than ten minutes. I did not stop, but let the car run quietly past. So far as I could see the house was dark and deserted, but I knew the sitting-room windows were not visible from the front.

On the street above I found a dark spot beneath the trees, and there I parked the car. With my knees knocking together I climbed to the top of the stone wall about the Doctor's garden, lay there listening for a time and at length dropped to the other side.

The night was hot and clammy. Perspiration dripped from the end of my nose, and my hair was matted to my forehead. Inside the garden the air was suffocating. It seemed to close in on me, making me gasp. So that for several moments I was forced to seek the support of the fence to regain my strength. My courage, too, for I trembled all over. I felt no fear for myself, but a premonition weighed me down, premonition of revelations for which I was not prepared, for which there was no way to prepare myself. It was like wandering into a dark cave where anything might happen.

Presently I set out toward the house. Somewhere ahead, through the trees and shrubbery, I caught a glint of light, and I picked my way carefully toward it. Then my advance was blocked by a sound. It was the soft strains of Doctor Millbrook's piano. I knew then that the door to the garden must be open, and, forcing myself forward, after a few steps I came within sight of the musician.

Doctor Millbrook sat at the piano, his agile fingers running dreamily over the keys. His head was raised, as I had seen him so often before. Were his eyes closed, in that rapt manner of his when the music had hold of him, or were they fixed on the revealing mirror on the wall before him? I had the answer in the listlessness of the melody-dreaming, perhaps, of the diary that had affected him so strangely, or of the time when he would be free of the ugly police tasks he was called on to perform.

Cautiously I went nearer. I had no idea what I expected to happen, and for the moment I had forgotten Larry. The music drew me on.

The window curtain was not drawn, and the door was propped open with a chair. But nothing would be visible from the street. The solitude that had been Doctor Millbrook's lot these many years was inviolate there.

At the edge of the shrubbery I stopped. Between me and the uncurtained window was twenty feet of open lawn. Dare I cross it? The light from door and window reached out revealingly across that short stretch of grass. And the Doctor had an unnerving habit of leaping suddenly to life.

As I stood hesitating Larry suddenly emerged from the shadows not forty feet away. There he stood motionless as a statue, as if he too were drawn by the music that gripped me. I edged nearer, remembering why I had come. Larry must not attempt it, he must not.

Suddenly the Doctor slid from the bench and trotted toward the garden door. But he did not come out. Instead he turned into the laboratory and the high windows of that curious room flashed alight. I waited. In a few seconds he was back, a thick pad of paper in one hand. Seating himself before the desk, he spread the paper before him and, lifting sheet after sheet, read.

As he read a tender look came into that round face of his, and once he removed his glasses and wiped his eyes. I could see his shoulders rise and fall, as if sighing.

Once more Larry had been wiped from my mind. But not for long. Suddenly he swept across my vision, striding straight for the open door.

"Good evening, Doctor."

Doctor Millbrook bounded to his feet.

"Ah, you, Rockford!" With a sweep of his hand he crushed the loose sheets he had been reading into the drawer of the desk. He turned and walked slowly toward the door where Larry stood smiling at him. "How did you get there? And—what's this? I thought you were a casualty."

"That's what everyone thought—what I wished them to think," said Larry, stepping into the room.

A swift smile of understanding suffused the Doctor's face.

"I see. Another little lesson in the gentle art of amateur sleuthing, is it? Would it ruin the climax if you were to explain? Don't tell me if the police must not know. I've enough on my conscience now without that."

Larry seated himself. The Doctor strolled back to the desk.

"That's what I came to tell you," said Larry. "It's part of my plan to run down the murderer of Vance Horton."

"Yes, I gathered that. But—"

"I'd have failed without my little ruse."

The Doctor's eyes beamed with eagerness. "You don't mean you've—you've got him—beaten Scotland Yard?"

"Yes, I've found the murderer."

I could see the pair of them, Doctor Millbrook leaning forward from his chair, his eyes fixed on Larry's face, Larry lounging back in another chair.

"You're prepared, of course, for the police to know, Rockford. Don't forget I'm still an official." He rose and walked nervously to the piano and leaned an elbow on it.

"The police must know, of course," said Larry. "I'm telling you."

Larry's hand moved swiftly to his pocket. But he was not quick enough. Doctor Millbrook's hand darted to the wall beside him. Next moment the room was in darkness.

XXXVIII The Trail

A SHOT rang out. It came, I thought, from Larry's gun. Someone rushed from the shrubbery where I had seen Larry first, then a moment of utter silence. It drummed dizzily in my ears, as I hesitated what to do.

From the room came a jeering, raucous laugh that filled the darkness with horror.

"I could blow you to hell where you stand, Larry Rockford! If you value your life, go as you came. I can see you against the window. I don't know why I give you a chance. Go—quickly!"

Then, suddenly as they blanked out, the lights snapped on. Against the wall, just inside the door to the hall, stood Barbara Venell. One hand pressed the switch. In the other an automatic pointed straight and steadily at Doctor Millbrook's breast.

The light shot across the grass, and someone—something—darted swiftly from its path into the shadows.

The round eyes behind the Doctor's glasses blinked into the muzzle of Barbara's gun. Larry, too, I could see, was equally surprised.

The Doctor laughed. "Good enough for the pictures, isn't it?"

Larry said: "Go away, Barbara. I'll see he doesn't do it again." He had his gun ready.

Barbara crept back to the hall and closed the door.

"I shouldn't have been surprised," said the Doctor calmly. "Mary Dignum turns out to be Barbara Venell—as both Scotland Yard and I knew. It seemed to be a providential opportunity to keep her under our eyes. But don't imagine she can get away. Every door in the house is locked tight. This room is full of traps."

"That was why you were so sure you could blow me up," said Larry.

"A bit of drama, Rockford, that's all. As a police official I've found it well to protect myself."

"You might have thought too late—this time," said Larry.

The Doctor chuckled. "I don't think so. I was safe. You weren't. If I even suspected you were one of the many who have reason to get rid of me I could block you right now, gun or no gun. But I've never thought you murdered young Horton. With Miss Venell it's different. We don't know."

I could remain apart no longer. Crossing the grass, I pushed through the door.

"Stay where you are, Larry. It's Dill. But what the hell—"

Larry's eyes never left the Doctor. "Keep your hand on your gun, Dill. Doctor, I said I'd found the murderer. His name is—Doctor Millbrook! Or that's what he calls himself. We have the proof—the police and I."

The smile on the Doctor's face did not alter. Seating himself in the nearest chair he stretched out comfortably.

"Yes," carelessly, "I'm the murderer. I shot Vance Horton. You have the proof—though I don't quite understand what it is."

"The bullet you professed to take from Vance's body, Doctor, was extracted instead from the leg of the table where he sat when you shot him. Your bullet killed him. The other, fired by another hand, missed him entirely. It entered the open drawer, passed through the bottom, and lodged in the leg. It was Barbara Venell fired that other shot. She was not the murderer!"

The Doctor nodded. "Damned good work, Rockford! But how did you work it out?"

"It was Dill here gave me the clue. When he looked into the billiard-room, just after Miss Venell had fired at the dead body, he saw an open drawer in the table. There was no drawer in sight when the police arrived. Because in the meantime you had turned the table around.

"Vance had gone to the billiard-room to meet you. You shot him. And while you were still in the room the two sisters entered from the garden—the way you entered. You heard them in time to conceal yourself. Vance looked so natural, there beside the table, that they did not know he was dead. Barbara shot at him to save her sister. Then, when we were all gone, you rearranged the room. You had no time to think of the possible consequences of that, but you counted on the silence of the three who saw the murdered man and ran away.

"Later you had another thought, and you sent to the police that anonymous letter involving them all."

"Quite true—quite complete," said the Doctor. "I slid the letter into the police station; it was too early for a delivery. What more?"

"Just that I want those sheets you put in the table drawer. I know what they are—the pages you tore from Vance Horton's diary."

For a moment I thought the Doctor was going to defy him, but after consideration, with a shrug of his shoulders he went to the desk, opened the drawer, and took out the pile of sheets I had seen him reading.

"It's no use trying to hide the story now," he sighed. "But I had hoped—even if luck turned against me—to conceal my reason for murdering him. When you read those pages, Rockford, you'll know I'm—just a murderer. I misunderstood Vance."

He tossed the sheets on the table beside Larry, whose gun never wavered.

"No need of the guns, boys. Were I so minded, they'd be powerless to save you. I could blow us all up, and you couldn't stop me. I won't. One murder on my soul is enough—when there's nothing to conceal. You have the rest of the diary, Rockford."

"I wish I had," said Larry. "I'll have to ask you—"

"I have it, Larry." I drew the book from my pocket.

The Doctor had seated himself again, legs outstretched, his hands clasped over his stomach.

"What you have there, Fullerton, tells part of the story, the part that makes what I did so—terrible, so unforgivable." An involuntary shudder ran through him. "You'll know how mistaken we were about Vance. You, too, Rockford. I saw that night the two Inspectors came that you'd had the diary from the shelf there. You'll know Vance was not the scoundrel we all thought him."

His voice had dropped to a sigh.

"Poor Vance! He never had a chance. I see it now—too late. That taint in the family—he could not fight it."

"But why," inquired Larry, "does that concern you?"

"I'm his brother, the one who ran away and was reported killed in Brazil. It was Vance who drove me out—mother's foolish adoration for him, her hatred of me. He was a dozen years my junior. He always hated me—and his hatred became mother's. They treated me like a pariah. They were not—normal. Vance had everything, I nothing. It has rankled all these years.

"I didn't come back to kill him. I returned just— to see. . . . You know what I saw. My brother was a brute, a fiend . . . crazy . . . ruining everyone he met, as he had me. Or almost. I stood it as long as I could. It was not the brother who hated me, who had driven me from home, that I shot, but the man the world would be better without. . . . And then, too late, I read in his diary how I had misunderstood, how terribly he had suffered through it all."

He jerked himself to his feet and commenced to pace the room, his hands writhing together behind him. I pitied him. Pitied him for his own suffering, more that it was undeserved. For the brother who had been driven from home had not read what I read in the diary—that Vance had not tried to fight, that he had accepted defeat before he thought of fighting—even that he revelled in the thought that he was helpless.

Doctor Millbrook stopped before us.

"Yes, I shot him. I had talked with him before, several times. That night I called him by telephone to meet me in the billiard-room. I was driven mad by his excesses, and the awful orgy that night was too much for me. . . . Perhaps I, too, have inherited the taint. I threw in his face the things he had done, was doing. He laughed—taunted me. But he saw how furious I was, and he took a gun from the drawer in that desk and ordered me away. . . . I took the gun from him. . . . I shot him deliberately.

"I saw the two girls come in, and I hid. I saw Fullerton. . . . I was called in by Inspector Emerson, and when I was alone in the room I found the diary. The police had locked the room up, but I unlocked that French window. I thought there might be more in the room that I didn't wish the police to find, and I planned to return next night and search. . . . Or perhaps it's true that the murderer always returns to the scene of his crime.

"That night I came on you two there. And I knew you had discovered that drawer. That was why—I thought to wipe both of you out and save myself. I'm glad now the dynamite failed, Rockford. I planted the gun in your house, Fullerton. It was I followed you that night to 'The Elms' and shot at you in the dark corridor. I called the police right away.

"I changed the bullets. I thought I had everything covered perfectly by that."

"And," I said, "when you failed to turn the police on Larry and me you tried Effie Shannon. Her automatic fired neither of the bullets you had."

"It looked so simple, Fullerton. I realized how my ruse had failed—hiding the gun in your room—and I pretended it was not the gun that fired the bullet. But Miss Shannon's automatic seemed to offer what I needed. As a matter of fact, the automatic I hid among your shirts was Miss Venell's, the one that had fired the bullet I gouged from the table leg. By the way, you noticed I'd blackened the hole over afterwards. Well, I found her gun where she threw it as she left the billiard-room. When you brought me Miss Shannon's gun it was easy to exchange the two in the laboratory. Even had Inspector Rountree tested it himself he would have found the bullets the same. As for the guns themselves, they were exactly alike, of course."

But Larry did not lower his automatic.

The Doctor sighed. "I don't blame you, Rockford. But what would be the use for me to do anything now? I look on things so differently. . . . If only I'd tried to help Vance, instead of just accusing him! You know," with a pitiful smile, "I scarcely know why I'm telling you all this. I suppose it's because I've been such a lonely man all my life, brooding, nursing my wounds. You're the first friends I've made, the first to whom I could unburden some of the weight that's crushed me since I was old enough to think. I don't think I could injure you now, even if it was to save myself. It's helped a lot to talk to you.

"You remember where Vance says in his diary: 'Some day I must meet my God.' So must I. Vance and I will be there. In that day it will be Vance who accuses *me.*"

He stood with legs braced, hands locked behind his back, staring with unfocused eyes over our heads.

"If you don't mind, Rockford, how did you know? I thought I'd covered my tracks, even with all my mistakes. More and more I'm leaning to the truth of an old police contention, that the less a murderer does to cover his tracks the less they have to lead them to him."

Larry laid the gun on the table. All the grim watchfulness of the last few minutes was gone from his face.

"You're right, Doctor. You did too much. First I wondered how you could have made such a mess of the body in the post-mortem. I'd seen a few, and you're a good surgeon. You did it, of course, to hide the real calibre of the bullet that killed him. And you saw yourself how unreasonable it was that the bullet you professed to find should have been so crushed against a rib. I remembered then how, the night of the murder, there in the billiard-room you acted more like a detective than a cold-blooded police surgeon. I knew from what Dill saw that someone had rearranged that room between the time he saw the body and the arrival of the police, and that, I knew, must have been the murderer. It meant that he was there when Dill looked in, for he would not have dared to return.

"Of course, it could not then have been the Venell sisters who did it. And that brought me back to you, and the growing conviction that you were not telling all you knew."

The Doctor listened intently. "I feared for that," he said. "It's why I had you here that night. I thought my interest in the diary would explain."

"And the night after the murder we saw you in the billiard-room," Larry went on.

"But how could you? You couldn't see through my torchlight. I had two with me, a dimmer one for my own work, the bright one to blind anyone who came on me. I thought I kept you both covered."

"You did, with the brighter one. But I knew before. I had found the drawer of the table turned to the wall. Then I discovered the bullet hole in the bottom of the drawer, and the blackened tear in the back leg where you had cut it out. How, I asked myself, had anyone been able to do all that when the house was in the possession of the police? The answer was that it must be someone connected with the police.

"I was still a long way from the truth until I discovered where pages had been cut from the diary, and I knew it must be you who had done it. Why? I had no answer to that. But it sent my mind back to the night before, when we came on each other in the dark billiard-room. Against the torch you used first I had seen your legs—those baggy pants, the cuffless bottoms, the very way you moved, your feet."

The Doctor's face lit up. "By jove, Rockford, that was clever." He seemed to have no idea what it meant to him.

"After that," said Larry, "it was only a case of adding this and that. You fitted in everywhere. The problem was motive. That evaded me all through. That's why I came to-night. I wanted those pages from the diary, for I knew they would tell the story."

"The amateur beating the professional," mused the Doctor. He stood, swaying dreamily from heel to toe.

"Your gun, please, Doctor."

Doctor Millbrook seemed to waken. From a pocket he drew an automatic and handed it to Larry, butt first.

"I've another here."

From the drawer of the desk where he had hidden the loose pages he took a police revolver and laid it on the table beside the other. He waited, the faintest of smiles on his face, almost pitying Larry, I thought, not himself.

Larry put the three guns in his pocket and rose.

"To-morrow," he said, "we must decide what to do. Of course, the police must know. There are too many living in terror to let them continue the search." He took a step nearer the Doctor and looked straight into his eyes. "That's what we're going to do. What are *you* going to do?"

Doctor Millbrook smiled, that kindly, gentle smile. "Leave it to me, Rockford. The case is closed—for all of us."

Larry turned to the garden door. I did not move.

"Miss Venell is going with us," I said.

Doctor Millbrook sighed, and a slight flush swept into his round face.

"Of course, Fullerton. She's as safe here as—But, no, you must take her with you. It will be—a long night for me."

He went to the wall and pressed a button. I opened the hall door and called. Barbara entered before the echo had died away. She was dressed for the street, and her eyes were wet with tears. But a joyous light shone in her face. She carried a suit-case. Doctor Millbrook touched her lightly on the shoulder as she passed.

"Brave girl!"

He had turned back to the piano by the time we reached the door. And the last we heard of Doctor Millbrook was the soft touch of his fingers to the keys in a slow Rondo. I looked back, just one quick, frightened glance. He sat with his head thrown back, his shoulders high, and his eyes fixed dreamily on the mirror. But the hall door was closed. The mirror could tell him nothing. Just memories—memories!

As we crossed the grass to the shadow of the trees Larry left us for a moment. He overtook us before we reached the gate. I was carrying Barbara's suit-case. Her hand was caught in my other arm, and I felt it tremble; then her fingers closed gently on my muscle, and she laid her head for a moment against my shoulder.

We dropped her at her flat, while Larry and I went on to my place. Neither had spoken a word. Cuddy opened the door before I could use the key, and his face was red with confusion. He would not look at me, but to Larry he made a sign back toward the library.

Larry patted him on the shoulder. "Great boy!" he said. "Cuddy, it's all over. You played your part like an old trooper. And you had a hard role."

"I hope, sir, you don't think—" Cuddy began, looking at me with twitching lips.

"Certainly he doesn't," laughed Larry. "That's what made him so valuable. We had to fool him."

In the library Inspector Rountree was waiting for us. He was smoking—in the chair I always considered my own. His face was twisted to an unhappy smile.

"I was afraid we'd got you into trouble, Rockford," he said. "When those lights went out I think I added a few grey hairs. I'm glad I didn't have to interfere. I heard it all." He laid his pipe on the table and leaned forward, his eyes fixed on the carpet. "Poor Doctor! We lose a clever officer. The world loses a fine man. D'you know, I believe if he'd been less fine his brother would be alive to-day. It's been an unhappy case for me."

"So," I asked, "you and Larry were working together?"

"Yes, at the last. We needed each other. We had to leave you out; it was part of the plot that won in the end."

"Poor Dill!" Larry poked me playfully.

But I was in no mood for playfulness. The picture of the Doctor at the piano hovered over me. I shuddered.

"It was really one of the simplest cases I ever handled," said the Inspector. "I was here in the early morning following the murder, and a clue or two fairly stuck out from the first. The conventional evidence of a struggle did not deceive me. I couldn't imagine a man shot through the heart falling flat on his back, arms and legs so carefully placed. There was, too, no such expression on his face as I would expect to be there if things were as they seemed. Horton, I decided, had been shot by someone suddenly, without a struggle, someone he did not expect to shoot.

"The hidden drawer gave me my next clue. I happened to glance along the wall, as I stood in the French window that was found open by the police, and I saw the knob. And so I traced the bullet Miss Venell fired. At first I thought it a first bullet that had missed, but in that case Horton's face would have told the story. And if that were so, why did the murderer try to cover it up? A moment's examination of the wound convinced me that the bullet was larger than a .25, yet the hole in the drawer was made by a .25, or some smaller bullet. It meant that two guns had been fired.

"In the ash-tray were burnt matches and a cigarette stub and ashes, and from that I deduced that someone had sat there for some time smoking. Yet Horton himself had been there only a short time. Thus someone must have waited there for him. It could scarcely have been one of the guests, for that would have been too risky, too easy to trace. Then the telephone message meant something, and the open French window was not a blind.

"I had found the French window unlocked, though Inspector Emerson assured me he had locked everything up the night before; and only he and four policemen, and Doctor Millbrook, had been in the billiard-room since. What, I asked myself, did it mean? Plainly that someone wished to use that door when the police were off guard."

He paused and chuckled at us across the room.

"When I saw you two mooching about that room in the dark that night I felt like the rawest amateur. Every part of the structure I had built seemed to tumble about my ears. You had been pointed out to me that day on the street by Inspector Emerson, with the story of the anonymous letter. I watched you, hidden behind that large cabinet in the comer, the whole room under my eyes from a hole bored in the back.

"And while I waited to see what you wanted that other entered. I too saw those baggy pants, the cuffless legs, the feet, but at that time I had not seen the Doctor."

"I wonder you didn't come out and arrest us all," I said.

"What good would that have done? You all couldn't be guilty.

The case against one would have acquitted the others. . . . In the meantime Inspector Emerson was keeping an eye on the other suspects, and we were quietly searching for the two girls. I concentrated on Doctor Millbrook from the moment I met him. I tried to trace his history, and found that, beyond five years in England, no one knew anything about him. His diploma is Canadian, and he has studied in Vienna. After all, what went before had little bearing on the case, except to provide a motive. That we could trace when we had enough to warrant arresting him.

"But I did not neglect you two. I knew you were hiding something. I read it in your faces the night I met you at Doctor Millbrook's. When you, Rockford, were blown up I went carefully over the ground. There was no blood, and from the condition of the garage and of the crock Doctor Fleury made of you I knew something was wrong. What settled that conviction was that each time I visited you your boots under the bed showed fresh use."

"But," puzzled Larry, "Cuddy polished them each morning after I came back to the room."

"That's what I noticed. If they had not been used he wouldn't have had to do that. Each time they looked a little different. I managed to make a mark on them with my foot at each visit. When I put it up to you—You can tell all that to Fullerton later.

"What gave me the proof I sought against the Doctor was his manipulation of the guns. I had noticed on the one Inspector Emerson found in your room a slight scratch on the under side of the butt. He professed to find that it had not fired the fatal bullet, though in reality it had. He had planted it on you, but when he was caught in the house there was nothing to do but pretend it was not the gun we wanted. When he gave me the automatic you said you got from Miss Shannon I found the same scratch. He had interchanged them, as he explained. Why had he done it? To fix the crime on another, of course. And that could mean but one thing."

"But," I said, "someone tried to kill the Doctor, too, in his own garden."

"Oh, no, he didn't. That antiquated dodge of frightened guilt didn't help him. It was perfectly arranged, but for one thing—the cord he used. Both Inspector Emerson and I had seen a ball of that cord in his laboratory four days before. It disappeared. To-night Rockford and I made our final bid for the truth. It succeeded. I had other means of learning the truth, but—but—well, just but." He smiled sadly.

"Surely," I said, "you can't intend to let him escape —not Scotland Yard!"

"Doctor Millbrook will not escape," Inspector Rountree assured me solemnly. "I've stretched a point. But there's a limit."

I'M not sure that I slept at all that night. Such a medley of sadness and joy, of pleasant and painful anticipation, flooded my thoughts, that I think I must have rolled about the bed until Cuddy crept into my room with my morning tea.

Barbara!

Yet in the midst of the ecstasy that made me breathe fast and deep Doctor Millbrook intruded. And I saw him as I had seen him last the night before, head thrown back, his fingers gliding over the keys, the melody of the Rondo driving me hurriedly toward the street.

Larry walked whistling in as Cuddy set the tray on the table beside the bed. He was fully dressed.

"Is it golf to-day, Dill? I just got Jordan out of bed to arrange a foursome. Peter Davenport and you will take on Jordan and me."

I set the cup back untouched and scowled at him.

"I don't like this, Larry. It's not like you."

Larry whistled two bars of the Wedding March before replying.

"Get your mind off everything else, Dill. I'll be best man. And I'll expect—"

"Stop it!" I stormed. "You're disgusting. You're heartless."

"Not heartless. Ask Willo. This is a new day, old chap. The Vance Horton murder was yesterday—nothing but history. The last chapter is written. When the police went to arrest Doctor Millbrook this morning he was gone."

"Gone? Did Scotland Yard let him—"

"Scotland Yard had no wish to stop him—where he went. He's gone to meet his God—and Vance. Just an empty glass—and a written confession. Now forget it. Get your clothes on. It's golf, if I have to carry you."

The telephone beside my bed rang. Larry reached it first, and a broad grin spread over his face as he listened.

"Yes, Barbara, he's here." He held me off as I struggled for the instrument. "He's just asked me to be best man at the wedding. . . . Certainly. He has it all planned. Willo there? . . . Fine—fine! Tell her Dill has consented to be best man at *our* wedding. How about a double one? . . . Yes, of course. And we've ordered a table at the Trocadero to-night for six. The two Inspectors will be there. . . . Yes, here's Dill. Cuddy has just managed to waken him. I hope you can train him to more regular hours."

THE END